"I CAN TELL SHE'S IN THERE, BUT SHE DOESN'T SEEM TO HEAR ME AND THE DOOR'S LOCKED . . ."

"The door's locked? That's funny," Diane said as she came up next to me and peered through the window too. "Let me get the keys."

Back she went to the reception area, returning with a full ring of keys. She tried a few before she got the right one. When she did she pushed open the door and went in, repeating the call of Steffi's name along the way.

I followed behind but there was still no acknowledgment of us or our uninvited entrance.

Diane headed around the desk to the rear of the chair.

"Hey!" she said more loudly, nudging the leather back slightly, playfully.

There was still no reaction from the other side of the chair and by then I was feeling the hairs on the back of my neck stand on end. Not a good sign.

I mimicked Diane's path around the desk from the other direction, getting a profile of the chair just as Diane turned it toward the desk. Too quickly for me to warn her.

That was when Steffi's arm fell limply off the chair's armrest to dangle along the side.

And when Diane saw what I had seen a split second before—the bloody mess that was the side of Steffi Hargitay's head.

Dell Books by Victoria Pade

Divorce Can Be Murder
Dating Can Be Deadly

Dating
Can Be
Deadly

Victoria Pade

A Dell Book

Published by
Dell Publishing
a division of
Random House, Inc.
1540 Broadway
New York, New York 10036

ISBN: 0-440-22642-2

Printed in the United States of America

Published simultaneously in Canada

October 1999

10 9 8 7 6 5 4 3 2 1
OPM

Dating
Can Be
Deadly

Chapter One

DATING? ME? IT had all the appeal of a root canal. Without Novocain.

But there I was, on an overcast Saturday morning in the middle of January, headed for the New You Center for Dating to learn how to get back into the swing of things.

Some Christmas gifts are just a pain in the butt.

I'm Jimi Plain, writer for hire for newsletters, pamphlets, brochures, assembly instructions, manuals, and—at the moment—a catalog for the home chef. Technically, I'm a freelance technical writer.

I have two kids—daughters both—and a schnauzer named Lucy. We share a house with my maternal grandmother, Rose Nell, and my cousin the cop, Danny Delvecchio, in a suburb northwest of Denver, Colorado.

I love them all and I know my grandmother and my daughters meant well when they pooled their resources to give me the whole Get Back on the Horse series that the New You Center for Dating offers. But when the tally gets taken, after fourteen years of marriage and another eight divorced—a full twenty-two years since my last date—I was beyond rusty. I was corroded. And not really interested in getting back on that particular horse again.

I'd been dragging my feet about the whole New You deal. So much so that my personal counselor, Steffi Hargitay, had called to say that if I was unable to come in today, my spot would be given to someone on the waiting list and I'd go to the end of that list, meaning it would be at least six months before I could hope to reach the top again.

As far as I was concerned, they could put me at the bottom of every list from now till kingdom come. But I didn't want to hurt my family's feelings, so I took a deep breath as I pulled into the parking lot and told myself to make the best of it. After all, going to the Center, attending their classes and beauty makeovers, didn't mean I'd actually ever have to date anyone.

The building that housed the New You Center was a single-story red-brick affair built across the street from the high school in a neighborhood that was a strange conglomeration. A development of nice single-family homes surrounded a few four-plexes, a not so nice two-level apartment building, a small office building, Walgreen's drugstore, and a fast-food Chinese place that had once been a Tastee-Freez.

When the New You Center was being built, rumor had it that it was a school for accelerated learning. I guess it didn't end up too far off that mark except that the learning that goes on there isn't academic. Instead the Center is a full-service organization guaranteeing to make getting into the dating scene a breeze even for the most inept.

Besides the Before video I was finally on my way to tape, what I was in for were classes with names like How and Where to Meet Your Magnificent Mate—and First Date Do's and Don'ts; The Lost Art of Flirting and How to Recapture It; If You've Never Danced Before, It's Time to Start; Tickle Your Partner's Funny Bone and Be a Socko Conversationalist; Sex, Singles, and How to Save Your Life While Still Having a Rollicking Good Time; and my favorite, Tiramisù and Tetrazzini, Too—What Every Dater Needs to Know About Fine Foods and Wines.

There were also exercise classes; a sauna and weight room that could be used to buff up; private counseling for advice on how to improve hairstyles, makeup, and clothes; mixers; evening and weekend excursions in groups; and After videos that went into a library of other After videos and made up the dating service that the Center also offered.

If you were serious about whipping yourself into marketable shape, there didn't seem to be a better place to do it. But I couldn't help thinking of the whole thing as dating boot camp.

I'd dragged myself to my orientation meeting with Steffi on Thursday. Steffi was one of the five people who ran the Center. As soon as she and I finished my Before video this morning, I was scheduled to have brunch with the other new recruits who had—again according to Steffi—already begun using the facilities and attending some of the counseling sessions to become New You's. Apparently I was the only slacker, but I still couldn't put a skip into my step as I crossed the parking lot and went up the walk to the double glass doors.

The doors were locked. No surprise. It was half an hour before opening. But Steffi had said she'd meet me there to let me in. I didn't see her waiting as I reached the doors, but there were two other people just inside, standing at the reception counter to the right of the cavernous entry.

The reception counter ran the full length of the side wall, acting as a barrier to protect the floor-to-ceiling shelves where the After videos were displayed. Maybe to inspire slackers like me with all the tempting possibilities for the New You.

I wasn't tempted.

One of the two people at the counter was restocking videotapes while apparently keeping up a conversation with the other, who was merely leaning against the gray marble top. It struck me just how attractive both people were.

The young woman replacing videos had a body like a Barbie doll's—tall, thin, all legs and breasts in a merciless white Lycra knit dress with a scoop neck and a hem that didn't reach more than two inches below the tightest tush I'd ever seen. She had red hair—the deep, rich burnished color red, not the carrot-hued kind— thick and silky, swinging around her shoulders in a cascade that looked as if every strand would fall back into place no matter what was done to it.

The man, who was also probably in his mid-twenties, stood at least six feet tall. There was no doubt that he was a bodybuilder. He had biceps no sleeves could contain, a neck so brawny it was the same width as his head, a sharply V'd torso, and thighs that swelled to the limits of the white jeans that matched his white polo shirt.

He had sandy hair cropped close to his head and the face of a male supermodel—all high cheekbones and chiseled planes. I don't routinely turn all heads when I walk into a room, but small children don't shriek in fright either. In comparison to the two people inside, though, I suddenly felt every bit of my age and imperfections.

Neither of them noticed me, so I knocked on the door. They both glanced my way, but it was the man who crossed to the entrance.

"We aren't open yet," he called through the door in a deep, polite voice.

"I have an early appointment with Steffi," I called back.

He raised his chin in a nod of understanding, unlocked the door on the right, and then bent to pull up a second latch that plunged into the floor for added security.

"Steffi was supposed to meet me," I added as I stepped from the frigid winter air into the heat of the building.

"I saw her car in the parking lot when I got here but I haven't seen her," the man informed me.

"She's in her office," the young woman offered.

"Okay. Shall I just go there or do you need to announce me?" I asked.

But rather than answer, the man held out his hand for me to shake and said, "I'm Gary Oldershaw and that's Diane Samboro. We're counselors too."

"Nice to meet you. I'm Jimi Plain. Steffi is making my Before video."

Diane Samboro gave me a warm, amused smile. "Jimi Plain. I've heard that name. You're the one who hasn't been too anxious to come to the Center."

Great. My reputation had preceded me.

"The enrollment was a Christmas gift," I said as if that explained it.

"Well, don't be nervous. You'll see, you'll have a good time."

I just smiled.

"You will," Gary Oldershaw seconded as if he saw through me. "It's just kind of hard to get yourself out there sometimes. But that's why we're here—to make it easier."

They were both being so nice and nurturing and encouraging, I couldn't very well tell them that I didn't *want* to be *out there* again.

"Are you recently divorced? Never married? Just broke up with your significant other?" Diane probed in a friendly way.

"Divorced but not recently. Eight years ago. Going on nine."

"And since then?" Gary asked expectantly.

"Since then I haven't dated."

"All those years divorced and you haven't *dated*?" Gary again.

I had the impression that something a little racier than dinner and a movie was what he was considering that I'd done without for all that time.

With amazement in his tone and expression, he said, "How come?"

I just laughed. "No time. No guts either."

"I'll bet you had kids to raise or a career to concentrate on," Diane guessed kindly.

"Both."

"But now your kids are busy with lives of their own and the career is on track and it's time for you."

That sounded like the title of one of their classes.

"No, now my daughters and my grandmother decided I should *get myself out there* again as you guys put it."

"So here you are, but you don't really want to be."

Diane was a perceptive person.

"Oh, what the heck. It couldn't do any harm," I said, not wanting to sound like a total spoilsport.

That seemed to bring the conversation to an end, so I repeated my earlier question. "Shall I just go ahead to Steffi's office?"

"Sure," Gary said, looking at me now as if I were some alien life-form. "Steffi's office is right around the corner, second door on the left."

I knew that from my orientation meeting but I didn't tell him. I just said thanks and it was good to meet them.

"We'll be seeing more of each other in the classes and sessions and things," Diane assured me as I tried another phony smile. "It won't be as bad as you think."

I just nodded and went in search of Steffi.

The place was so quiet that even my soft-soled shoes echoed down the hall. I was glad it wasn't a long walk to Steffi's office.

Hers was the first one after the door marked STEVE STIVIK—OWNER AND MANAGER.

There were large windows beside each office door

and when I passed the owner's I could see he wasn't in yet. No lights were on. No one was inside.

But beside it the yellow glow of electric light said Steffi was in hers even before I reached the door. Through her window I could see a plain, serviceable oak desk with a chrome and leather visitor's chair facing it. Behind the desk a high-backed leather chair was turned to the wall, but an elbow on the armrest was visible, letting me know she was there.

I took a quick scan for the phone, wondering if she might be talking to someone and had swiveled her chair around for an added bit of privacy. But the receiver was in the cradle, so I felt free to knock.

The Center really was quiet. There was no way I wouldn't have heard her say "Come in." If she had. But she hadn't.

I thought I'd knocked with enough force but maybe not. I tried again, putting some muscle into it.

Still nothing.

Maybe she'd fallen asleep waiting for me.

I tried one more knock—a real *bang-bang-bang* on the door this time. But again there was no response and the elbow in view didn't budge. It reminded me of trying to get through to my youngest daughter, Shannon, when she has earphones on.

I considered going back out to Diane and Gary in the lobby and telling them I thought Steffi was asleep or plugged into earphones or something. But if she was asleep on the job, I didn't want to get her into trouble. Besides, it seemed dumb to go through all that just so someone else could wake her up.

I did another series of power knocks on the door, but when it still didn't rouse her, I tried the handle.

Locked.

Okay. Now what?

"Steffi?" I called through the glass.

That didn't have any effect either, not the first time or the second or third. But by then the commotion I was making had brought Diane down the hall.

"You were right, I can tell Steffi's in there," I said by way of explanation for my antics. "But she doesn't seem to hear me and the door's locked so I can't poke my head in."

"The door's locked? That's funny," Diane said as she came up next to me and peered through the window too. Then, as if I hadn't done it right, she, too, tried knocking, knocking harder, calling Steffi's name, turning the door handle.

But her methods weren't any more successful than mine had been.

"Hmm."

I gave her my earphone theory, adding, "When my daughter's using those things I have to be standing practically on top of her, pulling them off, for her to know I'm there."

"Let me get the keys," Diane suggested.

Back she went to the reception area, returning with a full ring of keys. She tried a few before she got the right one. When she did, she pushed open the door and went in, calling Steffi's name again.

I followed behind, but there was still no acknowledgment of us or our uninvited entrance.

Diane headed around the desk to the rear of the chair. "Hey!" she said more loudly, nudging the leather back slightly, playfully.

There was still no reaction from the other side of the

chair and by then I was feeling the hairs on the back of my neck stand on end. Not a good sign.

I mimicked Diane's path around the desk from the other direction, catching a glimpse of Steffi's profile just as Diane turned the swivel chair toward the desk. Too quickly for me to warn her.

That was when Steffi's arm fell limply off the chair's armrest to dangle along the side.

And then Diane Samboro saw what I had seen a split second before—the bloody mess that was the side of Steffi Hargitay's head.

Chapter Two

THERE WAS NOTHING I could do for Steffi. It was obvious by the glazed and fixed stare of her baby blue eyes that she was dead. But when Diane saw her, she let out a gasp followed by a little whimper and down she went like a chiffon scarf in a breeze.

It was the most graceful faint I'd ever seen. Except that as I ran back around the desk to grab her, I realized it wasn't so much a faint as a swoon. She was conscious, her knees just must have given out on her. Or maybe she would have liked to pass out to escape the gruesome sight of her co-worker's once beautiful head smashed in like a Halloween pumpkin, brain matter oozing out of a wide-open, jagged split in her skull that looked as if she'd parted her blond hair with a meat cleaver. I know I could have done without seeing it.

"Let's get out of here," I said to Diane as I helped her to her feet.

That suggestion seemed to put the starch back in her legs because she left me in her dust as she ran screaming for Gary. I was barely two steps out of the office when he charged into the hallway from the lobby and nearly collided with the fleeing Diane.

"It's Steffi! It's Steffi!" Diane shrieked.

"Dial 911," I advised.

But rather than heading for a phone, the body-builder jogged around us as if he were Superman to the rescue.

"Don't touch anything!" I called after him in no uncertain terms, not knowing if he'd pay any attention.

In the lobby again I ignored the EMPLOYEES ONLY sign on the half-door that kept the reception area sealed off from everyone else, went behind the counter to the phone, and did the honors. Once the 911 operator had taken the pertinent information and hung up with a promise to send the police, I called home for my cousin Danny and told him I was sitting on a mess more tailor-made for his skills than mine.

About that time Gary returned from his visit to Steffi's office, his skin almost as white as his clothes. "Is Steffi dead?" he asked, almost trancelike.

"Yes, she is," I answered, not unsure about it.

Diane started to cry as if she hadn't realized what she'd actually seen until that moment, somehow managing to shed tears without so much as a red nose or a single streak of mascara running down her face.

I could hardly comfort her by telling her everything was okay because it wasn't. So instead I went out from behind the counter and urged her to one of the four chairs that lined the opposite wall like seats in a hospital waiting room.

Just then, with sirens blaring and red and blue lights flashing, two police cruisers raced into the parking lot, pulling to a brake-slamming stop at the curb outside the front of the building. Four cops in uniform rushed the doors. Since Diane was lost in her sobbing and Gary was staring into space with almost as dull an expression on his face as Steffi had had, I unlocked the locks and let in the authorities.

I told them why they'd been called, and no sooner had I finished than Danny showed up too.

Since Danny is a homicide detective with a highly regarded reputation he'd brought home with him from a stint in Los Angeles, the uniforms deferred to him and all of a sudden he was in charge. Gary was dispatched to a room with one of the officers while Diane was left to sit where she was with another of the cops standing behind her.

She was in better shape than before, though. Danny's arrival had helped stop her crying. He was a good distraction. He's a strikingly attractive guy. Tall, lean, well built, with dark mink-colored hair, darker brown eyes, a Cary Grant cleft in his chin, and a great patrician nose.

I saw a few extra heaves of Diane's bosom even after her eyes had dried up, but I didn't hold it against her. Not many red-blooded women didn't perk up around Danny. His looks and appeal to the opposite sex were his blessing and his curse, leaving him three times divorced but never without female companionship when he wanted it.

As usual he seemed oblivious to the attention he'd

drawn and focused on the business at hand—asking me
what had happened—but not before he'd taken me off
to a corner, out of earshot of Diane. Cops don't question witnesses or potential suspects where any other
witnesses or potential suspects might hear the answers.
Sometimes discrepancies in those answers solve cases.

I didn't have much of a story to tell, so it didn't
take long. When I'd told it, Danny left to go to Steffi's
office, still not aware of the influence he'd had on
Diane.

Other people started arriving about then. More
cops. The crime scene unit. Two people who weren't
police—a man and an older woman—both garbed in
the sporty whites that were apparently the dress code
of those employed at the Center. I had to admit it
helped make the already attractive staff look as polished and perfect as the crew on a cruise ship, which
was probably what anyone joining the New You Center
was supposed to aspire to.

The man was short and stocky—maybe five feet
eight—and all muscle, though not as out of proportion
and exaggerated as Gary was. He was nice-looking,
too, slightly less Adonis-like than Gary, but still his features were strong and sharp around blue eyes darker
than Steffi's. His hair was a darker shade of blond, too,
and streaked in a way I didn't think the sun had accom-
plished. He looked like a surfer gone entrepreneur, and
when he introduced himself to the cop who met him at
the door as Steve Stivik, the owner of the Center, I realized I was right about the entrepreneur part.

He tried hard to take charge, but the cop wasn't giving way and would only allow him a chair separated

from Diane by an end table and a lamp, telling him he'd have to wait for Detective Delvecchio.

The woman who had come in at the same time as Steve Stivik appeared old enough to be his mother, but there was no resemblance to lend credence to any such relationship, and in short order Steve Stivik told the cop she worked for him as one of his counselors.

She, too, was a handsome woman even for her years. She was no more than my height without an ounce of extra fat on her. She had glistening white hair cut in a chin-length bob, lovely green eyes, skin that looked like satin even with a few wrinkles here and there, and the sort of refined features that would have made her as photogenic now as she no doubt had been in younger days.

Her name was Irene Oatman and she was banished to yet another chair pulled away from the wall to sit alone and apart from both Diane and Steve Stivik.

Information about what was going on had not been offered, so the Center's owner and Irene Oatman were left curious. The owner didn't like that any better than he liked not being in control, and about every five minutes he demanded to be told what the hell was happening.

In between, both he and the older woman shot glances in my direction where I stood leaning against the reception counter. I hadn't met anyone but Steffi before this, but I assumed it was obvious I wasn't a cop, so they were no doubt wondering who I was and what I was doing there. I knew who I was, but I was wondering the same thing about what I was doing there.

We stayed cooling our heels like that for half an

hour that seemed more like three days before Danny
finally came back out into the lobby.

"Are you Delvecchio?" the Center's owner demanded
the minute he spotted Danny, shooting out of his seat
and meeting my cousin head-on.

"Yes, sir, I am," Danny confirmed.

"Well, I'm Steve Stivik and this place is mine. I want
to know what's going on."

"Looks like one of your employees—a Steffi
Hargitay—was killed here sometime in the last twenty-
four hours."

"Killed? Here? You're joking."

"No, sir."

"You mean there's a dead body back there?"

"Yes, sir."

"Oh, for Christ's sake."

"I'm not sure whose sake it's for, but we'll be need-
ing to talk to everyone who works here and whoever
might have had contact with her recently. We'll also
need a list of friends, relatives, anything you can tell us
about—"

"I've got new members coming in here any minute.
Can you get those cop cars pulled out of sight and the
rest of this under cover? I don't need them scared away."

Business first. Even if someone had just lost her life.
It was good to have priorities.

Danny remained unflustered in spite of the other
man's tone. "I'm sorry, sir, but at the moment we have
our hands full and moving cars is not at the top of the
to-do list. How many people are due here?"

"It's a small group—four or five—but I don't want
them turned away."

"Any of them know Ms. Hargitay?"

"She does—did—the orientations so they all would have met her at least once. Depending on what else they might have done since their orientation, maybe more than that. But I don't want them bothered with—"

Danny returned the favor of cutting him off. "They'll all have to be questioned. But beyond that group I don't want anybody else let in here. Consider yourself closed until further notice. And we'll need a room for interviews. A place where everyone can be comfortable while they wait."

"There's supposed to be coffee and sweet rolls in the conference room for this morning's breakfast for the new group. At least if you put them in there they'll have something to eat and drink and won't be able to see what's going on out here. You can use one of the classrooms to talk to them if you have to."

Begrudging cooperation. Better than no cooperation at all.

Danny turned to me. "Jimi, maybe you could take care of the folks coming in for that breakfast. Just make sure there's nothing but friendly chitchat. I'll send one of my men in too."

In other words, play hospitality committee but keep my mouth shut about what was really going on. And just to make sure of it, he'd send a watchdog in with me.

"Or I could just go home," I offered amiably.

"You know better than that. We'll have to take your full, formal statement—"

"Just who are you, anyway?" Steve Stivic interrupted.

"She's Jimi Plain—one of those new members due to come in for your breakfast this morning," Danny supplied.

The owner's tune changed.

"I'm sorry. I didn't mean to be rude," he said, holding out his hand for me to shake. "You were coming in for Steffi to film your Before video, weren't you?"

"That's me."

"She and I are who found Steffi," Diane put in from her chair. Maybe I was mistaken but I thought drawing some of Danny's attention might have spurred the confession.

Ignoring Diane, Steve Stivik went from Mr. Friendly to Mr. Compassionate—toward me. "I'm so sorry. Are you okay?"

"I'm better than Steffi."

"I can't imagine what's happened here. It had to have been some freak thing. A break-in or something. Nothing like this has ever—"

A knock on the glass doors stopped Steve Stivik's words and drew all eyes there. Apparently we'd run into the hour for the breakfast meeting because outside were three people peering in at us as if we were all on display at the zoo.

The uniformed cop standing near Diane looked to Danny, who gave him the go-ahead with a nod. The cop crossed to the doors then, unlocked them, and opened up to those three and an elderly gentleman who hurried in behind them.

Danny played host, introducing himself and telling the newest arrivals that there had been a slight change of plans. As if they had a choice, he asked that they all allow him to spend a few minutes with each of them so he could explain what was going on and ask a few standard questions. In the meantime, he invited them to enjoy the continental breakfast they'd come for, even if the program wouldn't be what they were expecting.

He was good, I had to hand it to him. No one was alarmed or could have had any inkling that there was a dead body down the hall. Instead he had smoothly captured everyone's interest and enlisted their help. Then he asked Steve Stivik for directions to the conference room and ushered me, one of the uniformed cops, and the rest of the group out of the lobby.

The building was T-shaped and the conference room was the first room on the left wing of the T. It wasn't fancy. In fact it was just three solid walls with a few motel-quality pictures hung here and there, and a fourth interior wall of windows that looked out onto the hallway.

The only furnishings were a big oval glass-and-brass table surrounded by fifteen leather director's chairs, and a small stand in one corner with a coffeemaker on it. A bakery box was at one end of the table, along with a grocery sack filled with paper plates, napkins, Styrofoam cups, sugar, and powdered cream. But nothing had been set out yet.

That job fell to me as Danny made coffee. He knew from experience what my coffee tastes like—and apparently my cousin didn't want to risk a mass exodus by leaving that chore to me.

Then he excused himself and there I was, with four pairs of eyes expectantly on me. This just got better and better.

My appetite even for donuts was nil but at my suggestion everyone else helped themselves. When the coffee was ready, they all took a cup of that too.

"Can you let us know what's going on here?" the older gentleman asked.

The cop standing near the door gave me a look that warned me not to say anything revealing.

I settled on "Detective Delvecchio will have to tell you that when he talks to you. For now, maybe we ought to just introduce ourselves. My name is Jimi Plain," I said, going on to tell them what I do for a living.

But even after I'd explained it the same man said, "So you're not with the police?"

"No, I'm one of you. I came to make my Before video this morning and then I was going to have breakfast with you all."

The elderly man pointed a knobby thumb at the door. "That detective seemed to know you, though."

"He's my cousin."

I didn't offer any more on the subject, but that seemed to satisfy the elderly man, who finally took the spotlight off me and introduced himself. "Well, I'm Bert Chumley. I'm a retired salesman and I just moved here from Arizona."

He was a dapper old guy, about five feet ten with a barrel-like body in a tweed suit, white shirt, and bow tie. He had a full head of salt-and-pepper gray hair, bushy eyebrows, a small mustache, and extremely large ears that stuck out like the handles on a baby's sippy cup. And as he talked he periodically made a slight sucking noise through his dentures.

"Most people move *from* here to Arizona to get away from the snow and cold," I said. "Do you have family in Denver?"

"No, no family at all. I was married years and years ago—briefly—but there were no children. I just didn't like the heat of Arizona so I thought I'd try Colorado. And the New You Center sounded like a good way for someone like me to meet people."

I wondered if I'd insult him by telling him there was also a nice senior recreation center not far away but decided maybe I should save that for later.

An empty chair stood between Bert and the woman to his right. She was a woman I'd seen around town but didn't know personally. I'm not sure if all suburbs are the same, but my particular one is a fairly small community. Not so small that I'm on a first-name basis with everyone, but small enough so that it isn't unusual to run into people I'm familiar with or at least know by sight.

I didn't know her name, but I knew we'd gone to the same high school. She'd been a year ahead of me and she hadn't changed much. She'd aged—*matured* was probably a better word—the way we all had, but not so much that she wasn't recognizable. Especially when her unique style of dress hadn't changed in all that time.

She was taller than me—maybe five seven—not too thin, not too heavy, with waist-length, coffee-bean brown hair and unremarkable green eyes. I'd never seen her dressed in anything that didn't have a Hawaiian print motif somewhere—in her blouse or skirt or dress or pants—and she wore one side of her hair pulled back with a large flower.

I didn't have the foggiest idea why she opted for that particular fashion, but she'd gone all the way through school—day in and day out, while the rest of us wore jeans and T-shirts—looking like a middle-aged Maui tourist.

Today she had on an out-of-season bright blue and white dress and the flower in her hair was a gardenia the size of a man's fist.

"I'm Delia Grant," she informed us, taking her turn. "I'm a travel agent—well, Brenda and I both are—over at The World Is Your Oyster travel agency at the Plaza mall."

Delia glanced at the woman sitting beside her—the only two among us who hadn't left an empty chair between them.

On cue, that woman said, "I'm Brenda Merchant and I'm thirty-three years old."

She said it so timidly it was barely a whisper and I wondered why she felt the need to tell us her age. Maybe it was the only other thing she could think of to say.

She was an average-size woman—medium height, slightly pudgy, with dull brown hair that hung limply to her shoulders and bangs so long they obscured her eyebrows and looked as if she wanted to hide behind them.

Of course, she looked as if she wanted to hide behind Delia too.

She wore absolutely no makeup, as opposed to Delia's somewhat overdone cosmetics. Without so much as blush or mascara her face was washed out and her pale blue eyes were lost. But then maybe the invisible look was what she was going for.

When Brenda didn't offer any more information about herself, the man to my left sat up a little straighter and pointed to his mouth as he chewed a bite of donut, letting us know he'd be right with us.

I put his age at late twenties. He was a tall, lanky drink of water with a bad haircut that left a cowlick spiking his ashy-brown locks at the crown. His features were very pointed, from the shelf his brow made over his eyes to a nose that tapered dramatically at the end, to a chin that could nearly enter the room before he did.

He had a goatee, which I thought only added to the severity of his face, and hazel eyes that had a bit of a squint to them. When he smiled, it helped light up his face and in spite of his not being terribly attractive he seemed to exude a happy kind of energy that was just what the room needed.

"I'm Carl Cutler," he announced enthusiastically. "I own Cutler's Corner."

"I just heard about that place," Delia said. "It was on the news last week. They reviewed you. It's a restaurant and bar but it's also like a video arcade for grownups, isn't it? In downtown Denver?"

"That about sums it up," he beamed. Then, pointing at me, he said, "If I'm not mistaken, we don't live too far from each other. I'm up at the cul-de-sac at the end of your block. I have to drive your way to get in and out and I've seen you bringing your trash to the curb and shoveling snow."

Oh good. When I shovel snow, I dress like Nanook of the North. It's not a pretty sight.

"I haven't been here long and I haven't really met many of the neighbors," I said.

"Well, I'm one of them," he answered cheerily. "I haven't been in my house long either, though. I just bought it last month."

Delia asked a question about the restaurant then and Bert Chumley chimed in too. That seemed to get the ball rolling among three of the four of them at any rate, letting me off the hook. I was grateful because the morning was taking its toll on me and I was more than happy just to fade into the background the way Brenda Merchant seemed to want to do.

The trouble was, not participating in the conversation left my mind free to wander and the image of Steffi Hargitay slumped in her desk chair the way I'd found her, the side of her head crushed in, came back to haunt me.

So when I saw Danny motioning to me through one of the interior windows a few minutes later, I eagerly slipped out into the hall. Just as I did someone called for him, leaving him with only time enough to tell me that one of his men was ready to take my formal statement so I could go home.

I didn't bother to poke my nose back in the door and say good-bye to the rest of the new recruits, I just headed for the classroom where Danny had said Detective Fitzwilliam was waiting for me.

But along the way I couldn't help thinking that somehow it didn't seem like a good omen to have kicked off my return to the dating game by finding one of my counselors murdered.

Chapter Three

I COULD HARDLY believe it was barely noon when I pulled up to the curb in front of my house after leaving the Center. It felt as if I'd been gone from home forever. The sky was still a heavy gray backdrop, but the place looked warm and inviting against it and I was glad to be there.

It's a big old red-brick classic of a house, shaped like a wedding cake with a huge wraparound porch, another balcony from the second floor, and dormer windows at the attic level. I'd bought the place from Gramma a few months ago when financial necessity—translation: divorce and years without child support from a deadbeat dad—had forced me to sell the house I'd lived in for seventeen years. Gramma had offered me a deal I couldn't refuse.

There was an apartment in the garden-level basement that Danny rented. Gramma's domain was the ground floor. My daughters had the bedrooms on the second floor and I was in the attic—an open area with an outside entrance all its own, stairs down to the rest of the house, and space enough for my bedroom furniture, my desk, a love seat, and chair, a minuscule bathroom, and even a tiny kitchenette I rarely used for anything but boiling water to make myself tea or hot chocolate.

I'd had some qualms about communal living when the girls and I initially moved in, but so far it was working out just fine. In fact, I was looking forward to walking in that front door where everyone was alive and well and happy. Gramma would be whipping up something great for lunch, and even if the girls were arguing—the way they did more often than not—at least the vitality of it all might help wash away some of the grimness of the morning I'd just had.

"Lucy's gone!" Chloe greeted me with an edge of panic in her voice the minute I'd stepped across the threshold.

At nineteen, Chloe is my oldest daughter and she, my grandmother, and my younger daughter, Shannon—who had recently turned eighteen—were in the process of taking coats out of the hall closet.

"What do you mean the dog is gone?" I asked.

"We let her out and when Shannon went out to get her she wasn't there," Chloe explained.

"Was the gate open?"

"No, but we found a hole underneath the fence to the front yard," Shannon offered, more controlled than

Chloe but pale enough underneath her now all-black hair to let me know she was worried too.

"Since when does Lucy dig holes at all, let alone to get out of the yard?" Me again.

"I don't know, but she's gone," Shannon said.

"It'll be all right. We'll find her," Gramma put in reasonably. It took more than a lost dog to rile her.

Gramma is a roly-poly dumpling of a woman—not fat but a little puffy from her own incredible cooking. She—like Shannon now—dyes her hair jet-black. She combs it in a sort of bubble around a face whose cheeks you just want to pinch. She has dark brown eyes that literally twinkle and a nose any plastic surgeon would love to get hold of to reshape and trim off the bulb at the end.

She wears basically the same thing every day—a shapeless shirtdress she calls her housedress, as opposed to her housecoat, which is her bathrobe. Today's dress was lavender with white pinstripes. She also never goes a day without nylons that she keeps up with garters. Until they start to pinch, anyway, and then she rolls stockings and garters alike around her ankles.

For the current adventure she'd taken off the pink fuzzy slippers she ordinarily keeps her bunioned feet in and put on her black rubber galoshes. Now she was putting on her black coat with the fake fur collar.

"How long since you let Lucy out?" I asked.

"Just a little while," Shannon answered. "I'll bet she went up the street to Barney's house. Whenever I take her on a walk she loves to go up to the fence and see him."

Shannon's change of hair color from part maroon,

part black to all black flattered her. She has great hair—thick and shiny—that she wears in a pageboy that cups her delicate jawbone in front and angles to the hairline in back. She also has porcelain skin and the same big, dark brown, almost black, eyes that Chloe has, making the fair complexion against the black hair striking.

"Barney?" I repeated, not knowing who Shannon was referring to.

"The Doberman," Shannon supplied.

"He belongs to the doctor in that Tudor ranch three doors up. You know, the house you always say you like when we go past it," Chloe put in.

Chloe is slightly taller than Shannon, but they both have long legs that support bodies perfect enough to qualify as New You counselors. Bodies and faces too. Chloe's features are a bit more angular than Shannon's, but she's no less a head-turner with her glimmering sable-colored, naturally wavy hair to top it all off. Even dressed the way they were—in Saturday sweatpants and flannel shirts—I knew from experience that they'd draw stares.

"I think the guy is a dermatologist," Shannon put in.

I wondered how the girls knew so much more than I did about the neighbors, but there was no time to ask since by then Chloe had on an anorak fit for the Alaskan tundra and Shannon had on her corduroy pea coat, earmuffs, and gloves.

I just turned tail and out we all went back into the cold.

The neighborhood is an old one, though only Gramma and the residents of two other houses are originals to it. In the fifty years since most of the half-acre lots were sold and houses built in the centers of them, the rest have changed hands, some of them several times.

Each place was custom built to suit its owners, so no two houses are alike. But the one constant so far is that nothing has been left to decay. Yards are taken care of; the leaves that fall every autumn from the huge oak, elm, willow, birch, sycamore, and maple trees are promptly raked up; flower beds are artfully done; hedges are trimmed and paint is never left to peel.

Directly next door to our house is the white clapboard colonial that Danny owns. It's a two-story, 3,000-square-foot behemoth that he rents to a family of five because it's just too big for him alone. And because he likes the perks of living with us—the company when he wants it and home-cooked meals to die for.

On the other side of Danny's colonial is a sprawling honey-brick ranch and then the Tudor. It's a single-story used-brick beauty set farther back on the lot than either of the houses that border it. A cobbled brick path winds up to an oversize front door, and there's also a matching double driveway and another path from that around to the side of the house, adding to the Tudor tone. On the house the gables are painted white, the roof is shake-shingled, and a wrought-iron gate stands amid cedar fencing attached every five feet or so to brick posts that match the house.

We spotted Lucy at that gate, digging madly underneath it while a big black Doberman with golden-brown markings on his face sat regally on the other side, calmly watching her work.

"Lucy!" Shannon called in the commanding voice she'd used to train her.

Shannon has a way with animals and kids and had turned Lucy into a generally well-behaved pet who usually obeyed.

But not today.

Lucy went right on digging, letting fly dirt and lawn and some of the perennials from the borders around the gateposts.

"Lucy! Stop that!" I tried. To no more avail than Shannon.

We all trotted from the sidewalk across the yard, calling the dog the whole way. Lucy ignored us, and just as we got close enough to make a grab for her, she dived into the hole, scurrying up on the other side of the gate to sit next to the Doberman like a queen beside her king.

"Oh for crying out loud," I muttered.

"Look what she did," Gramma said, pointing to the mess Lucy had made.

The gate was about four inches off the ground, so she hadn't had to dig too deep in the nearly frozen earth, but in the process she'd unearthed several of the paving bricks that weren't cemented down and torn up a fair plot of the landscaping to boot.

I love that dog, but at that moment I wanted to shoot her.

"Damn it, Lucy!" I reached for the gate, thinking to open it and get her out, but no sooner had my hand touched the rail than the Doberman sprang up on all fours and started barking at me as if he wanted to eat me alive.

"Great," I muttered, pulling my hand away.

I didn't know what I was going to do about any of this, when the sound of the double-car garage door opening accompanied the barking. We all turned to see a brand-new hunter-green Lexus pull into the driveway.

Some days it just didn't pay to get out of bed. Not that I would have slunk off into anonymity and left Barney's owner wondering who had vandalized his place, but it would have been nice to have had the time to do some repair work before he had to see what Lucy had wrought.

The driver went all the way into the garage, but I knew he'd seen us. We heard the car door open and close and then, from around the corner, a man I guessed to be the doctor joined us.

He didn't look happy to see us.

"What's going on?" he asked.

I was getting sick of that question today.

"Hi," I said. "I'm Jimi Plain—your neighbor over a few houses. This is my grandmother—"

"I know Nell. Hi," he said to Gramma. Then he glanced at the girls and said, "And I know Shannon and Chloe too. Hi."

So everybody knew this guy but me.

And he didn't seem inclined to introduce himself. Instead he frowned down at the hole Lucy had dug, so I went from there.

"I'm afraid our dog dug her way out of our yard and into yours," I said over the noise Barney was still making. "I'm sorry about this."

The doctor finally yelled for his dog to be quiet and then hunkered down on his heels to survey the damage.

He was a decent-looking guy. About my age, I thought. Probably six feet tall, with a boxy build that made me think I might be able to smooth some waters with my new recipe for mud cake.

He had dark, dark brown hair sprinkled with gray—
mainly at the temples—cut neatly around his ears and
left a little longer on top. His face was pleasant enough,
with a nose that had a slight bump in the bridge. His
best features were his eyes, which were a bright blue
and probably looked a lot nicer when he wasn't just
arriving home to find his yard torn up by somebody
else's dog.

"Big mess for such a little mutt," he said when he
stood up again.

"I'll fix it," I assured him.

"Let's get your dog out of there first," he said, reaching for the same rail on the gate that I had. This time it
was Lucy who started barking at him. With all the
ferocity she usually reserved for the mail carrier.

"Maybe Shannon can get in there," Gramma
suggested.

Barney's owner got out of the way and Shannon
stepped up to the plate, schmoozing both dogs as she
slipped into the yard and finally scooped Lucy into her
arms to bring her out.

Barney tried to come, too, but the doctor ordered
him to stay and the animal complied.

With Lucy on our side of the gate again I dropped
down to my hands and knees to start shoving dirt back
into the hole. It really was torn up and I'm lousy at
yard work under the best of conditions.

Everyone's standing there watching me didn't qualify
as anything even close to the best of conditions.

Especially not when I was as embarrassed as the
time I had to face the leader of the church youth group
after Chloe and her friend Karen went to the Halloween party as doctors of hymenology.

Hmm. Maybe if I let him know he and Chloe were colleagues of sorts, the guy would defrost a little.

Probably not.

I managed to get the cold soil packed and then I reset the bricks as best I could. They ended up kind of lop-sided, uneven and lower into the ground than the rest.

"That's good enough," the doctor said about then, and I wondered if I was only imagining the slight edge of disgust in his tone. Again, probably not.

"It's too cold out here to do more than that," he added. "As long as Barney can't get out, that's the most important thing."

I was glad for the reprieve and I took it.

There was nothing I could do with the perennials Lucy had uprooted but gather them to cart away with me so I could throw them out. I did that before I stood to face my neighbor once more.

"I'll owe you some flowers in the spring," I promised.

He didn't say anything one way or the other.

"I really am sorry," I said again.

"It's okay," he finally allowed, but not so nicely that I believed him.

"Would you rather I pay a professional to come in and do something?" I asked, not sure who I'd call for a job that small.

"It's okay," he repeated, this time sounding more convincing. But not much more.

"I honestly am good for the flowers later on."

"I'm sure you are."

I didn't know what else I could do or say at that point, so I told him we'd let him get in out of the cold and we took out troublemaking dog and left the way we'd come.

"Thanks a lot," I whispered to Lucy as Shannon carried her down to the sidewalk. "This was just what I needed today."

But Lucy only looked longingly over Shannon's shoulder at the spot where the doctor was rearranging the bricks more to his liking.

Chapter Four

DANNY DIDN'T MAKE it home until late that afternoon. I'd told Gramma and the girls that there had been a problem that had kept me from making my Before video but that I'd met the other new recruits. Which was the truth. Just not the whole truth. But since I'd reached Danny on his private line no one knew I'd had anything to do with his being called out, and I didn't see much point in telling my family the ugly details.

I was up in my room, trying futilely to think of a witty description for a cast-iron frying pan, when I heard my cousin's car out front. I didn't bother hitting SAVE on my computer because there was nothing there worth worrying about. I didn't grab a coat, either, I just used my outside entrance and went down the wooden stairs in time to meet Danny as he came around the corner of the house to the rear.

"Hi," I greeted him.

"Hi."

"Are you just now getting back from the New You Center?"

He shook his head. "From the cop shop. Had to go there when I'd finished at the Center. I'll bet you came to pump information out of me, didn't you?"

"You make it sound so cheap," I joked.

Danny gave me a look that said he didn't think I was funny but wouldn't resist my nosiness, either.

He caught sight of the patch job I'd done on Lucy's escape hole under the fence about then, and pointed his chin at it. "What's that?"

I explained, but only briefly. It was too cold to tell the long version of the story.

We went in the back door to a landing where Gramma keeps the coat she wears to hang laundry on the clothesline outside on chilly days. To our left was a short flight of stairs that led up to an old cherry wood door with glass in the top half. Through that door was the kitchen.

In front of us was a longer flight of stairs to the basement. I followed Danny down that flight glancing up at the kitchen door to see if there was any sign of Gramma or the girls. There wasn't, even though the light that was on in the kitchen told me Gramma was probably getting dinner started.

Danny's apartment is an odd setup. His bedroom is to the right of the foot of the stairs. Directly in front of them is an open room where the furnace stands and from which his bathroom, another bedroom, and a small room we call the cool room jutted off.

The cool room is just that—a room without heat vented into it and with a small window covered only by a grate so that cold air can come in. It's like our own private deli storeroom. Gramma keeps extra jugs of olive oil and homemade wine vinegar in there, balls of provolone cheese, salamis, pepperonis, strings of garlic, and sacks of dried basil, parsley, and oregano.

When my grandfather was alive, he kept an elaborate vegetable garden. Now Danny cultivates a much smaller one for us all, but even though he produces less than Grandpa did, the cool room is still the best place to keep vegetables at the end of the growing season. Thanks to the cool room, things last longer. Some years we have homegrown tomatoes until Thanksgiving.

But rather than heading in that direction, Danny and I took a sharp left into his living room. I sat on his leather sofa while he kept on going into the tiny kitchen farther to the left.

"Want a beer?" he offered.

"No, thanks." I'd learned to drink beer, play poker, and smoke cigarettes from following Danny around like a shadow when I was a kid. He'd been my idol. Of course, then we'd sneaked cans of Coors out of the cool room. Now he came back with a long-neck bottle with a fancy label from a microbrewery.

He sat on his La-Z-Boy and let his head fall to the back of it, and I saw him begin to relax. It made me feel guilty for essentially making him bring his job home.

But I still said, "So what'd you find?"

"About Steffi Hargitay?"

I nodded.

"*Steffi*—do you know that's even on her driver's license? Not Stephanie, *Steffi*. I feel like I'm talking baby talk every time I say it."

"It's a little too cute for my taste," I agreed. But then wasn't everything at the New You Center?

"*Steffi* Hargitay. Age twenty-eight. Height five nine. Weight one hundred fifteen pounds. Eyes blue. Date of birth August fourth. Address—"

I cut him off before he recited the kind of deodorant she used or how often she clipped her toenails. "What happened to her?"

Danny drank his beer and then, in the same matter-of-fact tone of voice, said, "She was killed by a blow to the head. There were no signs of forced entry into the building and the only thing missing is a video camera she was apparently setting up in her office to film your Before tape, so robbery doesn't seem to be the motive. She was not raped. There was no struggle. No one we talked to told us much, including the people she worked with. Looks like death turned her into a saint. A saint who carried a dozen condoms and a fresh pair of underpants in her purse."

"Safe and hygienic," I pronounced.

"Or promiscuous.'

"She was a beautiful young woman. Maybe she just enjoyed the fruits of that. If we were talking about a man carrying a lot of condoms and a change of underwear you'd say he was a stud."

Danny conceded my point with a toast of his beer bottle and another swig. "But maybe being a stud-ess got her killed."

"If that's what she was. Maybe she was just headed for a romantic night with the guy she's been in love with since kindergarten."

Danny rolled his eyes at me.

"How about family? Friends outside of work?"

"Nothing on that yet, though I'm thinking the owner of the Center knew more than he was saying. Frankly, I think all her co-workers had more to say than they were offering up today."

"Nobody wanted to speak ill of the dead?"

"Maybe. The rest of those members you were with in the conference room all had contact with her in the last week too."

"I heard Steve Stivik tell you she handled all of the orientations for new members. Could that kind of interaction with Steffi have provided someone with a motive for murder?"

"Never know. Looks like this was a crime of passion, not premeditated. I'm guessing she argued with somebody or just pissed them off and that somebody picked up the nearest weighty object—probably the missing video camera—and beaned her with it. Last night, sometime late. Apparently she was the last to leave."

"Well, not the last and she didn't leave. Whoever killed her had that distinction."

"She was *supposed* to be the last to leave," Danny amended. "Stivik usually is but he had a *special* date so he handed over the reins to her. Apparently it was a rarity for him to do that so it isn't likely that anybody anticipated Steffi's being alone and planned to kill her after everyone else had gone."

"Are you thinking that one of the new members might have killed her?"

"Anything's possible. But I'm betting it's somebody closer to her than that. Maybe that boyfriend she was going to spend a romantic evening with—if there is one."

From upstairs Gramma called, "Danny? Are you here?"

"Yes, I am, Nellie."

"You eating with us tonight or going out?"

Danny smiled an ornery smile. "I don't know. What are you cooking?" he asked as if he were leery.

"Aay, I got a lasagna with béchamel sauce and marinara. You like that," Gramma said, taking the bait.

"I'll be home, then," Danny said with a laugh at her insulted tone.

"And Jimi, do you want salad?" she said then.

"How'd she know I was down here?" I whispered to Danny.

"She sees all and knows all," he whispered.

"Salad would be good, Gram," I hollered back. "I'll be right there to help."

I stood to leave, but before I did I retraced one of our conversational steps. "So Steffi could have been killed by anyone connected with the New You Center. Maybe I should ask for a refund of Gramma's and the girls' money and steer clear of the place."

Danny grinned. "Maybe you did the killing just to give yourself an excuse not to date."

"You caught me cold. Case closed."

"You mean even the electric chair would be better than dating?"

"That's what I'm thinking."

He shook his head. "You're not getting out of it that easy. Forensics should be finished with the crime scene by Monday so the Center can get back to business. It wouldn't hurt to keep your eyes and ears open but I think you can still go on to become the new you."

I gave him a dirty look. "Nothing wrong with the old me," I grumbled. "Couldn't you at least keep the place closed a few weeks?"

"Not without provoking a lawsuit for unnecessary loss of income. Sorry."

"Yeah, sure," I grumbled some more as I headed upstairs.

But no matter what Danny thought, I wasn't crazy about the idea of a killer being loose in my dating pool or among the counselors who were supposed to guide me into that pool. If I had to go through with this, I thought it behooved me to do a little more than keep my eyes and ears open. In fact, some snooping of my own didn't seem out of the question.

Just for the sake of my own safety and peace of mind, of course.

Chapter Five

By Monday evening, just after dinner, I was on my way back to the New You Center.

On Sunday, Steve Stivik had called me three times. I'd let the machine answer the first two calls and he'd left messages saying he hoped I was all right after Saturday's ordeal, to please let him know if there was anything he could do, and urging me to reschedule my Before video, which he wanted to film himself.

On the surface they were nice enough calls. But to me he sounded too concerned and sincere. Or maybe it was just that I couldn't get the image out of my mind of how uncaring he'd been over the death of one of his employees and how much more worried he was about the crimp her death might put in his business.

He'd caught me on the third call. Shannon had

answered before the machine picked up. Same spiel, only I'd had to respond as if I bought it.

He'd been very insistent about my going in to make the video, and I confess that it was curiosity that made me cave in to the pressure. I wondered just what made him tick and if he'd disliked Steffi Hargitay to such an extent that her death hadn't affected him. And if he'd disliked her that much, why? Going in to make my Before video would provide me with an opportunity to satisfy that curiosity.

When I got to the Center, I could barely find a spot to park. Apparently Monday nights were a big draw.

I ended up far back in the lot. It was well lit and there were other people coming and going, so I felt safe.

About halfway to the building I saw two faces I recognized. New recruits Carl Cutler—the second of the neighbors I hadn't known I had until Saturday—and Brenda Merchant, the melt-into-the-scenery friend of my old classmate.

They were standing near an ancient, faded brown Datsun—from the era when that particular brand was a Datsun, not a Nissan—with Brenda in the open lee of the door. Not that I would have expected the decrepit heap to belong to the prosperous owner of Cutler's Corner even if Brenda hadn't been half in, half out of it. I'd just read a small piece in Sunday's newspaper about what a booming business it was and how rich it was making Carl Cutler.

I thought it was nice that the outgoing Carl was attracted to the timid Brenda. They looked about the same age and I was glad for them if they'd connected. Maybe Carl could help bring Brenda out of her shell.

I wasn't going to stop to talk to them or even say

hello because I didn't want to distract them. But Carl caught sight of me and motioned me over.

"Jimi Plain, right?" he said when I reached them. "Remember us? From Saturday morning?"

"I do. Carl Cutler and Brenda Merchant. Hi."

"Brenda was just leaving as I was coming in."

"But my car wouldn't start," Brenda offered almost inaudibly.

I'd realized only as I'd joined them that the motor was running. Barely. The travel business must pay less than the freelance writing business.

Carl shot a nod toward the Center. "Looks like Saturday's events didn't slow anything down here."

"Business as usual, I guess," I said.

"Life goes on" was Brenda's contribution.

It was punctuated by a sputtering of her engine, which made her leap into the car and give it gas to keep it going.

"I should probably leave before this quits on me again," she said, sounding reluctant.

I was sorry that the car and I had both put a wrench into the works, betting that if I hadn't happened by and her car wasn't demanding attention, she would have lingered longer to talk to Carl. She kept casting glances at him, reminding me of the way Lucy begs for table scraps.

Carl didn't seem to notice. But he did say, "I'll run that business card by your office tomorrow. You really should give my guy a call. He's good and cheap."

"Thanks, I'll do that," she promised, smiling at him with more than passing gratitude.

She had a pretty smile. It lit her eyes, softened her features, pinkened her cheeks, and took away some of her drabness.

But it faded as she said good night to us both. Carl closed the door for her and waved as she pulled out of the parking spot. The Datsun made a terrible grinding noise and spewed a cloud of charcoal-colored smoke.

"I hope the guy you're putting her in touch with sells cars," I said as we watched the thing sputter out of the lot.

Carl laughed. "No, that would be my brother-in-law but we already talked about that. The card I'm bringing her is for my money man. I thought he could help her with a few things."

"So she can find a way to finance a new car," I guessed.

We set off across the lot together and as we did he said, "I'm glad you and I crossed paths tonight. I wanted to talk to you."

"About what?"

"Hiring you."

I might not have needed a new car—the Subaru station wagon was doing just fine—but I could always use work. "You need something written? Because I'm lousy at waiting tables, tending bar, or fixing video games, if that's what you had in mind."

He laughed again, a light chuckle that I thought might put Brenda at ease on a date. "I need a writer. Think you could do a prospectus for Cutler's Corner?"

"Sure."

"I'm planning to sell franchises. It's in the offing, anyway. But I'll need that kind of material to present when the time comes and when you introduced yourself on Saturday you said that was part of what you do."

"It is. Well, it's something I've done a couple of times before. And I'd be happy to do it again."

We'd arrived at the building by then and he held the door open for me.

"Let me give you a call when I have my schedule in front of me so we can set up a time to meet. Are you in the phone book?" he asked.

"Under J. Plain in the white pages. Residential listings. Nothing fancy. Or you can just drop by the house when you're passing by. We aren't formal."

Carl and I stepped into the warm white lights of the Center and that seemed to end the business discussion.

"What are you here for?" he asked.

"The Before video. Same thing I was here for Saturday."

"It's kind of creepy being here again, knowing what happened, isn't it?"

I was trying not to think about that, so rather than address it, I said, "How about you? What are you here for tonight?"

"Weight lifting." He seemed to shake off whatever dark feelings he'd had coming in and made a scrawny muscle in one biceps. "They tell me it takes a hard body to get a good date," he joked, laughing again, this time at himself.

"That's what I'm always hearing," I agreed, pleased to know he saw the lighter side of this stuff too.

Gary Oldershaw was manning the reception desk where returned videos were piling up and five people I'd never seen before were apparently waiting to view more. He spotted us both then, but only called to me that they'd let Steve know I was here.

"Guess I better get to work," Carl said. "I'll talk to you soon."

He gave me the same wave he'd sent to Brenda and headed for the wing off the left side of the lobby. Aerobic exercise music was coming from the same direction, along with the stomping and clapping of the participants and Diane Samboro's voice urging them to strive for more.

Several retirement-age people were gathered in the lobby. I assumed they were waiting for Irene Oatman to begin the class that was chalked on a blackboard propped against an easel like a restaurant's daily menu. The class was called You're Never Too Old to Shine and Show Your Stuff. Bert Chumley was among that group, but he didn't notice me. No wonder, since he was only one of two men in the group and the eight women seemed evenly divided to conquer.

I'd barely had time to take off my coat when Steve Stivik appeared from the right wing. He approached me as if I were royalty or a really big investor.

"Jimi!" he said with an expression of deep and abiding compassion and opened his arms as if he were going to engulf me in a bear hug.

Maybe that's what he'd intended, but my involuntary step backward changed his mind. He only took my hand in both of his.

"How are you?" he asked me earnestly, massaging the back of my hand.

"I'm fine, thanks," I said, unable to keep my suspicions of his bum's rush out of my voice. What exactly was the point to it?

"Come on back to my office," he urged in a conspirator's tone. "Can I get you something to drink? Coffee? Tea? Bottled water? Fruit juice?"

"No, thanks. I don't care for anything."

I have to admit that as he ushered me into his office my eyes wandered to Steffi's door just beyond it and I had a moment's pause as I experienced a flashback of what I'd found in there. But I fought the picture in my mind of her broken and bloodied skull and went into the owner's office instead.

It wasn't any bigger than Steffi's office and the furniture was identical, except there was a video camera set on a tripod in the corner.

"Is that the missing video camera or did you have more than one?"

"That's a brand-new one. The better to take a better video of you."

I nearly rolled my eyes at that but managed to refrain.

"Let's sit and talk a minute before we get started." He motioned me to the visitors' chairs as he rounded the desk to take the high-backed leather one behind it.

The sight of that chair that was just like Steffi's gave me more pause. I tried to cancel my mental images by keeping my focus directly on Steve Stivik. Certainly his dark blue eyes were honed in on me.

"Truthfully—how are you?" he asked with an even greater helping of concern, as if he'd reserved the full extent of it for the privacy of his office.

"Truthfully, I'm okay. It wasn't nice finding Steffi that way but it's over and done with. I'd think you'd be more upset than me. After all, she worked for you. I'd only met her once before. Or hadn't you known her long either?"

"Oh, no, I've known Steffi . . . I *knew* Steffi . . . for a long time. We met years ago when we were both working for a gym downtown. She was my only staff member when I first came up with the idea of the New You Center and started it in a storefront."

He leaned back in his chair then, far enough to tilt it as if to get a better view of me. "You're a nice-looking woman," he concluded. "Big hazel-green eyes. Good skin. Shiny hair. You must have signed up for the dating service. You certainly don't need the makeovers."

"I didn't sign myself up for anything. My grandmother and kids did it as a Christmas gift."

"Because you don't get out enough."

"According to them."

"Hard to believe guys aren't lining up to spend time with a woman like you."

Oh, come on. He was pouring it on more than a little thick. Sure, he and I were probably close in age. He might even have rounded the corner on forty. But I couldn't see him with the likes of me. My baggy jeans and turtleneck hide a short-legged body that's had two kids and no toning, tightening, or tucking. I just wasn't his type.

But I didn't deny the compliments. I knew if I did he'd just go further with this, as if I were fishing for more.

"Maybe we could have dinner sometime. You and I," he said as if it were a carrot he was waving in front of a donkey.

"Maybe," I allowed. I didn't have any desire at all to have dinner with this guy, but I also wasn't inclined to burn a bridge I might want to cross later on. Dinner with him would give me another opportunity to poke around in his head, which I might need if this encounter with him didn't succeed in slaking my curiosity.

"So, were you and Steffi partners?" I asked, not caring whether it was a smooth change of subject.

"No, I own the Center. But you could say that Steffi was my second in command."

"Then you were close."

"Yes," he agreed, turning on an expression that was supposed to convey grief. But he'd never win an Academy Award. In fact, something told me Steve Stivik wasn't all that sorry Steffi was out of the picture.

"I'd imagine that after a lot of years you must have had a relationship outside of business, too," I said.

"We were friends, if that's what you mean."

"You didn't date? Two attractive people like you?" I said, doing a little pandering to his ego this time.

"We dated early on, when we first met, but it just didn't turn into anything. So we became friends instead." And he didn't want to talk about it because he took a turn at changing the subject and leaned earnestly across his desk. "What about you? I looked over your personal profile and saw that you're divorced."

"Isn't everybody?" I joked lamely.

"Well, not *everybody*. Some of us have never been lucky enough to meet someone like you and be married."

Jeez, did anybody really fall for this stuff?

"Was Steffi married? Now or ever?" I asked.

"I think there was something quick when she was about eighteen. Over with by the time she was nineteen. She didn't like to talk about it." And neither did he. "I heard through the grapevine that you haven't dated in all the years you've been divorced."

"Nope. How about Steffi? I'll bet she dated a lot."

"I wouldn't know."

"You were friends and you didn't know if she dated?"

"Of course she dated, but not just one man. She

wasn't involved with anyone special. Anyone I'd get to know."

"Would you have minded if she had been?"

"No," he snapped.

Clearly I was not playing the game right. He was supposed to ask the questions and schmooze me and I was supposed to answer and be schmoozed, not ask questions of my own.

He backtracked quickly from that last nasty tone of voice and smiled a smile that didn't reach his eyes. "Would you mind talking about Saturday?"

"What about it?"

"It must have been tough on you to find Steffi that way."

"It wasn't pretty. But Diane was more upset about it than I was. . . . I could hear her voice coming from the exercise class when I came in—does that mean she's doing okay?"

"It was a shock for her but she and Steffi weren't exactly friendly. I don't think they liked each other much. Besides, Diane is a drama queen. Probably some of what you saw as her reaction to finding Steffi was for show."

Steve Stivik went serious on me, beetling his brow. "Can I ask you something about your finding Steffi or would it be too painful for you to rehash?"

"I can probably stand it." Especially since I had the feeling we were finally getting down to the nitty-gritty of why he'd been so eager to get me here tonight.

"When you first went into her office—did you see a small notebook anywhere? On her desk? On the floor? In her lap maybe?"

"A small notebook?"

"It's kind of a ledger. About eight by five inches big. Black cover. Somebody might mistake it for an address book."

Kind of a ledger?

I shook my head. "Sorry. I didn't see anything like that."

"Think about it. Picture her desktop in your mind. It probably wouldn't have really stood out."

I did picture the desktop in my mind. I remembered glancing there before going into the office, thinking Steffi might have been on the phone and that was the reason her chair was turned toward the wall and she wasn't answering my knock on her door. The desk had been bare of everything *but* the phone.

"I'm sure there was nothing there."

"You didn't accidentally pick up the notebook? Or knock it to the floor? Diane didn't pick up anything?"

"Neither of us touched a thing. There wasn't anything for us *to* touch. Or take."

He nodded, watching me as if trying to be sure I wasn't lying.

"Apparently the notebook was important?"

He shrugged. "No more so than any ledger. Just business, you know."

"But it's missing?"

"Unfortunately."

"Maybe somebody else took it."

"Steffi's the only one who could have. It was in my drawer here when I left. Locked up. She knew where the key to the drawer was and she was the sole person besides me to have any reason to get into it. In fact, nobody else even knew about the ledger. When I left, Steffi was here alone, so I'm thinking she must have come in, taken the notebook, and gone back to her office with it."

"And met up with her killer. Would anyone have reason to want the ledger?"

"No. I can't think of anybody. I told you, it wasn't all that important."

But it was important enough for him to go to the trouble of getting me here to talk about it.

"I would think all your records would be on the computer system."

"Oh, they are. Everything is on the computer. But the ledger had some other notes in it. Just reminders."

Reminders of what?

"Maybe the police have it," I suggested just to see Steve's reaction.

It didn't disturb him in the least. "I thought of that and asked. But the cops didn't find it either."

"Maybe Steffi took it out of your desk but left it somewhere else in the building."

"I've looked everywhere. For the last two days I've scoured this place. It isn't here."

"Do you think the killer took it?"

"I don't know why anybody would want it. Honestly, there wasn't anything in it of value to anybody but me."

"And Steffi?"

"I don't think you could say it was of value to her, either. She just helped me keep a record of a few things in it."

"So you don't think she was killed for it and nobody had any reason to want it, but it's still missing. I don't know why a killer would just pick up a notebook and take it with him—or her—for the heck of it. Do you?"

"No, I don't. I have thought—well, this is kind of

gruesome—but maybe blood got on it or something so whoever killed her took it to throw out."

Tidy killer. That didn't seem likely to me.

"Maybe the killer took it because he—or she—left fingerprints on it."

His eyebrows shot up. "Oh, sure, that makes more sense." He sighed and made a clicking sound with his tongue as if to say *that's the way the cookie crumbles.* "I s'pose that would mean it'd be lost forever, wouldn't it?"

"The police might find it when they find the killer. Or they might find it if the killer threw it away."

"But probably I'll never see it again," he said, sounding like that settled it for him. Then he perked up, pushed himself to a standing position with both hands on the desk, and headed for the video camera.

"Well, we should get down to business," he said. "Let me tell you what we're looking for in the Before video while I check for your best angle."

I didn't care much about what I was being coached to say on tape or what my best angle was. I only half listened as he talked about being myself, explaining why I'd joined the Center, what I was hoping to get out of the membership and classes, and what I'd like to change to become the New Me.

Instead I was wondering what parts of the things he'd just said and the emotions he'd shown were genuine and what parts were designed to make me believe something he wanted me to believe.

Was the *kind of* ledger a ledger, or was it something else? Just how important was it to him? And was it really of no interest or value to anyone else, or was it worth killing for?

And then something else occurred to me.

Maybe Steve's whole line of questioning was something other than what it appeared to be. Maybe there wasn't any notebook at all and he'd just invented it as a red herring to help make him look like a peripheral victim rather than something a lot more sinister.

Or maybe I just didn't like the guy.

Maybe it was the name.

The only other Steve I've ever known was the lying, cheating, stealing husband of a good friend I'd lost to an untimely death in the autumn. The other Steve had done such despicable things to his wife that I wouldn't be in the same room with him if someone paid me. So maybe the name just automatically triggered dislike in me now.

Maybe I wasn't giving this Steve a fair shake.

But I had a hard time really believing that.

Chapter Six

I COULD SMELL garlic and olive oil cooking when I went downstairs for lunch on Tuesday. During the day Gramma and I do our own thing, but we'd decided when I'd first moved in to have lunch together. It's a good way to touch base without anyone else around.

Gramma never fixes a meal that isn't delectable, but lunch is usually something simple, like Swiss cheese melted on top of marinated tomatoes on a slice of Italian bread or whatever might be left over from dinner the night before. So I knew when I went into the kitchen and saw her making one of my favorites—a dish we ordinarily have for dinner—that she wanted me to do something. And when I saw the bottle of holy water next to my plate I figured I was in for one of her regular attempts at soul cleansing.

The kitchen is a fairly large room divided down the middle by a breakfast bar. The table is to the left, the sink and appliances to the right. I went right and watched as Gramma drained capellini.

"Al'aglio for lunch?" I said.

"Sounded good."

We pronounce that *allya oil,* but my sister-in-law calls it oily noodles. Gramma cooks cloves of garlic in extra virgin olive oil then adds water and parsley. That goes over the thinnest angel hair pasta.

She drained the macaroni and drenched it in the olive oil mixture and sprinkled on a lot of Romano cheese, then we took the pot to the table.

I pour tomato juice over mine, something that always makes my grandmother roll her eyes at me and say, "I make this so you don't have so much tomato and you do that."

True to form. Sometime during this lunch I also knew I'd say how good it was and she'd tell me it was peasant food.

But for now, she just got down to brass tacks, pointing at the bottle of holy water near my plate. "Do with the holy water—the sign of the cross here, here and here." She demonstrated, making the sign of the cross over her forehead, her lips, and her breastbone with her thumb.

I opened the bottle of holy water, put some on my thumb, and did as I was told. It was a waste of time not to.

"And you better go to church with me and Danny on Sunday, too, to take that evil eye off you."

Gramma is big on the evil eye.

"Danny told you about Saturday morning at the Center," I guessed.

"Another dead body. God must be trying to tell you something."

A few months ago I'd volunteered to help lead a divorce support group and I'd found one of the members dead in his home.

"If I'd known, I would've never let you go to that place," Gramma added as we ate.

"It was just a fluke, Gram."

"Pretty soon they'll say where you go, death follows. You better go to church and get that evil eye off."

"Death was there ahead of me both times," I pointed out, having no idea who *they* were who would besmirch me with that reputation.

"We sent you to meet a nice man and look what happens."

"I met a man for you," I said to get us headed into a new direction.

"Me? Aay, what're you talkin' about?"

"One of the men who's just beginning at the New You Center the same as I am. He looks about your age."

"Thirty-nine?"

Gramma hadn't admitted to any more than that as long as I'd known her.

"I'd say he's in his early seventies." I was thinking about Bert Chumley. If there was anything left of him when the women surrounding him in the Center's lobby the night before were through with him.

"What do I want with an old buck?"

"You want a younger one?" I teased her.

"Who said I wanted one at all?"

"Who said I did?"

"You're young yet."

"There are quite a few older people at the Center. I'm thinking maybe we should join you up too."

She shrugged. "It wouldn't be so bad to have a nice man take me to dinner or to the movies. But no sex stuff. I'm too old for that."

I laughed. "What if I could get you Jack La Lanne?"

"Oh, maybe then," she said with a glimmer in her hazel eyes. "So who died over at that place?"

Nobody ever gets anything past my grandmother for long.

"One of the women who worked there. The one who was going to do my Before video."

"Danny says I don't need to worry that you're still going."

"I don't have to go. We could probably get your money back. Say I was too traumatized when I went in last night and I just can't do it again."

"Danny says he thinks you'll be all right."

In other words, even someone's being murdered wasn't going to get me out of this dating business.

"You don't want to be an old maid, Jimi," Gramma warned.

"Too late for that, Gram. Now I'm a divorcée. You can't be an old maid if you've ever been married."

"You don't want to be *alone* then. It's no good. I can tell you from before Danny and you and my dollies moved in—being alone is no good at all. I'm not going to live forever and those girls'll get married and move out. Even Danny could go. And then where will you be?"

"Traveling through Europe? On a beach in Maui?"

"Hah! Not you. You're a homebody. Only there won't be anybody home with you."

Maybe I'd rather talk about dead bodies.

"You go to that Center and find a man," Gramma said. "Just be careful."

My marching orders.

"Good al'aglio, Gram."

"Aay, it's peasant food."

I had an appointment late that afternoon with Diane Samboro, my new personal counselor. Before I'd left the Center after my meeting with Steve Stivik, he'd pressed me to arrange for my makeover consultation. I hadn't balked at the idea, even though I was tempted to. Just out of orneriness I'd thought about reminding him of his earlier claim that I didn't need to be made over, but I'd resisted the urge.

I wanted to talk to Diane about a lot of things and a consultation seemed like the prime opportunity, so I'd made the arrangements and at four-thirty I was sitting in her office.

Actually, it was an office she and Irene Oatman shared. It was a smaller space than either Steve Stivik or Steffi were allotted, with desks butted up against each other, head-to-head, against one wall to allow a visitor's chair alongside each and barely enough room to walk around.

I'm claustrophobic, and in order to stay in there I had to concentrate on the windows that faced out to the parking lot so I didn't feel so closed in. Then, too, it helped when Diane joined me and I could think about something else.

"Hi, Jimi. I'm sorry to keep you waiting."

"I've only been here a few minutes," I assured her because it was true.

She was dressed in white spandex again, this time a mock-turtleneck dress that almost didn't cover her rear end when she sat down. She had to tug at it to get it underneath her. The white suited her, though. It set off the dark burnished red of her hair like fire against snow.

"How are you doing?" she asked.

I could tell by the tone in her voice that she was referring to Saturday morning. But her interest in how I was faring after finding Steffi's body didn't come off as contrived as her boss's had.

"I'm okay. What about you?" I returned, also using the tone of comrade in arms.

She shrugged her pretty shoulders. "I'm okay, I guess. I'm having some trouble sleeping. Seems like when I close my eyes at night I can't get the picture of Steffi out of my mind. And when I do finally drop off, I keep dreaming about her. Except that in my dream she stands up from that chair with her head all bloody and caved in."

There were hints of purple crescents under Diane's eyes to support her complaint of lack of sleep.

"I'm sure you and Steffi were friends so it's doubly hard for you," I commiserated.

"I wouldn't call her a friend. But just knowing her and finding her like that . . ." A shiver punctuated the words that dwindled off.

"You and Steffi weren't friends? I thought being about the same age and working together . . ." I let my words dwindle off, too, hoping it would encourage her to tell me more.

It worked.

"Steffi didn't like me," Diane said a bit wearily. "I

tried to be friends with her, believe me. But it seemed like the more I tried, the less she liked me. I finally accepted that. Not everybody can like you, I guess. And at least she wasn't trying to get me fired the way she was with Irene."

"Steffi was trying to get Irene fired?"

"About two weeks ago we were all here just after closing. Irene and Gary and I were putting away videos and Steffi and Steve were in Steve's office. Pretty soon we could hear them both shouting. Steffi was saying how having Irene around looked bad for the Center. That we wanted to project a young, beautiful image and Irene was just an old hag. Gary and I were really embarrassed and poor Irene, she turned pale as a ghost. She needs this job. She doesn't have any retirement except social security and it isn't enough for her to live on. If she doesn't do this she'll have to be a clerk somewhere for minimum wage. It was bad enough hearing herself called a prune-face but I could tell Irene was really afraid Steffi would win that fight and Steve would let her go."

"So who did win the fight?"

"Steve said he wasn't firing Irene. That it was good to have an older person on staff to appeal to other older people when they joined and to talk to them later on. That old ladies didn't want me or Steffi telling them how to dress and do their hair and makeup, and that Irene was nice enough looking to appeal to the old men—which is true—she gets a lot of dates and I keep hoping some nice older fella will marry her and take care of her so she doesn't have to worry so much about money anymore."

"Did Steffi accept Steve's refusal?"

"There wasn't anything else she could do. But she didn't like it. She got even madder and started screaming that Steve owed her and she was sick of not having any power around here and that she wanted what she had coming to her and she was going to make sure she got it."

"What did she mean by that?"

"I don't know. And we didn't listen to any more. Gary and Irene and I stashed the videos to reshelve in the morning and left before we had to hear anything else. But I know Steffi's been mad at Steve ever since."

"Were they close before that?"

"Close? I guess you could say that, but it makes their relationship sound a lot nicer than it seemed. I know they'd worked together for a long time and they did a lot of private meetings that the rest of us have never been in on, but if I had to say they really liked each other, I probably wouldn't."

"Private meetings?" I repeated.

"It wasn't like they were having sex in Steve's office—I didn't mean for it to sound like that. It was just, well, almost like they were talking about secret things. He'd always lock his door so nobody could come in. But you could still see them through the glass and it looked kind of like they'd be bickering sometimes. I don't know, maybe they were discussing marketing strategy or something."

Behind locked doors?

"All I know is that Steffi and Steve are—were—two of a kind in a lot of ways—not really what you'd call nice people all the time."

Diane whispered that last part and then, as if she was uneasy leaving it at that, she added, "Not that

Steve isn't a good boss. He is. He's just . . . well, he isn't
very friendly either. Although to be honest, I haven't
tried to be friends with him the way I tried with Steffi. I
was afraid, you know, with a male boss, that if I tried to
be too friendly it might be taken as a come-on. I've had
problems with that before."

"So you didn't think Steffi and Steve were having
any sort of romance then?"

"Oh, no. She did see Gary for a while, though."

"Romantically?"

"They dated. That was up until a few weeks ago,
too, now that I think of it. I was surprised that she'd
date Gary—she saw a lot of our clients but there've
been a few guys who worked here before Gary who
were real hunks and they couldn't get her to go out
with them no matter how hard they tried. But something about Gary was different, I guess. She really
seemed to hit it off with him. In fact, when they broke
up, I even felt sorry for her. And believe me, it's not
easy to feel sorry for Steffi."

Belatedly, Diane seemed to remember what had
more recently happened to Steffi and she made the
kind of face someone makes when they've caught themselves in a social blunder. "Well, I feel sorry for her
now. But I mean, before Saturday it wasn't easy to feel
sorry for her."

"Did Gary break up with her?"

"No. He was crushed when she told him she wouldn't
see him anymore outside of work."

"So if she liked him and he liked her, why the
breakup?"

"I don't know. Like I said, Steffi and I weren't
friends. It wasn't like she'd tell me her problems. You

could just tell by the way she'd watch Gary when he wasn't looking that she still wished they were together. But Gary told me she dumped him. Without even saying why. Poor guy."

"He was really upset by it?"

"He was a wreck. I think he might have even loved her."

"Was he mad?"

"Mad, but more hurt, I think. You know how hard it is to tell with a lot of men. He just kind of got real quiet and serious and maybe a little impatient, and he worked out in the weight room even more than usual. Kind of like now, since Saturday. I think that's how he's dealing with her death too. He'll end up putting another inch or two on his muscles by the time he's gotten over it. Which isn't a bad thing when you think of how good he looks," she said with a smile that left me thinking Diane might have a soft spot for Gary herself.

She opened the file folder on her desk about then, and I was afraid it was the signal that she was ready to get down to the business of advising me on how to improve my appearance.

But I wasn't ready to move on to that. To forestall it, I pretended the sight of the file reminded me of something. "When I talked to Steve last night he wanted to know if I'd seen a notebook of some kind in Steffi's office when we found her on Saturday."

"I know. He grilled me about it, too. I told him I didn't see it. I can't remember seeing anything but Steffi." Another visible shiver shook Diane.

"Then you didn't know about it either?"

"No. I never saw what he described before Saturday and if there was a notebook around *on* Saturday, I didn't notice it. He acted annoyed with me and I know he's been tearing this place apart looking for it, but I can't help him out."

So much for how unimportant the notebook was to him. Again.

Steffi shuffled papers, and once again I knew she was on the verge of starting what she thought I'd come for in the first place.

But I still wasn't quite finished.

"Do you know of anybody who would have wanted Steffi dead?"

"No!" Diane said without thinking about it. "I mean, she wasn't a very nice person, but for somebody to *kill* her?" Yet another shiver shook the young red-head. "Who would do that?"

Good question.

And I was beginning to think it might not be an easy one to answer.

Chapter Seven

WHEN MY MAKEOVER counseling session with Diane was finished I rushed home. Carl Cutler had scheduled a seven o'clock meeting with me to talk about his prospectus and that meant that Gramma, the girls, and I were going to try to get dinner out of the way before that.

But even so, after I hung up my coat in the closet in my room I had to make a stop in front of the mirror on my dresser.

Diane's advice—in writing on two full pages—had been similar to what Chloe and Shannon usually gave me. But then Diane was closer to their age than to mine.

Cut my hair had been the first suggestion. Or at least wear it loose.

No to that one. My hair is thin. Baby fine, in fact. When it's short, there's nothing to it unless I turn it into a hair helmet and spray it to within an inch of its life. And as for wearing it loose? I look like some middle-aged broad trying to pretend she isn't.

Darker lipstick was the second tip.

Okay. Maybe I'd try that on my next trip to Walgreen's. And yes, I could use a manicure, but nail polish to match the lipstick? I'm not big on nail polish and I thought I'd leave that to Shannon, who has long, gorgeous nails and the time to take care of them.

Tighter, more feminine clothes had been another of Diane's recommendations.

I nixed that without a thought. Nobody's getting their hands on my turtlenecks and jeans, and I'm not wearing them as shrink wrap for anybody.

So all in all, on the makeover front, the advisory had been a bust. Not that I'd expected it to be much more. I can be kind of stubborn that way.

On the other hand, I had learned a couple of interesting things about Steffi Hargitay and Steve Stivik. And maybe about Diane herself.

I hadn't had the impression she was a drama queen, the way Steve had claimed, and she'd confirmed my own suspicion that the notebook/ledger Steve was looking for was more significant than he'd wanted me to believe.

I wondered if Danny knew about the missing notebook and the meetings or about the fight between Steve and Steffi, and I made a mental note to ask him. Then I gave my mirror a let-bygones-be-bygones shrug and went downstairs for dinner.

Steffi's murder was keeping Danny busy and away from home just as all new cases did, so it was ladies-

only for dinner. But we'd make sure there was a plate-
ful of Gramma's roasted chicken, glazed potatoes, fresh
tomato and cucumber salad, and homemade rolls waiting for him when he finally did come home.

"Lucy got out again," Chloe announced to me as we
sat down to eat.

"How?" I asked, exasperated because I'd hoped
Saturday's excursion would be a one-time occurrence.

"She dug another hole," Shannon said. "I found her
trying to get to Barney just like the last time."

I might have understood this better if Lucy was in
heat, but I'd had her spayed years ago and she'd never
shown any interest in any other dog before. In fact, she
was downright nasty to my brother's dog, Jerry, when
they were together.

"It's like Lucy and Barney are in love," Chloe
supplied.

"Did she wreck things there again?"

"I caught her before she could," Shannon answered.

"Did the doctor see her? You know he could file a
complaint with animal control if he wanted to."

"He wasn't home," my youngest daughter assured me.

"He wouldn't call the police anyway," Gramma put
in. "He's a nice man."

"Even nice men can get nasty when somebody else's
dog is tearing up their property," I pointed out.
"What's that guy's name, anyway? I wish one of you
had introduced us. I felt like an idiot."

"Ben. Dr. Barrows," Gramma said. "I thought you
knew."

"Nope. I'd never met him before and he didn't offer
his name when I told him who I was." Which didn't

help convince me of his nice-guy status. Although under the circumstances of Saturday anybody would have been ticked off, so I told myself to reserve judgment.

"And how did you two girls come to know him?" I asked my daughters as we all indulged in Gramma's cooking.

"Barney got out of his yard and came over here. That's how Barney and Lucy met," Chloe explained. She's the more romantic of the girls, and I could tell that that romanticism had come into play on this subject.

"We didn't know who he belonged to, so me and Chloe—"

"Chloe and I," I corrected.

"So I and Chloe went around ringing doorbells until we found his house," Shannon said. "Ben figured the lawn guys must have left the gate open. He wanted to give us a reward."

Ben? Shannon was on a first-name basis with the doctor?

"You didn't take it, did you?"

Shannon and Chloe both made faces at me.

"No, we didn't take it," Chloe said with exaggerated patience.

"And no, we didn't go into his house or anything, either, just in case he was a pervert," Shannon finished facetiously, anticipating my next motherly question.

"Aay, he's no pervert. He's a doctor." Gramma took up the gauntlet. She's of the old school that reveres anyone in the medical profession.

"Even doctors can be perverts, Gram," I pointed out, not as awed by his occupation as she was.

"Well, Ben's not. He keeps to himself, but he's not a pervert. He was married."

I refrained from the obvious comment about marriage not necessarily precluding perversion either. Gramma reveres that too.

Without my input, Gramma went on. "His wife was a lot younger than him. She ran off with his partner about three years ago. I heard at church that they stole Ben blind too. The wife emptied their bank accounts and even sold some paintings and things he had as investments, and his partner took from the business. Ben had to move into a smaller office by himself, and Marge across the street says he swore off women and partners. I thought of him for you, Jimi, but Marge said don't even think of it. He won't dirty his hands with another woman."

"I'm probably too old for his taste anyway. He probably has more of an eye for Chloe or Shannon," I joked.

"He can have Chloe," Shannon offered.

"Oh yeah, sure, I want some *old* guy."

"He's not old. He's forty, just right for your mother if some Jezebel didn't do bad by him and make him sour. I never liked that girl. She'd go out for the mail in the middle of the afternoon still in her nightclothes. He's better off without her."

That seemed to do it for the subject of the neighbor, so I said, "Did somebody plug up the hole Lucy made to get out today?"

"No, we left it there so she could get out again whenever she wants to." Shannon can be a smart-ass.

"I don't know what to do with her. Maybe one of us

is going to have to go out with her every time and scold her if she starts to dig. At least until she forgets about Barney."

"Or maybe we could just adopt Barney for her," Chloe suggested.

"Great idea. Just what we need—Lucy's very own Doberman love puppy." Okay, I can be a smart-ass sometimes too. "I doubt your Dr. Barrows would like to share custody of his dog with us. But if Lucy doesn't cut it out I might consider giving her to him," I said in a threatening tone aimed at Lucy, who always stays by my side during meals.

"Oh, sure, Mom," Shannon said, calling my bluff. "We'll just give Lucy away."

"Something has to be done to keep her from digging holes all over the place," I reiterated.

"We'll go out with her," Chloe promised.

"Good."

Because I didn't want to have any more dealings with the soured-on-women doctor.

"Now tell us what they told you at your makeover session today," Shannon said, changing the subject enthusiastically.

Maybe I'd rather have gone on talking about Lucy and the doctor.

"I was sent home with a sheet of beauty tips," I answered vaguely.

"I want to see them!" This from Chloe.

"Me too," Gramma chimed in.

"Me three," Shannon added. "Where are they?"

Oh good, an excuse for everyone to put in their two cents' worth.

"I think I threw it away," I lied, knowing full well it was still upstairs on my dresser.

Shannon gave me a sly smile as she stood. "I'll go look. I can get it out of your trash if you did," she said. Damn her anyway.

And off she went.

And I could have sworn Lucy smiled some kind of smug dog smile now that I was on the hot seat instead of her.

When it comes to cooking, it's a good thing we don't have to rely on my abilities. I make a few—very few—things that are edible. But as much as Gramma loves to cook, she hates to bake. And that's where I make up for my other culinary shortcomings.

For dessert and also to serve my potential client, I'd made a semisweet chocolate pâté that I served in a circle of custard sauce striped with raspberry puree.

Carl Cutler was a coffee drinker—I'd been the only one on Saturday morning to forgo the brew. But since I make lousy coffee, too, when he arrived Gramma made a pot.

While we waited for it Gramma had a long enough chat with him to promise him homemade spaghetti, to give him the history of his house, to tell him how to get his white shirts brighter, and to order me to find him the phone number for one of her sister's sons who could build Carl a shed like the one we have out back.

When the coffee was finally ready, I took it, the dessert, and Carl up to my attic loft. With cup and plate in hand, he settled in on the love seat while I sat at a ninety-degree angle to him on the overstuffed chair.

My space is pretty compact and a really big man wouldn't have fit in. But even though Carl was tall, he was so skinny he did just fine.

He was dressed casually but impeccably in well-tailored tan slacks and a beautiful blue cashmere polo-style sweater. It helped distinguish his otherwise not so attractive appearance with those very pointed features and the eyes that had a slight squint to them.

"I like your family," he said first thing. He'd met the girls, too, just before they'd both gone up to their rooms to study. "Your grandmother reminds me of my own."

"You're Italian?"

"Greek. Well, half Greek on my mother's side. But Greek grandmothers and Italian grandmothers are the same breed. Mine raised my sister and me after our folks were killed in a plane crash."

"Wow. How old were you when that happened?"

"Eleven. My sister was thirteen. Yaya's house was about three miles from here. She died a little over a year ago and Kim—my sister—and her family took over the house. I miss my grandmother. I'd like to scoop yours up and take her home with me."

I don't like even to think about anything happening to my grandmother. "I can't imagine how hard it must have been to lose both your parents at eleven."

He nodded his agreement as he tested the pâté. After he'd swallowed and given me his enthusiastic stamp of approval on the dessert he said, "I was an awkward kid anyway—homely as hell—big ears, big nose, too much chin, scrawny. I had one friend where we lived in Brighton, but when my parents were killed and I had to move here with Yaya, I was too far away for that friendship to go on. I never really connected with anybody else after that. Well, except maybe Steffi Hargitay."

"I didn't know you knew Steffi."

"Only as kids. I hadn't seen her since high school graduation. Couldn't believe my eyes when I went in for my orientation and there she was. And then to go back into the Center on Saturday and hear she was dead . . . God, I couldn't believe it. We were supposed to get together Saturday night to do some catching up."

"Did you date in school?"

He laughed and pointed to his physical features as he recataloged them. "Big ears, big nose, too much chin, scrawny body, remember? No, I was too big a geek for that. I had a miserable time growing up— which actually turned out to be a great thing for me because I spent all my time at an arcade near Yaya's house. My claim to fame was that I could beat anybody at any game. In a roundabout way that led to Cutler's Corner, which made me enough money to get my ears tucked and my nose reshaped. I'm still working on the scrawny part and the beard is supposed to hide the chin. But did I *date* Steffi back in school? Not hardly. She was a cheerleader. Homecoming queen. Prom queen. The stuff geek dreams are made of."

"But you were friends?"

"I tutored her in math—that was how we got to know each other. Those sessions were the highlights of my weeks. I thought she was an angel. And then, actually, she was."

"How so?"

"Most of the football team and the wrestling squad used me as their prime target for abuse. I was the kind of kid who got locked in lockers—among a lot of other things that were even less nice. One day a bunch of guys were giving me a hard time and Steffi came by. She put a stop to it. She stood up for me, made them let me go, even read them the riot act on my behalf."

That was a different facet of Steffi Hargitay than what Diane saw. But then maybe Steffi had a soft spot for underdogs and Diane could hardly be called an underdog.

"Did the abuse stop after that?"

"No, but it did get more confined to the locker room. None of my tormentors wanted Steffi Hargitay to know what pricks they really were. But after that it was easier for me to withstand it. Maybe it sounds crazy, but she'd told them all what stupid jerks they were and from then on, every time they bothered me I'd think about how Steffi Hargitay knew as well as I did that they were assholes." Carl laughed a little. "It was cold comfort but it was comfort."

"And then just when you meet up with her again, she dies."

He shook his head sadly. "I couldn't believe it," he agreed, the disbelief echoing in his voice. "God, what a waste. What a tragedy. Who could have done something like that to her?"

"I don't know. But I'm sure the police will find out."

Carl seemed lost in thought for a moment before he said, "You know what I keep thinking?"

"What?"

"That I wish I could have been there for her the way she was there for me that damn day in high school, to save her. I kind of feel as if I owed her and I let her down. That probably sounds dumb."

I could see shadows of a younger Carl in his expression and the sorrow he felt. I also imagined the fantasy that must have played out in his head about returning the long-ago favor and being Steffi's hero. It was too bad for them both that he hadn't had the chance.

"Did she say anything to you when you talked at your orientation meeting about any problems she was having with anybody or if someone was bothering her?"

Again he shook his head, this time in denial. "No. We just talked about things like the Milk Duds I used to bring her when we studied together, and how my nose was so hooked I could hold a pencil underneath it, and the time she stuck two pencils up her nose and pretended to be a walrus—silly stuff like that. Old times."

"Did you notice her giving anybody a strange look when she saw them or did you see a black notebook on her desk maybe?"

"You know, come to think of it, there was one thing. Remember that woman with us on Saturday morning—the one with the flower in her hair?"

"Delia Grant."

"She was waiting for Steffi when my orientation ended. She said she wanted to see Steffi, that she had a complaint. I just figured it was something to do with the Center. You don't suppose she was mad at Steffi herself?"

"When was this?"

"A week ago Monday."

"Did you tell the police about it?"

"I didn't even remember until right this minute. She probably was just peeved over a bad locker combination or something that didn't have anything to do with Steffi. It isn't like she stormed into the office and made a death threat."

"How about outside the Center? Have you ever heard anything through the grapevine about Steffi or what she'd been doing since high school?"

"Not a word. But like I said, I didn't come away from the second half of my school years with any friends. I haven't been in on any grapevines."

"How about a class reunion? You've probably been out of school ten years, haven't you?"

"As of last June. But I didn't go to the reunion. It wasn't as if high school was such a good time for me that I wanted to see those people again."

"Not even Steffi?"

Once more he shook his head. "I remembered her fondly but it wasn't as if I'd carried some kind of torch for her all this time. Meeting up with her at the Center was just a happy coincidence but I wouldn't have gone back to see the rest of those assholes for anything or anybody."

I couldn't blame him.

"You know," he said, squinting at me as if he needed to take a closer look. "You sound a lot like the police when they questioned me."

Oh, good, just the impression I wanted to give a new client—that I was interrogating him.

Well, okay, I *was* interrogating him. But I didn't want him to realize it.

"Sorry," I said with a little laugh. "It's this insatiable curiosity I have. Gets me into trouble all the time."

I was glad to see him smile and not take offense.

"You're good, though. You got me to remember more than I did for the cops on Saturday."

"Probably just because you're relaxed. I don't think anybody is calm when they talk to cops."

"Maybe they should hire you."

"I thought that was what you were here to do," I joked.

"I am. But not before you give me the name of that cousin of yours who can give me an estimate on building my shed."

I'd forgotten about that.

I did it and then Carl and I finally got down to business.

But it wasn't easy for me to concentrate on the list of things Carl wanted to include in his prospectus. There was lots on my mind that I wanted to talk to Danny about.

And then, too, I couldn't help wondering what my former classmate, Delia Grant, had been so upset about that she'd complained to Steffi.

Chapter Eight

MY MEETING WITH Carl Cutler ended at about nine-thirty. Once we'd gotten past talking about Steffi Hargitay's death his natural ebullience had returned, and by the time he left I'd felt as if we were old friends. It occurred to me that it wasn't only his appearance that must have changed since his high school geek days. His personality and his social skills must have changed, too, because he seemed self-assured and comfortable, and he'd put me completely at ease too.

And again it occurred to me that he'd be a good counterbalance for Brenda Merchant, who I'd encouraged him to ask out.

Carl hadn't been gone five minutes when there was a knock on my interior door. I knew it was Danny. He was the only one who knocked. I'd been about to go downstairs to see if he was home yet anyway, so this just saved me the trip.

"Come in, Danny."

He did. He'd changed out of his work clothes into a gray sweat suit, white socks, and no shoes. Which was a good thing because he went right across to the love seat and sat lengthwise on it with his back against one arm and his feet propped on the other.

"I hear we have chocolate pâté up here."

"And I thought it was just my company you wanted."

"That too."

I sliced him an inch of the rich confection, decorated it with the custard sauce and raspberry puree, and poured him a glass of milk to go with it—all out of the mini refrigerator in my mini kitchen. Then I took the same spot I'd occupied all evening on the overstuffed chair, kicking off my shoes too.

"Did you arrest somebody for Steffi's murder?" I asked, cutting to the chase.

Danny shook his head as he let the pâté melt on his tongue.

When it had, he said, "Not even close."

"Carl Cutler was just here," I offered. "I'm doing a prospectus for him. We had an interesting chat about Steffi before we talked business, though." I went on to tell my cousin what I'd learned from my new client.

Danny already knew everything except that Delia had been mad about something and wanted to complain to Steffi.

"Carl said he'd forgotten all about it until tonight but he didn't think Delia was necessarily mad at Steffi personally. And she didn't threaten her or anything."

"I haven't interviewed Delia yet but I'll make sure to ask about it when I do."

"But you have talked to Carl?" I pressed, curious to know what Danny's take on him was.

Danny nodded. "Energetic guy. Like Chloe."

"I thought the same thing. No wonder he's a success. Did he tell you anything you can use?"

"Not much, but why should he be any different from anybody else I've talked to on this case? He seems to be alone in liking Steffi Hargitay, so far, though."

"It seemed genuine to me."

"Yeah, me too. And he has an alibi."

I was glad to hear that.

"We have his voice time stamped on the answering machine tape at her apartment at about the time of death. He was calling to confirm their date for the next night. From Laddy's. With witnesses."

Laddy's was an Irish pub, the only bar in the community.

"Do you have anybody without an alibi?"

"So far? Everybody else I've talked to. Steve Stivik had a date with Brenda Merchant but had gone home to get ready for it and they didn't hook up until an hour and a half later—plenty of time for either of them to do the deed."

"Steve Stivik and Brenda Merchant had a date?"

"I know—go figure."

"I think Carl has a little thing for her too."

"I'm not so sure Stivik has a *thing* for her."

"What other reason would he have for dating her?"

"I don't know. I just can't see it. I mean, yeah, okay, maybe she and Cutler hit it off—they're more each other's type. But Stivik? He strikes me as an operator.

Not the kind who'd go for a chubby, limp-haired, meek little mouse."

I hated Danny's description of Brenda. Even if it was true, it was merciless.

"Steve Stivik came on to me," I told my cousin. "Maybe he's his own personal relations department. Maybe he does it with all the new female recruits to make them feel like the Center is money well spent because they've already drawn attention from the opposite sex."

"That I could see. Not that I don't think he could have been genuinely interested in you, Jimi."

"Nice save. But he wasn't. I'm not his type any more than Brenda Merchant is. Besides, I could tell he had ulterior motives. I just didn't know what they were."

"But somebody like Brenda Merchant—"

"Would probably just be flattered and think he really liked her," I finished Danny's thought. "Maybe he toyed with Steffi too."

"Something's strange there."

"Between Steffi and Steve?"

"He doesn't seem to have liked her. Yet not only did he keep her on, she almost seemed to be his partner. Even though she wasn't. Like I said, strange."

"I had the same feeling," I agreed. "Did Diane or anyone else tell you about the fight between Steffi and Steve a couple of weeks ago?"

"Diane did."

"Complete with Steffi hollering that she had something coming to her from Steve and she intended to make sure she got it?"

"Yep."

"Know what any of that means?"

"Nope. And Steve claims he doesn't have any idea who could have told me such a thing because it never happened. There never was an argument. Steffi had nothing coming to her from him but her paycheck and never demanded more, never said anything about making sure she got anything else out of him. *Nada*. I haven't talked to Gary Oldershaw or Irene Oatman about it yet for confirmation, but I will."

"And I suppose you know the fight started over Steffi's wanting Irene Oatman fired."

"Which Irene Oatman couldn't afford to have happen. Sounds like Diane has her story pretty down pat."

"You think it's only a story?"

"Don't know. And won't until I talk to some other people about it."

"Who else have you interviewed beyond the preliminaries on Saturday morning?" I asked.

"Diane Samboro—obviously since she told me about the fight. She didn't like Steffi Hargitay. I get the impression they were rivals."

"I know they weren't friends. What were they rivals for?"

"Men, would be my guess. Hunters after the same prey."

"And Diane may have her sights set on you."

Danny made a face. "She's too young for me."

Maybe Barney the Doberman's doctor dad would like her.

But I didn't say that. Instead I said, "Did Diane have an alibi?"

"She was getting ready for a late date, too, but was home alone at the time, so no. Bert Chumley was the last to see Steffi alive. Well, except for the killer. Unless he was the killer."

"Bert? That nice old man? I was thinking of him for Gramma."

"I'd think again if I were you. He seems more inclined toward younger women. Seems as if he was with Steffi, asking her out."

This time I made the face. "He's old enough to be her grandfather. Maybe even her *great*-grandfather."

"Uh-huh."

"Think she turned him down, he got mad and beaned her?"

"Maybe. But he says she agreed to go out with him."

"Gross."

"Uh-huh." Danny set his empty plate on the coffee table and clamped his hands behind his head. "Besides, Nellie is sweet on the butcher and the butcher is sweet on her. Haven't you heard her say he saves her that veal pocket roast when she smiles at him?"

"She's been smiling at the butcher for the past twenty years and it's never gone beyond that."

"And if she's going to push you to date then you want to push her to, too."

"Hey, why should I be the only one to suffer?" Then I went back to the subject at hand. "What about outside the Center? Did Steffi have family? A boyfriend?"

"She has a sister in Georgia who didn't seem all that broken up about her death. Said they'd never been close. Her father's in California but he hadn't seen her in over ten years. Her mother's dead. As for a boyfriend—there doesn't seem to have been anybody special but she has a date book that's a mile long. It's going to take more man-hours than I want to think about to get through it."

That reminded me of two things. I told Danny about Steffi's former relationship with Gary Oldershaw.

"Didn't know about that," he said as if he found it very interesting.

Then I said, "And speaking of books—" I told him about Steve pressing me for information about the notebook/ledger.

"He asked me, too, and half a dozen cops on the scene. But there was nothing like that on her body, in her purse or office, or at her apartment."

"Do you think it has anything to do with her murder?"

Danny shrugged. "Don't know. Stivik claims no. That there was nothing in it anybody would want. But he's sure hot to have it back. Makes me wonder."

Danny swung his legs off the love seat and sat facing me. "And that's about it for now," he said like a news-caster wrapping up the evening report. "You aren't going out with Stivik, are you?"

I rolled my eyes. "I don't want to go out with any-body, but even if I did, it wouldn't be with him."

"Carl Cutler?"

"No. He's ten years younger than I am."

"Women do it too. You know Nellie says you should marry them young and raise them right."

"She said that about Grandpa because he was two years younger than she was. I like Carl but I'm not attracted to him and I wouldn't go out with him even if he was my age."

"You're going to drag your feet about this, aren't you?"

"I'm just not going to do anything more than go through the motions at the Center for Gramma and the girls' sake."

"Maybe it would do you some good to really get into the swing of things there and actually go out with somebody."

"Or maybe it wouldn't," I said amiably.

"A little wining. A little dining. A little sex . . ."

I closed my eyes, sighed, and shook my head to convey my long-sufferingness. Then I said, "Go home."

"I am home."

"Go to your room, then."

He stood to do just that. But not without first saying, "Seriously, Jimi, it wouldn't hurt you to get out a little, have some fun for a change."

"So I keep hearing. That's why I was thinking of joining a luge team."

"Great idea but the outfits are pretty tight."

"Oh, too bad, guess I'll have to come up with plan B."

He gave me the you're-not-funny look and finally said good night, leaving me to wonder why it was that everybody thought I couldn't be happy without romance in my life.

Especially when even murder was less complicated.

And probably not quite as painful.

Chapter Nine

I SPENT WEDNESDAY morning doing some preliminary work on the prospectus for Cutler's Corner. I organized the notes I'd taken the night before while Carl and I had talked, and did a quick outline.

By lunchtime I had a pretty good idea of what I'd say to make the establishment appealing to people looking to buy a franchise. So, when Gramma started to talk about what she wanted to give her sister Soondy—a childhood nickname for Susanne—for her upcoming eighty-ninth birthday, the wheels in my head started to turn in a different direction.

At a quarter after one we were headed for The World Is Your Oyster travel agency.

Gramma thought a plane ticket for Soondy to visit her son in Arizona was a good birthday gift.

And I thought the trip to the travel agency would give me a good opportunity to talk to Brenda Merchant and Delia Grant.

As it turned out, when we got to the small storefront agency in the Plaza strip mall a few blocks from home, only Delia was there.

She had on a loosely flowing, ankle-length tank dress made of lightweight cotton with an all-over pattern of big flowers in shades of pumpkin orange and banana yellow. In deference to the January temperature she wore a white sweater underneath it, turning the sundress into a jumper. And her long coffee-bean brown hair was pulled back on one side by a calla lily.

She seemed delighted to see us, delighted to meet my grandmother. But before we could do more than the introduction a deliveryman came in with several packages Delia needed to sign for.

As she did that at the entrance to the office Gramma whispered, "Ooo, she's a pretty girl, isn't she?"

"She has a pretty face," I agreed. It was true, she did. But I thought that the luau attire detracted from it.

On the other hand I had the feeling the flower in Delia's hair and the clothes were just what my grandmother liked. For the most part Gramma has good taste. But sometimes she surprises me. For instance, she has a perfectly nice chenille bedspread on her bed. But where other people might decorate it with throw pillows as a finishing touch, Gramma props a teddy bear that plays "When the Saints Go Marching In" and a Barbie doll against the headboard.

I thought that Delia's chosen style of dress might fall into the category of the music-box bear and the Barbie doll—an appeal I didn't exactly understand.

While Delia was busy I took stock of the office.

It was nothing fancy. Two identical gray metal desks stood side-by-side facing the front wall of glass that looked out on the parking lot—the other desk with Brenda's nameplate on it. Besides the two visitors' chairs pointed at each desk there were four more chairs that looked as if they'd come from a garage sale where someone had sold their Early American dinette set. Those formed a waiting area along the glass wall. There were also two tall filing cabinets and a coffee stand, and the three solid walls were papered in travel posters promising fantasy vacations. All in all, serviceable but not what you'd call plush.

"Can I get you coffee or tea?" Delia said to announce her return.

"None for me, thanks," I answered.

Gramma declined the offer too.

"My grandmother wanted to get a plane ticket for a birthday gift and I remembered that you and Brenda were travel agents," I said to explain our being there.

Gramma chimed in then with the details. More details than Delia actually needed to know, like the fact that Gramma came from a family of nine sisters and two brothers and where in the birth order she was and how many of those brothers and sisters were living and how many were dead and how close she was with some and not with others.

Delia was not only patient with it all, she actually seemed interested, which won her a lot of points in my book.

"Are you Hawaiian?" Gramma asked when she was finished with the family history. "I mean, is that where you come from and why you wear that flower in your hair?"

I cringed a little at that one. I wasn't too sure if Delia would be offended by it or not.

But she didn't seem to be. In fact, she and Gramma were hitting it off like two old cronies.

"No, I'm not Hawaiian. It's just how I see myself. Floating along a path through a tropical forest in the moonlight. It's how I want other people to see me too."

"Well, you're so pretty. I just thought you were a beautiful Hawaiian girl," Gramma said.

Delia beamed at the compliment, turning to include me as she said, "It's so nice to meet people who have some appreciation for uniqueness. I thought when I got out of high school I'd seen the last of small minds and lack of imagination but here I am, running into it again."

"At the New You Center?" I asked, trying not to appear too eager for the opening I hoped she'd just given me.

"I don't want to be a *new* me. I like the *old* me. I joined for the tips on dating and the dating service and hopefully to connect with some new men, not be insulted."

"You were insulted at the New You Center?"

"By Steffi Hargitay," Delia confided in a whisper, as if there were someone else in the place to overhear.

"Is that the girl who got murdered?" Gramma asked.

Delia nodded. "And I'm not surprised. She wasn't nice at all."

"Did she make fun of you?" This from me.

"She was very nasty. Right from the start she looked down her nose at me. We—Brenda and I—went in on our lunch break the week before last for our orientation. Steffi did mine and Steve Stivik—the owner—did Brenda's, and—"

I had to interrupt. "Steve said Steffi did all the orientations."

"She didn't do Brenda's. Steve did. And it was more than an orientation. He put the munch on her."

"He asked her out?" I asked, just to be sure I knew what putting the munch on someone was.

"He said a lot of flattering things to her and then yes, he asked her out."

The tone in Delia's voice said she didn't approve of his actions. Even though I agreed, I said, "Is that a bad thing?"

"There's just something about him that I don't like. Of course, maybe that's because I overheard him make a smart-aleck comment about the flower in my hair when he didn't know I was standing behind him, but still, as far as I'm concerned he's no better than Steffi was."

So much for personal relations.

"What kind of grown man does that? It sounds like something a bad boy would do," Gramma said, outraged on Delia's behalf.

"Well, grown man or bad boy, he's the kind that I'm afraid will hurt someone like my friend Brenda," Delia answered, aiming it at Gramma and then going on to explain. "Brenda is so shy and she hasn't had much experience with men. Especially not men like Steve Stivik—I think he's just a piranha looking for his next meal. But what can I say about it? I can't hurt Brenda's feelings and tell her I don't think he likes her for herself, can I?"

"No, you can't tell a friend that," Gramma commiserated.

But I was thinking that again Steve Stivik seemed to have an ulterior motive.

I wanted to explore that, but Delia was obviously very fond and protective of Brenda and I didn't think it was wise to agree too strongly that Brenda's appeal was a mystery. It was apt to put Delia off and I didn't want to do that.

"Did you say that Steffi was insulting to you during your orientation?" I asked.

Delia adjusted her flower hair ornament. "Steffi said the Leilani look definitely had to go if I ever wanted a date because she knew for a fact that Don Ho wasn't in the video library of available men."

Another strike against personal relations.

"And that's not the worst," Delia went on. "She threatened me."

"She was probably just jealous of you," Gramma put in.

"How did Steffi threaten you?" I asked.

"Well, I've been going to the exercise class that Gary Oldershaw gives—have you met him yet?"

"He let me into the building on Saturday morning."

"I just really like him and I guess I've been flirting a little with him and I sort of let him know I'd like to go out with him. Steffi must have seen us talking or something because she cornered me in the locker room last week and told me to stay away from him. She said I was nothing but a joke and somebody like Gary would never want anything to do with me and I should stop bothering him. And if I didn't, she'd make me sorry I was ever born."

"What did you do?" I asked.

"I called her a bitch," Delia whispered again.

"Good for you!" Gramma cheered.

"And then I reported her to Steve. But that only made it worse. He talked to her but he didn't *do* anything about it. She said there was nothing he *could* do about it. And then she started calling me at home. Late at night. Every night until I'd take my phone off the hook."

"Did she call you to talk or—"

Delia shook her head firmly at my suggestion of anything remotely amiable.

"She called me names, and told me how stupid and ugly I am, how she and Steve and Gary all had a good laugh over my clothes and hair, just awful things. Like I said, I'd have to take the phone off the hook. I even went into her office one day to tell her I was going to file a complaint with the phone company if she didn't quit it. But all she said then was that I'd better stay away from Gary or I was going to get more than a phone call from her."

"You should have called the police. Our Danny wouldn't have let her get away with that," Gramma assured.

I didn't remind Gramma that Danny was a homicide detective and wouldn't have handled a call like that in any event.

Instead I said, "You must have been kind of afraid of her. I think I would have been."

"I kept my doors locked, that's for sure."

"But you were still going to the Center?"

"I thought about stopping and demanding my money back. Especially since Steve hadn't done anything but make things worse when I complained to him. But, well, I really like Gary and I think he kind of likes me, too. And I'm working on him to get him to ask me out. I couldn't do that if I didn't go to the Center. Plus there's Brenda too. If I stopped going so would she and I'd feel guilty about that. In a way it would be good because maybe then Steve would leave her alone. But in another way, she wouldn't meet anybody else, either, and maybe that would be even worse because she'd glom onto Steve even more and pin her hopes on him. I decided to just keep going and maybe Brenda would meet somebody else she liked better and I could get things started with Gary and then we could quit." Delia shrugged. "But now that's not a problem because Steffi isn't there anymore. And I'm sorry, but I can't say it's a loss to the world."

It flashed through my mind to ask where Delia had been Friday night when Steffi was killed, but I couldn't think of a way to do that and not sound as if I was interrogating her without a license.

And then, before I had the chance to say any more at all, another customer came in.

Delia greeted the man, said she'd be right with him, and suddenly, as if the teacher had walked into the classroom and caught us gossiping, we were back to business.

Delia asked Gramma a few date-and-time questions, punched some things into her computer, then told us she'd shop around for the best price for Soondy's ticket to Arizona and give Gramma a call.

But rather than just leaving it at that, Gramma said, "Why don't you come to dinner at our house on Sunday night? You can bring the information with you."

I hadn't seen that one coming.

"Oh, you're so nice! I'd love to."

"Come at six o'clock," Gramma said, rattling off our address for Delia to copy down and insisting that Delia not bring anything.

Then Gramma shot to her feet like an energetic toddler and I had no choice but to follow suit.

We said our good-byes and Gramma and I left.

"Why did you invite her to dinner?" I asked the minute we were safely out of earshot.

"For Danny."

"For Danny? Danny can question her anytime. I don't think he wants it to be over dinner at our house."

"Not to question her. I thought she'd be good for him."

"To date? Oh, Gram . . ." I groaned as we got into the car.

But my lack of enthusiasm didn't register with her and she stopped me from saying any more by turning on the radio as soon as I started the engine so she could listen to the family therapist on the talk station.

Not that I had any illusion about changing my grandmother's mind once she'd set it on something.

So instead, I just settled into my own thoughts as I drove us home.

Those thoughts went back to our conversation with Delia as I wondered why Steve Stivik had done Brenda's orientation in the first place when there seemed to be no reason why Steffi couldn't have walked both Brenda and Delia through it at the same time. It was almost as if he'd known he was going to put the munch—as Delia had said—on Brenda before he'd ever set eyes on her. And why, having done Brenda's orientation, had Steve lied about it and said Steffi did them all?

People didn't lie without a reason, and that reason was usually to cover something up.

But what? Was it just that he didn't want to broadcast that he was hitting on Brenda Merchant? Or was there something else?

I didn't have any answers.

But I did have one more question.

What was Danny going to do when he found out that Gramma was trying to fix him up with Delia?

Chapter Ten

"**D**ELIA GRANT? YOU'RE trying to matchmake me with Delia Grant?"

Danny was not happy when he heard the news at dinner that night.

The girls had gone to the library after we'd eaten and Danny, Gramma, and I were sitting at the table having tapioca for dessert.

"You could do worse," my grandmother insisted. "She's a nice girl with that pretty long hair."

I'd thought the membership at the New You Center was bad. But at least everything beyond my enrollment had been left to me. Gramma's arranging a blind date for Danny with someone of her choice was worse.

Danny turned diplomat. "I can't date a suspect, Nellie."

"A suspect? That nice girl? She couldn't hurt a fly."

"Steffi Hargitay was tormenting and bullying her. She was cruel to her. She was trying to interfere in a relationship Delia wants to cultivate. Delia was at the Center Friday night. No one knows when she left. She claims she was home by eight—long before closing and the time of death—but she was alone, didn't speak to anyone on the phone or see anyone who can verify that. She fought with the victim twenty-four hours before the murder and was threatened by Steffi. Believe me, Delia Grant is a suspect."

"No matter what you say, I know that nice girl didn't do anything wrong. And I already invited her to dinner Sunday night."

Danny put his head in his hand. "Nellie . . ." he said, part groan, part warning.

"She didn't do anything," Gramma repeated. "And I can't uninvite her, now can I? Just get to know her a little, Danny. You'll see."

"How about if I ask Carl and Brenda to come too?" I suggested. "Then it'll seem more like a get-together than a setup."

Danny looked at me as if I'd lost my mind too. "You're doing the same thing, aren't you? Trying to fix those two up."

I shrugged. "Brenda and Delia seem to be close and I hate to see Brenda with Steve Stivik. I think Carl likes her, so what harm can it do? Who knows, it might even help your investigation. Everybody will be more relaxed, they'll feel as if you don't really suspect them, and you never know what you might find out."

"The Jimi Plain method of investigation," Danny said, in a tone of voice that indicated he was no more pleased with me than with Gramma at that moment. "But the truth is, you don't think any of the three of them did it or you wouldn't want them over here any more than I do."

I shrugged again. "I don't know who did in Steffi Hargitay, but we'll keep our video camera under lock and key so we'll all be safe, just in case. Or you could wear your gun to dinner."

"You better not wear your gun to my dinner," Gramma warned, missing the fact that I was just being as facetious as Danny had been.

He stood just then, letting me know he'd had about enough of the whole conversation. "I think I'll go downstairs and catch a little TV," he said, heading for the cherry wood door.

But before he disappeared down the steps, he stopped short and turned around again. "I almost forgot. My car's on the fritz and I had to leave it with the mechanic this afternoon. Can I use yours tomorrow, Jimi?"

"Sure. I'm just working all day. I won't need it. Or if something comes up I can use one of Gramma's." Danny didn't like the old Nova or the '57 Chevy that spent their life in the garage because they'd belonged to my grandfather and Gramma didn't drive. "I'll bring you the keys after we do the dishes."

"Great, thanks."

"You make sure about Sunday night," Gramma called after him as he left.

Danny just waved a hand over his shoulder at her and disappeared down the stairs.

"You don't think that nice Delia could kill anybody, do you?" Gramma demanded of me after Danny had gone.

I gave her a raised eyebrow. "Danny makes a good circumstantial case against her. You never know."

"Oh, you're both crazy. And that Carl didn't do it, either, so go ahead and ask him to dinner too. Along with that Brenda. I'll make a big bowl of rigatoni. Everybody likes rigatoni."

Chapter Eleven

I'D DITCHED THE class on how and where to meet my magnificent mate, but I had my own reasons for wanting to go to Tiramisù and Tetrazzini, Too on Thursday night. And not because I didn't know what tiramisù or tetrazzini were.

Luckily, after having my car all day long, Danny got it back in time for me to leave early for the seven o'clock class. I drove to the Center through a light snowfall that floated from the sky on angel's wings, hoping it wouldn't start to snow like the devil before I had to drive home.

The Center was as busy on Thursday night as it had been on Monday. Maybe more so since the video counter was surrounded at least two-deep and poor Irene Oatman was working her tail off trying to fill demands for what I could only guess were last-ditch efforts at weekend dates.

The Center's two classrooms were down the left wing along with the conference room, the exercise room, the weight room, the locker room, and the sauna. I'd barely turned the corner to get to classroom number one when I ran smack-dab into Steve Stivik.

"Well, if it isn't Mizzz Plain," he said, hissing like a snake.

"Hi, Steve," I returned the greeting, debating with myself suddenly about whether to pursue the new set of questions I had for him—mainly about his lies—or to bypass him so I could reach my real goal of the evening.

"You're just the woman I wanted to see," he said before I'd decided. "Have you heard anything about my ledger or thought about where it might be?"

He made that sound casual, off-the-cuff, again as if it were no big deal, as if he were just wondering. But also as if I had some obligation to find the notebook he seemed to think I knew more about than I did.

"How would I have heard anything about it or know where it might be?"

I got a shrug and a wink in response to that. I knew the shrug was so he could go on seeming as if the notebook wasn't important to him. I didn't know what the wink was for.

"I heard that detective—what's his name? Del something or the other?"

"Delvecchio."

"Delvecchio. Is your cousin."

I should have kept my mouth shut on that score.

"Yes, he's my cousin. But that doesn't mean he tells me about police business."

"My ledger is police business?"

I'd struck a nerve.

"Must be or you wouldn't be wondering if my cousin has it."

"Does he?"

"I know as much as you do."

"Mmm."

That mere muttering was as close to being called a liar as I'd ever come. Right back atcha, guy.

Then he said, "And you haven't thought about maybe seeing it yourself? Or remembering seeing somebody else take it?"

"I can't remember what I never saw or saw happening."

He raised his chin as if he were going to nod but instead stalled on the upsweep and looked down his nose at me. "But you'll, uh, let me know if you do hear anything or remember anything."

I didn't like the undertone of intimidation in his voice.

"Can't imagine that I would hear anything or remember anything, but you'll be the first to know if I do," I assured with my own undertone of facetiousness.

Then I made a quick decision that I didn't want to spend any more time with Steve Stivik, so I tapped my watch face. "Sorry I can't talk more. Food class, you know."

"Sure," he said as if I'd just made him all the more suspicious of me.

But I didn't wait for him to say anything else.

He was standing in my way and whatever intimidation he was employing apparently kept him rooted there like some mighty brick wall. I just went around him and continued on my way to the classroom Steffi had shown me on the orientation tour.

But before I went inside I glanced over my shoulder to see Steve Stivik standing in the same spot, watching me.

I had an inordinate urge to flip him off.

Instead I winked at him.

Let him wonder.

I'd wanted to get to the Center early because I was betting that that was just what Brenda Merchant and Delia Grant would do so Delia could have a few minutes to work on project Get a Date with Gary Oldershaw before class. I wasn't sure if that's where she was, but where she *wasn't* was in the classroom with Brenda. Brenda was there all by her lonesome, just as I'd been hoping she would be.

She was sitting in the farthest corner seat of the last row, looking as if she wished she were invisible. As I went in I pretended to be surprised to see anybody else there already.

The room wasn't large and was set up with thirty folding chairs—five rows of six—all facing a podium at the front. Three of the walls were bare, the fourth had a large cork bulletin board on it announcing the Center's classes, services, and upcoming social functions.

I headed down the second-to-last row, sitting in the folding chair directly ahead of Brenda. I was reasonably sure the one beside her was meant for Delia and I didn't want to get us off on the wrong foot by taking it.

"Hi, Brenda. Remember me? Jimi Plain?" I said, turning sideways on my seat so I could see her.

"Yes," she allowed in that near whisper of a voice. "Hi."

She had on brown polyester pants and a fisherman's knit sweater that had a frayed edge around her right wrist where she grasped it with her fingertips and worried it against her thigh. Her hair was just as it had been on Saturday morning—hanging loose and limp, the bangs at half-mast over her eyes.

She didn't want to make conversation and so looked down at her lap as if that erased my presence.

But I'm not that easily ignored. At least not when I don't want to be.

"Did Delia tell you my grandmother and I were in at the agency yesterday?"

"Yes."

"Delia's helping Gramma with a plane ticket."

Nothing.

"I wanted to talk to you, too, though. Gramma and I are having a few people over for dinner on Sunday night and I wondered if you'd like to come."

Brenda raised her head a fraction and hazarded a glance at me. "Who all will be there?"

"My family—including my cousin Danny. Delia. Carl Cutler—I spoke to him on the phone this afternoon. And you."

"Bert Chumley?"

There was something steely in even the soft utterance of the elderly man's name. Something steely and laced with contempt. It surprised me.

"No, not Bert Chumley. Just Carl, Delia, and you."

"Carl's definitely going?"

The steely dislike evaporated and a lighter note chimed in her voice, this time maybe with a dash of hopefulness. And I even thought I might have seen a twitch at the corner of her pale mouth that I could count as a smile. If I really stretched the point.

"Carl's definitely coming," I confirmed.

"And it's Sunday night?"

"Sunday night."

She seemed to consider it. Then she said, "Okay."

"Great. Hopefully this weekend will end up better than the last one."

I knew it wasn't much of a lead-in. But I was getting no help from Brenda, so I was on my own with this one.

I paused just a moment to signal the subject change I was about to make and then said, "I only met Steffi once. During my orientation. But after talking to Delia it sounds like I was lucky not to have had any more contact with her. She really gave Delia a bad time, didn't she?"

"Very bad."

And that was it. Even when I waited for more, she didn't offer it.

"Was Steffi that nasty to you too?" I tried again.

"She didn't do my orientation."

"Had you even met her?"

"I'd met her."

This was like pulling teeth.

"Was she nicer to you than she was to Delia?"

"You couldn't call it nice."

"Did she do your makeover counseling or something?"

"No."

Still nothing, even when I again waited for more.

I decided to try another tack.

"I understand Steve did your orientation."

The corner of her mouth twitched again and I considered it encouragement.

"And you two hit it off," I said, one old chum to another.

I actually got a real smile for that. A shy one. But a smile. And a nod along with it.

"Have you been going out?" Me again.

"Twice."

"Good dates?"

She smiled for real again. "He took me to two of the fanciest restaurants I've ever been to."

"That's nice."

She agreed with a nod. "I wouldn't even care if we didn't go to such fancy places."

"Hey, I say sit back and enjoy it."

"It's hard to enjoy it when it's so expensive and I know he can't afford it," Brenda said, looking at her knees rather than at me.

"Can't afford it? I don't know, from looking at this place, I'd say it's doing well enough. And Steve is the sole owner."

"I don't think the school is doing all that well."

"Why is that?"

Her face turned the color of blood plums and she let silence fall.

Finally she said, "Both times we went out to dinner his credit card got rejected."

"Ouch. That's embarrassing." I wondered if Steve

had turned as red in the face over it as Brenda had just thinking about it.

"It is," she agreed softly.

I don't know what made me think to ask my next question, except that somehow I couldn't picture Steve Stivik embarrassed. "Did he end up having to write a check or did he have enough cash with him to pay the bill?"

She shook her head solemnly.

"You had to pick up the checks?" I guessed when she didn't offer the information.

She nodded her affirmation. "I felt awful for him."

"Did he reimburse you later on?"

"He said he'd make it up to me—that's what the second date was for—to make up for the first."

"And now he has to make up for the second?"

Again the nod. "That's how Steffi was nasty."

Brenda had lost me. "How was Steffi nasty?"

"She made some comments to Steve when he was asking me out the second time and then after that, too."

"What kind of comments?"

"About telling me the truth."

"Comments like that Steve should tell you the truth?"

"No. Like she would. I guess like she would tell me he wasn't doing very well financially. He got mad. It wasn't as bad as what she did with Delia but, well, Steffi was . . . a pain."

That steeliness sounded in Brenda's voice again, and again I heard contempt. Along with maybe a note of jealousy.

"Do you think Steffi and Steve were personally involved?" I ventured.

Brenda shrugged a bony shoulder. "He said they weren't."

"Did Steffi ever tell you to stay away from him like she told Delia to stay away from Gary Oldershaw?"

"No. But she wouldn't leave us alone. She was even at the same restaurant we went to on the second date."

"Coincidentally?"

"I don't think so. It was like she was waiting for us. Like her being there was supposed to be some kind of reminder for Steve."

"A reminder of what?"

Another shrug. Another "I don't know." And another ring of steel as Brenda said, "I only know I didn't like her being there."

I took a closer look at Brenda Merchant because while she might have been painfully quiet and shy, I was beginning to see another side of her. A side that made me think that had Steffi decided to tangle with Brenda over Steve she might have met with a stronger foe than she had in Delia. A side that made me wonder why Delia was so protective of Brenda.

And speaking of Delia, she came in then, along with a swell of other people including Diane Samboro, who was giving the class.

Brenda looked up as Delia took the chair beside her and seemed grateful to have my attention diverted.

There wasn't much I could do to continue our conversation and I had to be satisfied with what little I'd learned from Brenda. I exchanged a few words with

Delia and then turned around in my seat as the class began.

But all through the lecture on new fads in food and who-paid-for-what etiquette, I couldn't get the thought out of my mind that there was more to the timid Brenda than met the eye.

Chapter Twelve

I WENT BACK to work when I got home. Overlapping projects call for late hours sometimes and since I'd neglected the kitchen catalog to do the preliminaries on Carl's prospectus, I wasn't as far along as I should have been with the catalog. I'm not against burning the midnight oil anyway. I'm more of a night person than a morning person.

I kept the computer fired up until a little before midnight, when I hit a good stopping point. Then I decided to call it a day.

It was snowing like crazy and I was hoping Lucy would stay snoozing on the overstuffed chair rather than want to go out. But the minute she saw me turn down the quilt on my bed, she headed for the outside door, letting me know she wanted one last doggy whiz of the night.

It was miserable outside. I was tired. I still needed to wash my face and get into my pajamas and all those nightly ritual things that close out the day.

Translation: I did not want to go outside to keep an eye on her and make sure she didn't somehow get out of the yard.

I thought that surely she was ready to turn in, too, and would trot down the stairs, do her business, and come right back. She never stayed out in the cold for long anyway, so I opted for opening the door and just watching her prance outside.

"Don't you leave the yard," I warned.

But apparently I'd used up all my good luck on getting Brenda Merchant alone before the food class at the Center. Because even though I only gave Lucy the time it took me to undress and take a towel and washcloth out of the closet, when I stuck my head outside to call her in again, she didn't come.

I whistled. I made that kissing noise dogs seem to like. I called her name as loudly as I could without waking the dead.

But the little stinker never reappeared.

That's what I get for being lazy. Instead of two minutes standing on the landing I had to drag on my sweat suit, jam my feet into my snow boots, and go looking for her.

Damn dog. I love her but sometimes . . .

I grabbed my keys and slipped quietly out my door, trying to navigate the creaky wooden stairs without making too much noise.

Once I hit the snow-covered ground I did another round of calling, whistling, and kissing air into the darkness of the backyard. Just in case.

But Lucy wasn't there.

At least I knew where to look for her and I didn't think she'd been out long enough to do too much mischief over at the doctor's place. But there was no escaping a trek up the street after her.

The gate to our chain link fence squeaked a little when I opened it, something I never noticed in the daytime. I hoped Danny didn't come charging out to shoot me, thinking I was a prowler.

He'd left my car at the curb since Chloe had nabbed my side of the driveway for herself and her girlfriend's car had been on Danny's side. I was half tempted to use my keys to get into the Subaru and take out one of my Hal Ketchum tapes to listen to while I fell asleep when I got back. But I was afraid the time that would take might give Lucy all the more opportunity to do damage. So I just slipped my hands and my keys into the kangaroo pouch of my sweat suit and headed up the street.

I kept watch for Lucy as I passed sleeping houses and streetlights that provided spotlights for the swirling snowflakes. It would have been nice if she'd stopped along the way to anoint a bush or a tree so I could have caught her before having to go all the way to the doctor's house.

But my luck really had run out for the night.

Like the rest of the block, the doctor's Tudor was dark inside and out. And unless he didn't like his dog, I guessed that Barney was probably snuggled inside too.

I wasn't sure if that was good or bad. If Lucy hadn't found the Doberman of her dreams outside, I was afraid she might have kept going, complicating my finding her after all.

I tried calling her from the sidewalk in front of the doctor's house, hoping she'd just run out to me from there, wagging her tail. But she didn't. Not that that meant she wasn't back there—schnauzers are stubborn dogs—and since it was too dark around the house to see if she was digging her way into the yard, I had no choice but to tramp up the driveway.

I'd barely taken three steps before I triggered motion-sensitive lights and the night was suddenly flooded like a prison yard during a breakout. I half expected alarms to sound but was thankful that didn't happen. And at least the light let me see Lucy digging like mad again to get under the wrought-iron fence.

"Lucy!" I whisper-shouted.

She opted for making a break for it and dived into the hole she'd only just begun.

In case it was bigger than it looked, I dived after her, trying to catch her before she could make it to the other side. I overshot and sliced the back of my hand on one of the iron pickets, letting out a none too nice epithet about the same time I heard a door open from the rear of the house. Barney charged outside barking and baring his teeth, and the doctor appeared in his plaid flannel bathrobe and bare feet and legs.

"What the hell is going on out here?"

It wasn't exactly *Hi, neighbor!* But what could you expect?

"It's just me—Jimi Plain from down the street? My dog got out again," I said in a hurry, in case Danny wasn't the only one on the block who might be armed.

Ben Barrows gave Barney a command that stopped the Doberman's barking, but even though I had Lucy in my arms by then, she was putting up a terrible fuss.

I had to clamp my hand around her muzzle to make her stop.

As I was using my foot to push dirt back into the hole she'd started to dig I said, "I'm sorry. Again."

When he glanced down at the ground, I thought it was to assess the damage Lucy had wrought this time. Until I followed his gaze and saw the blood my hand was dripping onto his nice white snow.

Then he looked up for the source.

"How did you do that?" he asked pointing to my hand.

"On the gate when I reached for her. It's no big deal."

"You better come in and let me take a look at it."

Oh sure. This was just what I warned my daughters about. I didn't know this guy from Adam. No one had any idea that I wasn't at home in my nice warm bed or where I might have gone. I could go into his house, he could shove me down his stairs, lock me in a cage in the basement, no one would ever see me again and be none the wiser.

"Thanks, but I'm fine and it's late. I'll let you go back to bed and I'll just take care of it at home."

"You're bleeding a lot and I want to at least clean the wound. I wouldn't want it to get infected. You're liable to sue me."

"I'm not going to sue anybody, don't worry about it."

Maybe my stepping backward when he stepped forward—even though his gate was between us—gave him insight into what was going on in my head because he said, "Fine. You don't want to come in. Then wait until I put some pants on and I'll walk back to your place with you so I can take a look at that cut."

"It's no big deal. Really."

"My place or yours."

Great, an ultimatum.

I wasn't going to make the guy go all the way back to my house to look at my hand. Gramma, the girls, and I were doing our best to keep him from blowing his stack about Lucy's antics. The last thing I wanted to do was to make one of those antics even more troublesome for him.

"Okay. I'll come inside and let you look at it here," I finally conceded.

But I never got inside.

Because about then a huge boom broke through the night, and so much light blazed to life that it was as if a switch had been thrown open on the sound stage of our block.

I spun around and ran toward the sound of the explosion to find out what had happened.

Just in time for me to see my car to turn into a ball of fire.

Chapter Thirteen

I CAN SAY without a doubt that it was a night like no other I'd ever spent.

Lights went on in the houses shaken by the explosion. Fire trucks, police cars both marked and unmarked, and the bomb squad all arrived within fifteen minutes of the blast. My family and neighbors up and down the block were evacuated. And I watched my Subaru station wagon—or what was left of it—roast to a charred black mass of molten metal.

Nobody got too close, even the fire department only sprayed water on the flames from a distance, and once the fire was out, the bomb squad opened both ends of the car with a mobile cannon that blew the locks to make sure no undetonated bombs were left.

I didn't know how there could be, but no chances were being taken. Not a soul was allowed anywhere near the area until it was judged safe. That included a check by the bomb squad of Chloe's car in the driveway. Her rear window had been blown out by a piece of the Subaru flying through it, but beyond that it seemed fine. Danny was lucky his car was still in the shop, and fortunately the house hadn't been damaged at all.

I have to admit that I walked through the hours after the explosion in a kind of daze. Time passed and people came up to me, and I know I talked to them, but besides the fact that my family was okay, most of what registered were the goings-on around my car and the fact that Ben Barrows took care of me, the girls, Gramma, and even Lucy.

When we were allowed back as far as the doctor's house, he put the two dogs in the backyard and led Gramma, Chloe, and Shannon inside to get them out of the cold. Then he brought his medical bag and a cup of steaming tea out onto his front lawn, where I had stayed to watch what was happening. He bandaged my hand as I sipped the tea, leaving me to the melee of my own thoughts and offering only silent support and comfort—something I appreciated since I wasn't feeling particularly sociable.

It was nearly four before the police allowed us to reenter the house. My entourage and I did that while Danny remained in the midst of the cop–firefighter brigade where he'd spent the rest of the time and the good doctor stayed home.

I exempted the girls from school, so they decided to

go back to bed, but neither Gramma nor I could sleep. Instead we got busy making coffee and a buffet breakfast for the investigators who had to wait for my car to cool down and daylight to dawn in order to actually begin their work.

Once the food and drinks were under control, I went upstairs to get unready for bed.

I took a quick bath, put on my day's makeup, and trussed my hair up in an elastic ruffle.

By then it was all of a quarter to six.

When I returned to the kitchen, I talked Gramma into lying down since the cops and firefighters had moved outside to get the investigation started. When she'd gone off to her room, I cleaned up, realizing that I was going through all the motions as if I were walking in heavy fog.

Then I put on my snow-shoveling gear and went out onto the front porch, where I sat on the top step.

I wasn't sure if it was lack of sleep or shock, but I felt numb and removed from everything that was going on right before my eyes. I thought witnessing the process of investigation and cleanup might snap me out of it, but it wasn't having much effect. The whole thing still seemed surreal.

Uniformed cops and investigators alike did a wide search for debris, bagging everything they found and effectively removing even the small amount of litter that had been on the street and yards before. I couldn't help thinking that the haphazard circle in which my car stood looked like a giant cigarette burn surrounded by once pristine white snow that was now pockmarked and sooted and trampled by footprints and tire tracks.

Extensive photographs were taken, detailed descriptions were written up, and sketches were made that included a map of the neighborhood. A lab expert, an explosives specialist, and an arson investigator directed the collection of evidence and I was questioned three different times by three different people.

The first order of business was to clear the street because no cars could be allowed past the scene until every bit of detritus that could be collected was collected. Since our block curves and ends in a cul-de-sac, that meant no one above us could get in or out.

By about seven-thirty a narrow strip of the street in front of the house was finally opened. I hoped it was in time not to make too many of my neighbors late for work.

It did allow for looky-loos though, in a steady stream.

At about eight o'clock Carl Cutler drove down from around the bend, slowing as he passed. When he spied me on the porch, he pulled his car over to the curb just beyond the corded-off perimeter, parked, and hiked back to where I was sitting.

"What happened?" he asked in greeting, looking around at the one-ring circus going on in my front yard.

"My car blew up."

"No . . ." he said as if I couldn't possibly be serious.

"Afraid so."

"How did that happen?"

I was pretty sure he expected me to tell him about some mechanical mishap. After all, who comes upon a charred car and automatically thinks bomb? Even I hadn't until Danny had told me this was no gas leak that had ignited on its own.

"I'm not sure how it happened," I answered, partly because I wasn't completely sure what *had* happened and partly because I didn't know if I was supposed to let word out that someone had planted something in my car to blow it to smithereens.

Carl propped a foot on the bottom step and turned sideways so he could look back and forth between me and the crime scene. "What a mess."

"You can say that again," I agreed. "The explosion didn't wake you last night?"

"Something woke me but I couldn't say what it was. Then I remember hearing a lot of sirens close by but you know how that is. I figured somebody had a heart attack or a furnace caught fire or there was a bad car wreck—nothing I could do anything about—and I just went back to sleep."

I did know how it was. I would have gone through a mental rundown of where Chloe, Shannon, Gramma, and Danny were, breathed a sigh of relief that they were all at home, and gone back to sleep too.

"And it was your car, did you say?"

"Yep."

"I hope you have insurance."

"I do." Although I wasn't sure if bombings were covered.

"Still, this is just terrible," Carl commiserated.

"At least no one was hurt. It could have been worse."

"True. Thank God for that."

We all had in one way or another. But it was unnerving to think how close I'd come to getting in the car for my Hal Ketchum tapes just minutes before it had blown.

"Did you know there was something wrong with the car?" Carl asked then, still assuming this had been a more natural occurrence.

"No, no idea," I said, leaving him to his assumptions. We spent another moment watching the investigators taking and recording measurements.

"Guess you'll need a new car," Carl said then, laughing a little as he stated the obvious.

"Probably. I don't think even a good mechanic can fix this."

"You know, I own part of a Toyota dealership with my brother-in-law," he said tentatively.

"I remember you saying something about that that night in the Center's parking lot when Brenda had trouble starting her Datsun."

"I'd have to talk to my brother-in-law, but maybe we could work out something to help you get a new car. If you want a Toyota."

I hadn't even thought about a new car. But of course I'd need one. I was reasonably sure the insurance would just about cover a down payment and I didn't have anything budgeted for impromptu car buying, so any discounts I could get were discounts I couldn't afford to pass up. "That would be great."

"I'll call him today, run it by him."

"Thanks."

"No problem," he said as if I'd embarrassed him.

"I'll throw in your prospectus for free," I countered.

He laughed. "Okay. But don't tell my brother-in-law or you'll be doing his ad copy for nothing for the rest of your life."

"Deal."

Carl took another long look at the remains of the

Subaru, shook his head in disbelief, and said, "God," under his breath.

"Yeah," I seconded it.

We both just stared at the destruction for a while longer, and then Carl said, "I guess I should get going. If I were you I'd report this to your insurance company ASAP so you can start those wheels in motion. I'll call as soon as I get hold of my brother-in-law."

"I'd appreciate it."

"In the meantime, if you need a lift somewhere . . ."

I thanked him again, we said good-bye, and he walked off, keeping an amazed eye on the proceedings as he went.

Because I was watching Carl leave I didn't see Ben Barrows come up from the opposite direction.

"Hey," he said to announce himself.

"Morning," I answered.

He looked as if he were headed for work, just as Carl must have been, because he had on charcoal-colored slacks, a plaid shirt, and a knit tie underneath a deeper gray knee-length camel hair coat that made his fit physique all the more formidable. His dark brown hair was neatly combed and there weren't any signs of the sleepless night that had left smudges under both my eyes. His were as bright a blue as ever. In fact, he looked as if just a few hours rest was all he'd needed and he was ready to take on the day. I figured I was his morning rounds before he went to the office.

His hands were in his pockets and he brought one of them out, producing my keys as he did. "I found these by the side of my house. You must have dropped them last night before the fun began."

"Probably when I lunged for Lucy," I said, taking them and thanking him.

Even though I didn't invite him to, he came up the porch steps and sat beside me on the top one. "How's the hand?"

Yep, morning rounds all right.

"It's fine. I cleaned it out again a little while ago and put some antibiotic ointment on it. It's not bleeding anymore."

"Want me to take a look?"

"No, thanks. If I take the bandage off I'll have to wrap it all over again."

"How's the rest of you?"

"Okay. Long night."

"Did you get any sleep at all?"

"Not yet. Did you?"

"A few hours. Felt like I was back in residency. I'll catch thirty winks during lunch."

I could feel his eyes on me and I turned my head to find him studying me. Clinically, I thought.

"You really should try to get some rest too," he advised.

"Maybe later," I said, figuring I must look pretty bad.

"How about Nell and your kids? How are they holding up?"

"The girls went to bed as soon as we got back in the house. I just convinced my grandmother to lie down about half an hour ago. But I can't tell you how shook up everybody is, if that's what you mean. We haven't really talked about it. I think everybody is just grateful it was only the car."

"Good way to look at it." He poked his chin in the

direction of the curb. "Anyone saying what happened yet?"

Again I wasn't sure I should repeat what little I'd been told—mainly that the car was blown up on purpose—so instead I joked. "No, but I was wondering just how mad you are about Lucy tearing up your yard."

"Not *that* mad," he countered with a smile and a wry chuckle.

I think it was the first time I'd seen anything but a frown on his face. It took about five years off his features and improved his looks. Plus I'm always glad when somebody gets my jokes.

"Actually," he said, "I was thinking maybe you were just sick of driving the Subaru so you dropped a match down the gas tank on your way to my house last night."

Ah, he could give as good as he got. I liked that. "Don't say that to the insurance company, I want the check." I held up my hurt hand. "And don't forget, I could still sue."

"Never mind then. I won't say a word," he said in mock terror.

I didn't know what about the night before had relaxed the guy, but it was a vast improvement and I hoped it would help with any future contact we might have to have over Lucy.

"Well, if you don't need my expert medical attention, I should probably get to those who do," he said then.

He stood to go, but before he did I said, "Hey. Thanks for everything you did last night."

"Just earning my Red Cross badge. Take care of the hand."

"Sure."

He waved and walked off across the yards back to his house, his long coat flapping behind him like a cowboy's duster.

I noticed Danny watching him go before my cousin took his turn at joining me on the porch.

"Everybody's curious," he said with a nod in Ben Barrows's direction.

"Including me," I said. "I haven't been leaking word that it was a bomb, though."

"Ben's no dummy. I'm sure he put two and two together and came up with four."

"Well, I didn't say it to Carl anyway. So what's up?"

"Looks like it was dynamite. Not more than one stick. Close to the fuel line to make things interesting."

"Where would somebody get dynamite?"

"A lot of places. Landscapers sometimes use it to blast big tree trunks. Construction sites use it to clear the land. We'll check for thefts of it from places like that. Trouble is, if it was another kind of explosive it would likely have had a chemical signature the manufacturer puts in to make it identifiable. Helps trace it. But dynamite doesn't usually have anything like that in it. The detonator or the timing device may be trackable. We'll just have to see."

"Any way of telling when it was put there?"

"Not much. But they tell me that when dynamite gets wet and separates it gets as touchy as nitroglycerin, so chances are I wasn't driving around all day yesterday through the snow and slush with it or it would have blown all by itself. They're thinking it was planted last night, after you came home from the Center. But that still doesn't tell us if whoever set it was sending a message to you or to me."

"You don't think it was intended to hurt anybody?"

"No. It would have been rigged differently if it was. And it wouldn't have been set to go off in the middle of the night."

"Must not have been a message to you or why would they have blown up my car?" I suggested.

"I was driving it all day yesterday and it was parked in front of where I live. Could have been mistaken for my car. Could be somebody followed me home and just waited for their opportunity. Seems more likely that somebody's pissed at me than at you."

I knew he meant that as comfort, but I didn't like the idea of Danny's being the target any better than my being it.

"Do you think this is connected to Steffi Hargitay's murder?" I asked.

Danny shrugged. "Maybe. Maybe not. It's not the only thing I'm working on, just the most recent."

"And what you spent yesterday doing?"

"Not completely. I made a few other stops to talk to some other people about two other cases."

That wasn't going to help narrow the field.

"I suppose somebody has asked you this already," Danny said then, "but did you notice any footprints around the car when you went after Lucy?"

"I wasn't looking for any but no, I don't remember noticing anything. It was snowing hard, though. There could have been footprints around it fifteen minutes before I went out and they'd have been gone."

"That's what we figured, too, but I thought I'd ask just in case."

Neither of us said anything for a moment.

Then Danny said, "I'm sorry, Jimi."

"Wasn't your fault."

"But it was your car."

"Cars can be replaced. I've already got a lead on a new one." I told him about Carl's offer.

"Great. But I want to help out with the money. I know you can't afford—"

"Let's worry about that when the time comes," I said to put him off. I wasn't taking his money one way or another.

"They're about to erect the tent over the car to protect what's left of the crime scene—they would have done it earlier but there's been some trouble getting it here. There won't be anything to see once they do that, so why don't you go in and get some sleep?"

Weariness was settling in on me again.

"Maybe I will," I said.

Besides, the thought of my nice quiet attic room was getting more and more appealing and I wasn't doing any good sitting on the porch watching other people do their jobs.

"Go on," Danny urged, giving me a shove with his shoulder.

I lumbered to my feet and returned his shove with my knee. "What about you? When are you going to get some rest?"

"Haven't you heard? There's no rest for the wicked."

"Mmm," I said dubiously, wondering if whoever had sent this particular message—whether to Danny or to me—had lost as much sleep over it as we had.

Chapter Fourteen

I SLEPT MOST of the day, and by the time I got up my car had been towed to the county lab for closer study, the investigation team was gone, and the only thing left at the curb in front of the house was the charred shadow where the Subaru had met its demise.

The extended nap had done me good, though. It's funny how a little sleep can help clear your head. I still didn't *like* the fact that someone had blown up my car. But I'd tried to think of any reason anyone I knew would do it—or would even have the wherewithal for it—and I hadn't come up with anything. Which led me to be more inclined to agree with Danny that it probably didn't have anything to do with me. And that made me feel more removed from someone's evil intent.

On the other hand, the trouble with sleeping all day

is that I got up full of energy. And without an outlet for that energy. Since it was Friday night, Chloe and Shannon were both going out—Chloe with her boyfriend and Shannon with a group of girlfriends. My grandmother was scheduled to play pinochle next door. I didn't know where Danny was, but I knew it was likely he wouldn't be home anytime soon. And I wasn't really in the mood to call a friend.

It was looking as if I was going to end up working even though I felt too antsy to sit in front of my computer for any amount of time. And then Carl Cutler called.

He said he'd been thinking about me all day and just wanted to check on me, see how I was doing. I told him I was fine, with the exception of a little cabin fever. He said he was planning to go to the Center to work out with Gary Oldershaw and asked if I wanted to go with him.

I was so desperate, I jumped at the chance.

And believe me, I had to be desperate. Exercise is just not my thing and Gary Oldershaw struck me as someone who wouldn't agree with my start-slow-and-taper-off theory of fitness.

But I'd been wanting to talk to Gary about Steffi Hargitay and using a workout as an excuse for that seemed a lot more appealing than sitting home alone, thinking about whose feathers Danny might have ruffled enough for them to blow up the car they thought was his.

Carl wanted to pick me up on his way out, but it had stopped snowing and a nice stroll to his house in the bracing January air seemed like a good start to expending some of my energy. Besides, I was curious about which house was his. So I told him I'd walk up and meet him.

After a quick dinner during which no one seemed the worse for wear from our previous night, I suited up in my sweats and Shannon's tennis shoes, and took off.

Carl's house was around a curve our street makes to the west. It was a large two-story built with a Spanish influence in the stone that faced the lower level, the stucco on the second, and the red tile roof. The surrounding yard was landscaped with a fair amount of rock to cut down on maintenance. Two tall iron lamps that had to have come straight from Mexico stood like pillars on either side of the walkway that led up to a heavy, carved walnut front door that looked as if it had been pilfered from a monastery.

Carl must have been watching for me because he opened that monastery door before I had the chance to ring the bell.

We exchanged hellos in a huge entryway floored in shiny, irregular Mexican tile the color of rust.

"Nice house," I said as I glanced around.

"Want the tour? Down here, anyway, I had to hire a decorator because I don't know the first thing about that stuff and she hasn't started on the bedrooms upstairs yet. They're just empty. All but mine, and mine isn't worth climbing the steps to see."

I agreed to the tour of the ground level and followed him through room after room of tasteful decor in a Southwestern style that used a lot of clay pots and gourds.

We ended up in a kitchen at the rear of the house that was so high-tech, I wasn't sure either Gramma or I could have cooked in it. As it was, Carl had to point out the refrigerator because its front was exactly the same dark oak wood grain as the cupboards and I couldn't tell the difference.

The back wall of the kitchen was a series of French doors opening into a huge patio and a rock garden beyond it.

"I'll bet this is nice in the summer," I said, stepping up to one of the French doors to look outside.

"I hope so."

Carl came to stand beside me and pointed off to the left corner of the yard. "That's where Vince is putting my shed."

I could see that the cousin Gramma had recommended to Carl had already put up the wooden forms for the cement slab he'd pour as the foundation.

"Vince called and told us you'd given him the job. He's just a jack-of-all-trades handyman but he does good work," I said. "That's going to be a big shed."

"More like a small garage. I want to be able to keep the lawnmower and the snowblower out there along with any patio furniture I pick up so my real garage doesn't have anything in it but my car."

"That'll be nice. Our garage is so crammed it's hard to get my grandmother's cars in it at all."

"Vince is going to make the shed a replica of the house. He thinks he can get the same stone for the bottom half and match the paint for the stucco on the top. And there are enough extra shingle tiles stacked in the basement to do the whole roof."

"So you'll have continuity and it won't end up being an eyesore," I guessed.

"Right," Carl confirmed. "I wasn't sure Vince'd be able to put it in that part of the yard because there's a slight grade to it, but he leveled it out pretty well."

True enough. All but one corner of the site looked as smooth and flat as granite.

"As soon as the weather warms up he'll come in and finish that last little rough patch and then we'll be able to pour the concrete," Carl said.

"I'm glad Vince is working out for you."

"He's great. He'll do whatever I want."

With the nickel tour complete we went through a door in the kitchen that led us into the garage. Carl owned a Toyota 4-Runner, and as we got in and he started it up we began talking about Toyotas. It came as no surprise that Carl was a big advocate of them.

"I was hoping we could go into the dealership tonight and pick one out for you," he said. "But when I called my brother-in-law his secretary told me he went on some kind of weekend trip with his buddies. He won't be back until Monday. I hope you can wait that long."

I assured Carl I could.

"Maybe you'll want to shop around for other cars at other dealerships before then. Don't feel tied to this idea."

"I don't. I appreciate your help," I told him honestly.

"I'm thinking we can at least do fleet price. Maybe better."

"That would be great." Plus I was hoping to avoid the hassle of dealing with high-pressure car salesmen, but I didn't say it out loud.

And that was just about the amount of time it took us to get to the Center.

The New You Center was much quieter on a Friday night than on the other two nights I'd been there this week. Maybe that meant their dating service worked.

Steve Stivik was manning the reception counter when we went in, and neither Carl nor I received a hearty, warm welcome.

I knew why Steve was cool to me—apparently he was still fostering fantasies that I knew something about his missing ledger and was just refusing to tell him for some reason.

But his snide hello to Carl, accompanied by an inexplicable snicker as he looked him up and down, made me think that if we'd been on a beach, Steve would have come up and kicked sand in Carl's face. Or thrown him naked out of the locker room the way those bullies Carl had told me he'd faced in high school had. And *that* I didn't quite understand.

Until it occurred to me that maybe Steve had somehow heard of Carl's interest in Brenda and, in sizing up the competition, was trying to demoralize him.

Carl ignored it, but I wondered if Brenda knew there were two men at odds over her. It would probably do her self-esteem some good if she did.

"Hey," Steve called as we headed toward the left wing after brief hellos.

Since it wasn't clear which of us he was heying, both Carl and I turned.

Steve jutted his chin in my direction. "I hear your car blew up."

"How did you hear that?" I asked, surprised.

He gave a cocky, I-know-everything shrug before he said, "It was on the news."

"It was?"

"I didn't see that," Carl said as if he doubted it.

"Yeah, well, I did. On some channel or another," Steve answered, smug and vague at the same time.

I hadn't watched any of the evening news reports and hadn't seen any reporters at my house either. At least not before I'd gone to bed. But I supposed that didn't mean some hadn't shown up while I was asleep.

"What did they say?" I asked.

"Just that there was an explosion of a car belonging to Jimi Plain and that investigators were looking into it. That true?"

"True enough," I said.

"Tough break," Steve countered with a grin.

"Yeah," I agreed, not enjoying the idea anywhere near as much as he seemed to be.

"Come on, let's get to the weight room," Carl suggested in a quiet aside, steering me out of the lobby. Then he muttered so only I could hear, "Jerk."

I couldn't find any fault with the assessment of Steve's character.

Before getting all the way to the weight room at the end of the corridor, we passed the classrooms and then the largest room in the place—a big, empty space where aerobics and dance classes were held. The locker rooms just beyond that were accessible to both the aerobics/dance studio and the weight room on the other side of them.

I hadn't particularly cared for the arrangement of the locker rooms when Steffi had shown them to me. There were two separate areas, complete with showers, for men and for women. But between them was a utility room where towels and supplies were stored, and there were doors on either end that opened into each locker room. The doors weren't kept locked because the only access to the saunas was in the utility room too. But all I could think of when I'd seen the setup was that it was too easy for either sex to peek in on the other from inside that utility room.

Maybe I'm just a prude, but I'd made up my mind then and there that I would not be using that particular facility.

The weight room was about half the size of the aerobics/dance studio with all four walls covered in floor-to-ceiling mirrors. So not only did you have to sweat, you had to watch yourself do it.

The room was equipped with four stationary bicycles, two benches complete with barbells at their heads, jump ropes and chest pulls hanging from hooks, two mini trampolines, and one universal gym with more gizmos than I could guess uses for.

Since I hadn't been in the gym except during the orientation when it hadn't been in use at all, I didn't know if it was commonly or uncommonly empty. But tonight only Gary Oldershaw was in it, doing arm curls in front of one of the mirrored walls to watch the enormous bulge of his biceps in the process.

"Hi, Gary," Carl said to announce us when the other man's concentration seemed so intense, he didn't appear to have noticed us come in.

Gary didn't return the greeting. He merely set down the weights and turned to face us with a bland expression on his handsome face.

"This is Jimi Plain," Carl introduced me. "I don't know if you two have met."

When Gary took a closer look and recognized me, his expression went from bland to disturbed and what popped into my head was that if he hadn't been a tough guy he might have burst into tears. Apparently I was a reminder to him of Steffi's death. I felt bad about that.

"I know her," Gary said in a deep, pained voice. "Hi."

"Hi," I said, grateful for the courtesy in spite of the memories I'd apparently raised in him.

"Better warm up," he advised Carl. Then, to me, he said, "Can I help you with anything?"

"Mostly I just came to get out of the house."

He nodded. "Oh, that's right. I heard your car blew up."

"You did? From Steve or on the news?"

"Just around. Sorry."

"Me too."

As Gary laid out a series of things he wanted Carl to accomplish on the universal gym, I picked up the lightest hand weight I could find and mimicked the curls Gary had been doing when we came in.

Or at least I thought I was mimicking them until he moved to stand halfway between Carl and me to tell me I'd damage my elbow if I didn't change what I was doing.

He showed me the right way and I used the opportunity to say, "I understand you and Steffi were close. I imagine this has been a hard week for you."

"Harder than you think havin' to come *here* every day."

"Because this is where she died."

"Because I can't get any of the answers I should be gettin'."

"To what questions?"

He readjusted the angle of my arm curls, scowling too darkly to be only disapproving of my lack of physical ability. "I want to know why Steffi was here alone that night when she shouldn't have been. *If* she was."

"What do you mean?"

"I mean, where was Steve? He's always the last one to leave. He won't let anybody else lock up. He schedules us to do the cleanup work, sits in the sauna for a last steam, and then when we're finished, we have to wait for him to come out, check on us, and he walks out with us so he can turn on the alarm and lock up. So why not last Friday night?"

"Good question. I heard he left to get ready for a date."

"Yeah, I know. With that new girl he's workin'."

"Working?"

Disgust shook Gary's head and contorted his handsome face. "Pity fu . . . Well, you get the idea. He picks somebody, pours on the charm, does 'em, then laughs about it behind their backs and calls it pity you-know-whating."

Lovely. And not a good thing, I thought, for Carl to hear when he no doubt knew Brenda was the most recent object of Steve's attentions.

I glanced over at Carl, but he seemed more intent on his sit-ups. I hoped he wasn't paying any attention to what we were talking about.

"Do you know who was scheduled to do the cleanup last Friday night?" I asked before Gary said more on the subject.

"Diane Samboro. And that's my other question. Where was she? Why wasn't *she* here either?"

"I heard she was home getting ready for a date too."

"Nobody ever left early for dates before. We work until we're finished no matter what we have planned for later in the evening. Well, Irene, Diane, and me, anyway. Steve would let Steffi slide if she had a date with a member. But none of the rest of us."

"Was it part of Steffi's job to date members?" I asked because that's how he'd made it sound.

"Sort of. Certain members. I never really understood it. She just said it was an arrangement she'd had with Steve from the beginning, before she even met me, to make nice with some of the more desirable male members."

I was dying to ask if Steve took care of the women and Steffi did the men, but how could I ask that of this man who clearly had had feelings for her? And I didn't want to get back into that pity thing in connection with Brenda and Steve either. But I did recall Danny saying there had been a large number of condoms and a change of underwear in Steffi's purse.

"By desirable do you mean attractive?" I asked.

"No. I never really knew the details. I just know Steve would pick out who he wanted her to butter up and she'd have to do it."

"She'd *have* to?"

"It wasn't like he twisted her arm or anything. But it was their arrangement, she said. She said it was her ticket to a partnership and she was going to make sure she got it."

"A partnership in the Center?"

"And everything else Steve had plans for."

So that was what she had coming and was going to

make sure she got. Somehow I couldn't see Steve easily complying with it, even if he had promised it.

"And Steffi had to date the *desirable* members even when she was involved with you?"

"Yeah."

And Gary hadn't liked the idea, if his tone was any indication.

"Is that why you broke up?"

"We broke up because Steve all of a sudden made a rule that there couldn't be any co-worker dating."

"Why didn't one of you go to work somewhere else, then?"

"I can't. I have a contract."

"Was Steffi under contract too?"

"No. But Diane and Irene and I are. And believe me, there's no way around them. Diane has tried."

"Diane wants out of her contract here?"

"She did. Bad. She even talked about suing Steve to do it. But I suppose things have changed now."

Disgust dripped from his voice and then disappeared as he coached me to switch arms if the one I'd been doing curls with was tired.

I'd actually just stopped. But I changed arms so I didn't lose his attention.

"Why wouldn't Diane want out of her contract anymore?" I asked.

"Let's just say that she's not sorry that Steffi isn't still around. Her and Irene both. I even heard them talking to each other yesterday, saying they wouldn't miss Steffi. Good-bye and good riddance is what they said."

"That must have been hard for you to hear."

"It's not like I didn't know they hated Steffi."

"Do you know why?"

He shrugged one of those enormous shoulders. "Steffi didn't pull any punches with what she thought."

"And she thought Irene was too old to work here," I put in.

"She is. She's just lookin' for some rich old geezer to support her. She doesn't pay hardly any attention to anybody else, which means she isn't doing her job."

"And what about Diane?"

"I don't know. Steffi called her Miss Goody Two-shoes. I think she just thought Diane was sickeningly sweet and fake. She probably let her know it."

"And what about you and Steffi? Had your relationship not gone far enough for feelings to be involved? Could you just stop dating and go back to being nothing but co-workers without any problem?"

Gary's jaw tightened as firmly as his biceps had been when we'd walked in. "I loved her. I would have married her."

"Did she feel the same way?"

"I guess not. She didn't have a contract with Steve, so she could have left if she'd wanted to and we could have gone on seein' each other. But she wouldn't do it. She said she had too much invested here."

More than she had invested in their relationship apparently.

"How were things between you and Steffi after the breakup? Were you able to stay friends?"

"I loved her," he said as if I'd asked him to eat worms. "How could I just be friends with her? I just wish I'd been here last Friday night."

"Where were you?"

"Home. Lifting weights."

"By yourself?"

He looked at me through eyes that squinted suspiciously. "Yeah, by myself."

I knew when I'd gone as far as I could go.

"You're right—it is too bad you weren't here so you could have protected her," I agreed.

"I wouldn't have ever let anything happen to her," he contended insistently, as if I'd refuted the claim.

"I'm sure," I said, trying to keep him calm when it suddenly seemed as if he felt challenged.

But apparently I hadn't completely convinced him of my support. He narrowed his eyes at me again and then turned his broad back to concentrate on Carl as if I'd left the room.

But that was okay.

Because I didn't want to get myself into any more trouble than I already had by wondering out loud just how much Gary Oldershaw might really have been hurt by Steffi's rejection of him in favor of a job.

And how else that hurt might have vented itself in some kind of action besides weight lifting.

Chapter Fifteen

THERE WAS A message from Delia Grant on my answering machine when I got home on Friday night. She'd heard about my car, too, hoped no one had been hurt, and asked if I wanted to ride with her and Brenda to the dance class on Saturday night.

I thought that was nice.

Even though Carl and I had stopped for coffee after our . . . his . . . workout, it was barely nine-thirty when I replayed the message, so I called Delia and accepted her offer. Dancing is something I've never learned how to do and always wanted to. I figured I shouldn't pass up the opportunity when it was staring me in the face.

I spent Saturday catching up on the work I hadn't done Friday, but by six forty-five that evening I had on my dancing shoes—a pair of root beer–colored penny loafers. And when Delia pulled up in front of the house in her Honda Accord and honked, I headed for my first lesson.

Brenda was in the passenger seat so I sat in back. She was no more talkative than usual, but it didn't matter. Delia asked so many questions about what had happened to the Subaru that Brenda's minimal participation wasn't too noticeable. Neither of them had heard about the incident from the news report. In fact, I still hadn't found anyone besides Steve Stivik who had. Instead, Steve had told Brenda, who had in turn told Delia.

I explained that the perpetrator was likely to have been someone Danny was investigating who had mistaken my car for his. But I also made a mental note to ask Danny if there really had been a news crew at the house sometime while I was asleep on Friday.

If You've Never Danced Before, It's Time to Start was a popular class. The aerobics/dance studio had at least thirty people waiting around its perimeter when we got there.

Besides Irene Oatman—who gave the class—and Diane Samboro and Gary Oldershaw who assisted, I didn't recognize anyone but Bert Chumley. He saw us come in, but he didn't motion for us to join him even though he was standing by himself, apparently not knowing anyone either. I wondered if, for some reason, he didn't like Brenda any more than she liked him.

Both Brenda and I followed Delia across the polished wood floor as she made a beeline for Gary Oldershaw near the front of the room. It occurred to me as we exchanged greetings once she'd hit her mark that he was considerably younger than either Delia or I. I doubted he was more than twenty-six. Maybe Delia liked younger men, in which case Gramma's trying to fix her up with Danny was doubly doomed.

For his part, Gary was courteous and reservedly friendly. But very reservedly. I didn't have the impression he was as enthusiastic about her as she thought he might be.

I hoped for Delia's sake that I was wrong, but the glances that kept straying to the cluster of miniature red carnations in her hair and the bright red-and-yellow-flowered wraparound skirt she wore seemed less than appreciative of Delia's style.

Still, I was glad he wasn't being unkind to her the way Steffi had been.

As for Brenda, she began scanning the room the moment we entered it and was too preoccupied to respond even when Delia directed comments straight at her.

I was reasonably sure Brenda was looking for Steve and wondered if he'd promised her he'd be there. When she didn't spot whomever or whatever it was she was looking for, she seemed to deflate, as if the evening ended for her right then.

I wished I could slip out and call Carl to come so he could step into the breach. But he'd told me last night that he wouldn't be attending the class tonight because he needed to oversee Cutler's Corner while his manager attended a wedding. I thought he was missing a prime opportunity to pick up the ball I assumed Steve had dropped, but there was nothing I could do about it.

Ten minutes after we'd arrived, Irene started the class. The first thing she did was separate us into those who knew a little about dancing and those who had never tripped the light fantastic.

I was in the second group.

Then she asked us to pair up, one from my group with one from the other, so that we novices would have some help from those who weren't.

There were far fewer men than women, which meant some women would have to be partners with other women. But Irene handled that with such good-natured aplomb that it seemed less awkward. In fact, she handled the whole class as if she were enjoying herself so much, it was infectious. It was a side of her I liked more than what I'd seen before. She was fun.

I ended up with Bert Chumley. By Irene's design. When an older woman from my group headed for him like a heat-seeking missile, Irene stepped in and steered him to me.

Apparently Irene viewed the older woman as more competition than she thought I was. I didn't know whether to take that as an insult or not.

But since I wanted to get to know Bert better anyway, I decided not to be offended.

The stocky elderly gentleman was about my height and dressed in tan, beige, and yellow plaid polyester pants, a brown sport coat, and a brown bow tie at the collar of his cream-colored shirt. It was not an outfit a more youthful man would have been caught dead in, but Bert looked very natty and I told him so, getting a red-cheeked smile for the compliment.

I could tell right off that he didn't need the dance class. In fact, he seemed to be a pretty good dancer—if I was any judge—and I told him that too.

"But coming gave me something to do tonight. For no extra money. It isn't easy to show a woman a good time when you live on your social security benefit, you know," he confided with a bit of impish delight that made me understand even less why Brenda disliked him so intensely.

"I imagine that's true," I said about his particular brand of dating woes.

Irene did a demonstration of a simple one-two-three, one-two-three step, then started the music and let our more experienced partners go to work on us.

Bert was so smooth, he made it look as if I almost knew what I was doing. And in the process he said, "Are you the young lady whose car was blown up?"

"I'm the one," I confirmed, thinking that the whole world must know by now. But then I guess it isn't easy keeping something like that quiet.

"That's quite a shocker," he said.

"To put it lightly."

"You must've made somebody pretty mad."

"Somebody must have made somebody pretty mad, but I don't know that it was me."

"You've been going around asking questions like you're with the police, haven't you?"

"Have I?" I asked, pretending I didn't know what he was talking about and wondering how he did.

He didn't answer my question though. In fact, he ignored it and went on as if I'd admitted to the unauthorized interrogations, leaning in to say confidentially, "You're not doing a very good job of it because you haven't gotten around to me and I was the last person to see sweet Steffi alive, you know."

"Except for whoever killed her. Unless that was you."

"Nooo ma'am. Wasn't me."

"How can I be sure of that?" I asked in the same vein of teasing he was using.

"I'd never destroy anything so lovely."

"Not everybody thinks Steffi was so sweet or so lovely."

"Well, I did. She was a tempting morsel all right."

"I understand you saw her that last night to ask her out," I said then.

He grinned a grin so big it made his cheeks turn into apples and his eyes gleam. "And you think she could have laughed in my face because I'm old enough to be her grandfather and I was so enraged I killed her? No, no, no. I've been turned down for dates before and homicide has never been my reaction. But she didn't turn me down, so it certainly wasn't what I did this time. She had granted me the next night for supper and believe me, I wanted her alive for that."

"Do you mind if I ask whose idea the date was? Yours or Steffi's?"

"I don't mind if you ask me anything at all. And to answer that one—I asked her out."

I wondered if Bert somehow qualified as one of the *desirable* members of the Center that Gary had said Steffi chose to date or if she'd actually been attracted to the elderly gentleman who was charming but elderly nonetheless.

"You know, she was seriously involved with Gary Oldershaw," I said, just to see Bert's reaction in case he was lying about Steffi accepting the date.

"Not anymore, she wasn't. They broke up," he said as if acing the test he seemed to know I'd been giving him.

"You're on top of things, aren't you?" I teased him.

He wiggled his eyebrows mischievously and said, "I learned a long time ago in the army to keep my eyes and ears open," he said. "You're good at that, it shouldn't surprise you."

"Were you career army?"

"Oh no, thank you very much. I did my stint as a demolition man during the war and took my discharge with glee."

"I guess that means you know a lot about blowing things up," I said, still in that teasing tone we'd been using all along.

"You bet your booty," he confirmed. Then he leaned in close to my ear and said, "But I didn't blow up your car, if that's what you're thinking. Had no reason to."

The first song ended and Irene used the natural break to demonstrate what some of us were doing wrong before she started another.

Bert advised me not to watch my feet and I obliged.

"Did Steffi do your orientation to the Center?" I asked then, curious as to how widespread Steve's lie might be about Steffi doing them all.

"She did. And I was sold the minute I laid eyes on her."

"Sorry." Not about Steffi having done his orientation. I'd stepped on his foot but good.

Bert was polite enough not to wince.

Irene came over to us then to tell Bert what a wonderful job he was doing and to warn me to let him lead.

When she'd finished, she squeezed his arm and smiled warmly at him as if they shared a private joke.

Then she moved off to the next couple.

"Now, she might have done it," Bert whispered when Irene had moved out of earshot.

"Really? Why is that?" I asked, even though I could tell he wasn't being serious.

"Jealousy over Steffi's youth and beauty? Or those two you came in with," he said, looking first at Delia—who was happily dancing with Gary—and then at Brenda where she sat on a folding chair against one wall and watched the door.

"Brenda and Delia," I supplied the names.

"They could be in cahoots. They seem to be joined at the hip. Maybe they worked together to thin out the competition."

I laughed at his speculation and the delivery of it that made him sound like an ornery little boy. "Or maybe Steffi was a spy for a chain of health clubs and Steve found out and killed her before she could reveal his secrets," I said, playing along with Bert's game of irreverent what-ifing.

"Possible. We all do have our secrets," Bert allowed like an overzealous Hardy boy. "Or maybe she discovered our Arnold Schwarzenegger wannabe was taking steroids to build those muscles of his and she was going to turn him in to whoever regulates those muscleman things so he had to stop her."

I had to smile at the Arnold Schwarzenegger wannabe part. "Gary? I don't know. I think drug testing is de rigueur now. Nobody needs to turn anybody in."

"Then maybe it was just because she threw him over."

I didn't want to get into anything that might actually be true. But stepping on poor Bert's foot again spared me from having to comment.

He gave me a few more pointers—probably in an attempt to spare his toes—and then said, "And then there's Diane. Just as beautiful, younger even, and so sweet, sugar wouldn't melt in her mouth. But underneath the veneer could beat the heart of a killer."

He still sounded like an overly imaginative child, only now he put so much melodrama into his voice, it came out like something from an old radio mystery program.

"You never know," I said, playing along.

"Or there's you," he suggested matter-of-factly.

"True. Everyone's a suspect. But if you say my motive was jealousy over her youth and beauty I'm stepping on your feet on purpose."

"Maybe Steffi was the other woman in a love triangle that tore your husband from your side and you just got even."

"Mine will be the last husband she steals—is that it?" I asked even more melodramatically.

"And now, because Schwarzenegger knows what you've done and wants to get back at you, he blows up your car."

Bert actually sounded as if he half believed that one.

I just laughed and repeated, "You never know."

He let his eyes sweep the room then in a slow, exaggerated glance. "Or it could be any one of the rest of them here tonight. No one we know or have any clue about."

"True."

"Or someone not here at all. Someone Steffi had never met before, who just struck out at her for reasons nobody knows." Again he used the radio voice.

"True too," I agreed, but only in keeping with this game Bert and I seemed to be playing.

"Or maybe," he said then, coming full circle on both our subject and the room, "I'm just lying and when I asked her out she really did laugh in my face and call me a shriveled-up old coot and I just snapped."

The added details of that same scenario he'd proposed at the start of our dance and conversation seemed to make it more of a possibility.

"Maybe," I said in that same tone of voice he'd used about me, sounding as if I half believed it.

That made him laugh, so I laughed too.

But just because I was enjoying the elderly man's company, it didn't mean I wasn't curious about how he knew so much.

Or what secrets he might be keeping since he was so sure everyone had them.

The music stopped again, and this time Irene announced that we no longer needed partners because we were going to learn to line dance.

But before Bert went to Irene's side in response to her invitation for him to stand next to her, he again leaned toward my ear to say, "Shame on us for making light of that poor girl's murder."

But whether it was the glimmer of delight in his eyes or something else, I didn't have the sense that Bert felt any shame at all.

Chapter Sixteen

I SPENT SUNDAY afternoon helping my grandmother with dinner preparations. Helping as much as she would let me help, anyway. Mostly I washed dishes and pots and pans so they didn't pile up.

Our formal dining room isn't connected to the kitchen. It's off the living room, which means that everything has to be carried through. It's inconvenient and more than once has resulted in food being dropped on the living room carpet. So we don't use it much. But for that evening's party, Gramma wanted to take the risk. Besides, the kitchen wouldn't seat as many people as we had coming.

Just when I thought everything was under control and I could go up to the attic to get dressed in peace, the real work began. On me.

Apparently my daughters and my grandmother had studied the suggestions from my makeover session at the Center and plotted that this was the day it was going into effect. Whether I liked it or not.

And I didn't.

But as with the whole dating thing, I was overruled.

They knew better than to get me new clothes, but they had dug out the black slacks and high-necked blouse I'd worn to Chloe's high school graduation ceremony. Not as comfortable as the black jeans and silk turtleneck I'd planned on, but I could live with it.

Then they sat me in a chair and proceeded to play beauty shop.

At least Chloe and Shannon did. Gramma just coached from the sidelines and kept all mirrors out of my hands in the meantime so they could have their way with me without my protests at what they were doing.

I had visions of coming out of this looking like Bette Davis in *What Ever Happened to Baby Jane?*

My pale brown hair was curled to within an inch of its life and so were my eyelashes—they tend toward the long side, but it's less evident when I don't do anything with them.

My skin is light and shows every freckle—covering them and evening the tone was the reason they gave for slathering me with makeup and then powdering me until they'd taken my breath away.

My hazel-green eyes were lined and shadowed and mascaraed. My lips were drawn in and colored with darker lipstick than I'd ever used before. My nails were buffed, decuticled, and polished. Gold hoops were jammed through the nearly closed holes in my earlobes.

They pulled my wildly curly hair back into a cascade

with a stretchy headband that looked like a ring of garden spikes connected together and felt as if it were accomplishing a mini facelift, it held my scalp so tight.

At that point I started worrying I was going to end up looking more like something out of *Fright Night* than *Baby Jane*.

But then my pit crew finally let me look at myself and I was pleasantly surprised. It was a change for me, no doubt about it. A big one. And way more trouble than I'd ever go to every day. But I had to admit—grudgingly, of course—that the whole procedure had whipped me into shape. I probably still wouldn't turn heads in a crowded room but I didn't look half bad.

Rich cooking smells welcomed me when I went back downstairs, just the way I knew they would welcome our guests. They were in for a treat. Gramma had made her favorite spaghetti sauce—or what she calls her stew. It's a thick tomato sauce full of fresh basil, Parmigiano-Reggiano cheese, garlic, meatballs, sausage, chicken breasts, spare ribs, and braciola—a thin flank or round steak that she tenderizes, seasons with cheese, garlic, and herbs, then rolls like a jelly roll, ties, browns, and finishes to cook in the sauce.

Chloe and Shannon had set the table with Gramma's good china and silver, and as I checked the job they'd done, I counted place settings. Three times. Then I rejoined my grandmother in the kitchen.

"You, me, Chloe, Shannon, Danny, Carl, Delia, and Brenda," I said, flicking a finger for each name I recited. "That's eight. How come there are nine places at the table?" I asked.

"Ben makes nine," she supplied as she filled a pot with water.

"Ben Barrows? Lucy's father-in-law?"

"Lucy has a father-in-law?" Danny said as he came up from his apartment just in time to overhear.

"She wishes," I said.

Gramma took the huge pot to the stove to boil for the rigatoni. "I asked him," she said in answer to my question about Ben Barrows.

"When?"

"Yesterday. After what he did for us Thursday night over the car, I wanted to pay him back."

I wasn't too sure if the invitation was as innocent as it sounded. Sometimes I just can't tell with my grandmother. She can be cagey. And with the extra effort of my makeover added in, I was doubly suspicious.

But since she'd told me before that she'd disregarded the doctor as a potential mate for me, I gave her the benefit of the doubt and wrote off the invitation as just what she'd claimed it was—gratitude for his hospitality and consideration while we were banned from our house the other night.

"Put some oil and salt in the pot and watch it, Jimi, while I go change my dress and fix my face," Gramma said then, leaving Danny and me alone.

Danny gave me the once-over, raised his eyebrows, and did a wolf whistle.

"I know. I look pretty hot, don't I?" I deadpanned.

"Too hot to handle."

"Good. I don't want to be handled. You don't think Gramma is matchmaking me with Ben Barrows, do you?"

"Why should you be any different?"

"She said he'd sworn off women."

Danny just laughed, as if I was crazy if I believed that.

"Maybe he'll hit it off with Delia and we'll both be spared," I suggested.

"Until the next time Nellie can think of somebody for either of us."

I added some olive oil and salt to the water and changed the subject because I didn't want to think about what I might have in store for me in the next few hours.

"So," I said, "it occurred to me last night that there's a definite difference between how men felt about Steffi Hargitay and how women felt about her. The men I've talked to loved her, the women hated her. Is that what you've found or am I mistaken? Are there any women who liked her?"

"None that I've come across."

"Does that mean you're looking for a woman as the killer?"

"There's certainly more of a stacked deck on that side than the other."

"Hitting someone with something besides a fist does seem like more what a woman might do than a man," I put in as I thought about it.

"Not exclusively but factored into how many women Steffi pissed off, I'd say you could lean that way. On the other hand, not *all* the men who knew her—or encountered her—liked her."

"Bert Chumley asked her out and thought she was sweet and lovely. Gary was in love with her. She saved Carl from embarrassment and made his life more bearable in high school and he thought she was an angel—his word. I still can't tell what was going on between her and Steve Stivik—is that who you think didn't like her?"

"I'm still not sure about that one way or the other myself. But there's also the good Dr. Barrows."

That surprised me. "Huh?"

"His name was in Steffi's date book."

"You're kidding."

"He joined the New You Center last September and apparently went out with her."

"So much for swearing off women."

Danny raised his eyebrows at me as if to say *I told you so.*

"Have you talked to him about it?" I asked.

"I was at his office on Thursday. It's one of the stops I made that day in your car."

"I asked him if he blew up my car over Lucy—just teasing. Do you think he might have done it over this, seriously?"

"I'm not betting on it, but—"

"You never know," I finished for him.

Danny shrugged his agreement.

"What you're telling me is that Gramma's trying to fix me up with somebody who could be a murderer and mad bomber?"

"She's doing the same thing to me—don't count Delia out. Her father owns a construction company. She could have had access to the dynamite. We know she hated Steffi. And when I went to that travel agency to talk to her on Thursday I met her as she was coming out, so she saw the car I was driving."

"Great," I said facetiously at about the same time the doorbell rang to announce the arrival of one of our guests. "Maybe we'd better frisk them all at the door before we let them in."

But the truth was, the evening I hadn't been looking

forward to a few moments before finding out our
neighbor, the doctor, could be a suspect suddenly had
more appeal for me.

At least that made the doctor interesting and gave
me something to talk to him about.

My suspicions of my grandmother's intent were
renewed when she told us all where to sit around the
table, pairing up Carl and Brenda, Danny and Delia,
and Ben and me, while she sat at the head of the table
with Chloe and Shannon on either side of her. I was
regretting not inviting Bert Chumley after all, to put
her in the same boat she'd put me in.

The meal was lively, though. Between Carl's energy
and exuberance, Delia's talkativeness, and Gramma,
conversation never lagged. In fact, Gramma even managed to bring Brenda out of her shell slightly and make
her laugh, which I counted as a miracle.

The food was a big hit. But then, I've never met anyone who didn't love my grandmother's cooking, and
the mud cake I made for dessert and served with
French vanilla ice cream and homemade hot fudge
sauce went over well too.

Apparently Gramma had made arrangements with
Chloe and Shannon ahead of time because once everybody was filled to the gills the three of them began to
clear the table. When I stood to help, my grandmother
insisted forcefully that all six of the rest of us stay right
where we were. That was when I knew without a doubt
that she'd put her matchmaking hat on with Ben Barrows's invitation.

I would have been more irritated with it if I hadn't been so curious about his connection to Steffi Hargitay.

Once the table was cleared and Gramma had us all sipping Rock & Rye liqueur, Carl and Delia honed in on their conquests.

Carl was definitely putting the moves on Brenda. I just hoped he wasn't boring her with all the talk about Cutler's Corner and his plans to franchise. I could tell he was a little nervous with her and thought he was probably talking too much because of that. But I wished he would find a topic she might be able to participate in.

Then again, maybe Brenda was too timid to participate no matter what the subject and it was just as well that Carl kept up a steady monologue on his pet project.

Delia was blatantly flirting with Danny, asking him endless questions about his personal life as if she were his biographer. Danny was using the opportunity to try to scare her off with tales of his three failed marriages. But it didn't seem to be working because the more he pointed out the perils of relationships with cops, the more determined Delia appeared to get. She moved her chair closer and closer to his, and she pushed at the gardenia in her hair as if it were a love charm she expected to work on him at any moment.

Since Carl and Delia had broken things up into couples, I was left naturally with Ben Barrows.

He'd come dressed casually in corduroy jeans and a camel-colored sweater with a white shirt collar sticking out of the crew neck. He looked particularly nice, I thought. He smelled good too. A little spicy. I liked it.

In fact, he was a pretty attractive guy all around. He seemed relaxed and as if he felt right at home, which I was also glad to see. In fact, he'd been the first arrival, and when we'd taken him into the kitchen with us he'd even lifted the lid on Gramma's pot of sauce.

Now he sat back in the chair he'd turned sideways to the table to face me, propping one ankle on the opposite knee. He was studying me the way he'd done on the porch steps on Friday morning and I wondered if he was making some kind of habit out of it.

I decided to ignore it and just launch into what I wanted to know.

"I understand you joined the New You Center yourself a while ago," I said, referring to the earlier part of the evening when I'd added the fact of Delia's, Brenda's, and Carl's memberships into their introductions.

"This last fall, when it first opened. They did a special promotion for professional people in the area and I thought why not give it a shot. But it didn't work out for me."

"You didn't meet your Magnificent Mate?"

"I didn't even meet a Dandy Dinner Partner."

"But you dated Steffi Hargitay?"

"One date," he amended, keeping his blue eyes on me.

"You didn't like her?"

"Not particularly. She was nice to look at but not what I'd call a peach. Besides, she had a different agenda than I thought she had, and I didn't appreciate it."

"How so?"

"I was on a date. She was on a recruitment."

"For a cult or what?" I asked, joking.

"Yeah, she wanted me to shave my head, wear a foil hat, and sit around chanting *new you, new you, new you* until the mother ship came to beam us all up," he joked back, winning himself a point in the sense-of-humor column. "No, she wanted me for the *team,* as she put it."

"Softball? Basketball? Squash?"

"Kickback."

"I don't think I've ever played that."

"Me neither," he said wryly. "She wanted me *on board* with the Center. She said she would start recommending plastic surgery during the makeover counseling sessions, send the lambs over to me for the slaughter—her phrasing, not mine—I could charge a little extra and give her a cut. Kickbacks."

"Ah. But I thought you were a dermatologist not a plastic surgeon."

"That's what I told her. I'm a board-certified dermatologist and I actually lobby against dermatologists passing themselves off as plastic surgeons and getting into that area when they aren't specifically trained for it. There are more and more who do it after a few quickie refresher courses but without having had a residency in it and without being qualified. I do peels, injections, minor procedures that fall within my specialty, but that's it. And I don't do kickbacks to anyone or want patients who've had their insecurities played upon to push them into anything."

And I was betting that was just how he'd told Steffi no—with a building vehemence by the time he'd finished that speech. A vehemence that clearly came from being insulted even to be asked such a thing.

"How'd she take the rejection?"

"She turned into a flaming bitch."

Nothing like telling it like it is.

"She'd started out with this very seductive come-on, falling all over me, throwing a lot of hints about what beautiful music we could make together. Then she did her pitch and when I turned it down the claws came out and she attacked me personally."

"You mean, like she hit you?"

"No," he said, cooling off enough to laugh. "She just told me I was a homely-looking, paunchy asshole who was going to have to wave my medical degree and my bank account around to ever get laid."

"Have you tried it?" I asked, joking again because as snits went, I thought I could come up with something better than that.

Ben laughed. "Have I tried getting laid or waving my medical degree and my bank account around?"

"Waving the degree and the bank account," I clarified.

"Not yet."

I refrained from asking if he'd gotten laid. Didn't seem like good after-dinner chitchat.

Instead I said, "Did she hurt your feelings?"

"You mean enough to murder her? No. But the whole deal wasn't what I needed to hear. I joined the damn club—or whatever you call it—because I was in the market for an ego boost. Right away this gorgeous young thing comes on to me and I think, great, just what the doctor ordered. But she blows me out of the water with the kickback proposal so I know that's what she was after from the get-go instead of being attracted to me. Then she frosts the cake with the nasty comments about my person. It put me back into hibernation."

I appreciated his candor about his own feelings and responses to Steffi. "Did she want the kickbacks for herself or for the Center?"

"I wasn't really clear on that."

"And that was it? One date that turned hostile?"

"She made a phone call to my house after that. To offer me Diane Samboro—"

"What does that mean—to offer you Diane Samboro?"

"To date, I guess. Steffi said she could probably persuade her to go out with me if I'd reconsider the plastic surgery referrals and kickbacks. When I said no, she got abusive again, said I smelled bad, even threatened to blackball me."

I took a sniff of him but all I smelled was that spicy-scented aftershave. "How was she going to blackball you?"

"She said there were always people who came in with bad skin or ugly moles that she recommended they have treated. Only since I wasn't cooperating, when she told them to see a doctor she'd make sure to tell them *not* to use me because people they'd sent to me before had had bad results."

"Nice."

"She was a sweetheart," he agreed facetiously.

"Did it sound like the kickbacks were something that went on with other people? I mean, who else was on the *team* she wanted you to join?"

"She didn't say but she alluded to the fact that it was common practice among people who had any amount of brains at all—as in: I didn't."

"Do you think she really thought she could intimidate you?"

"Seemed like it. But she thought wrong."

Apparently. Because thinking right didn't get you killed.

Chapter Seventeen

MY GRANDMOTHER DOESN'T interrupt me when I'm
working unless it's important. So when she knocked on
the attic door a little after eleven Monday morning, I
assumed there was a good reason.

Well, there was a reason, anyway.

"Jimi! Jimi! I got you a date!"

She also got my attention.

"A date?" I repeated cautiously, hoping I'd heard
wrong.

"With the butcher's boy. I was just at the store with
Amelia and there he was visiting his father and carrying
a brochure for the New You Center for Dating. That's
how we got to talking because I told him you were
going there too. He said he's looking for a nice girl so I
said you were a nice girl and he said he'd like to meet

you and I said you weren't doing anything for lunch today and since he was off work this was the perfect time."

Gramma's cheeks were red with excitement.

Unfortunately, I didn't feel the same way. In fact, the wheels of my brain went into instant overdrive trying to think of a way out of this.

"He'll be here in forty-five minutes," Gramma went on. "Can you get dressed up like you were last night?"

Last night. So much for Danny's being worse off than me because Gramma had arranged a blind date for him with Delia. Hadn't my having dinner primarily with the doctor been enough?

"Gramma . . ." I began.

"I know what you're going to say and don't say it. He's a nice boy. A butcher, too—like his father. And your same age and his eye only wanders a little. What can it hurt? Lunch. That's nothing. And just think, if you hit it off we'll be in for the best cuts of meat— maybe at a discount."

I knew she meant that innocently, that she wasn't really pimping me out for a good porterhouse steak. But I still didn't like it. Any of it.

I also didn't seem to have any more choice in the matter than Danny—or I—had had the night before.

I tried, believe me. All through her prodding to change clothes and put on the makeup the girls had applied on Sunday. All through Gramma's wielding of the curling iron and trying to work that headband contraption.

But when the doorbell rang at noon, there I was, dragged downstairs by my grandmother, being introduced to the butcher's boy.

Claude Hagenstreit.

Five feet two inches tall—shorter than I am. Wispy, dirty blond hair he'd lost half of. Brown eyes—one that wandered just enough to make it seem as if he were looking over my shoulder at something behind me. The tiniest nose I'd ever seen. Bright pink lips. A huge gap between his front teeth. And warts. The man had three warts the size of dimes—two on one cheek and another down on his jawbone.

And even though he pulled a bouquet of flowers out from behind his back as my grandmother ushered him in, the scent of feet wafted in along with him.

Just before he looked me up and down and grimaced as if he'd seen something he didn't particularly like.

Let's just say it wasn't love at first sight for either of us.

His favorite restaurant, he told me as we went out to his faded gray truck, was the International House Of Pancakes. So that's where he was taking me for lunch.

He didn't open the passenger door for me but went around to the driver's side, got in, and left me waiting while he put on his seat belt before he reached across the seat and unlocked the door on my side.

Over a bowl of vegetable soup and a grilled cheese sandwich Claude told me he was a thrill seeker. Bungee jumping, sky-diving, shooting the rapids—those were all things he was going to do someday. And despite the fact that he made his living as a butcher, he actually considered his occupation to be photojournalist. Even though he'd never had a picture published and only used those handy disposable cameras.

I spent a lot of time thinking how much more I'd

enjoyed Ben Barrows's company the night before, and was ecstatic when the meal was finished and we were headed home.

Neither of us talked much during that drive and as my house came into view Claude's "Maybe I'll see you around," let me know he wasn't any more interested in repeating this performance than I was.

The truck was still rolling slightly when I got out— he didn't have any intention of coming to a complete stop. But that was okay with me. I would have dived out at an even faster speed just to get away from the guy.

I didn't know how this would affect the flirtation my grandmother enjoyed with the butcher, but I thought we were probably in line for more gristle in our ground round. I figured it was what she deserved for putting me in that situation. The membership to the dating center was bad enough but this—

I was actually working up a pretty good head of steam from the curb to the front porch, but it got diffused suddenly with the sound of another truck pulling into the driveway.

I turned, half afraid Claude had come back, only to find my skinny cousin Vince arriving instead.

At our dinner party Sunday night Carl had asked if he could leave a check for Vince with us. Vince needed the money to buy the building supplies for Carl's shed and didn't want to go all the way into downtown Denver to Cutler's Corner to meet Carl to pick it up.

Neither Gramma nor I had had a problem with that, so Carl had written out the check. But we'd both figured Vince was likely to show up for it about midday, at a propitious moment for being invited to eat. He's no different than anyone else when it comes to my grandmother's cooking—he's wild for it—but he's also so tight he squeaks and a free lunch is a free lunch.

Inside, Gramma was ready for him with the kitchen table laden with food. Although this time it didn't turn out to be completely free because Gramma extracted a payback—Vince had to walk over to Ben Barrows's house with me afterward and put his handyman talents to work making the walkway under the gate into Ben's backyard look as if Lucy had never messed it up.

Well, practically. He couldn't fix the foliage the dog had dug up on the borders, but by the time he was through, every stone was level with every other stone and the dirt was hard-packed around them.

I hoped the doctor would notice when he got home.

Of course, Gramma could hardly wait until we were alone to ask about my midday date with the butcher's son.

"Let's just say please don't ever—*ever*—do that to me again," I said now that my head of steam had evaporated.

She was having some trouble not grinning. "He didn't look so good out from behind that meat counter," she admitted. "I thought he was taller and I didn't see those warts on his face from the distance. And he smelled a little, too, didn't he?"

"Like feet," I said with a bit of my pique sounding.

"I'm sorry, Jimi," Gramma said with a full-out laugh by then. "I guess I just got carried away. The butcher's nice."

"Well, his son isn't. Next time make a date for yourself and the butcher and leave me out of it," I said as I headed for the attic.

But I could hear my grandmother giggling to herself behind me.

At least one of us had gotten a kick out of it.

After a productive afternoon that left me with the police report on my car faxed in to the insurance people to help speed payoff on my claim and with the kitchen catalog at the halfway mark, I got roped into going to the New You Center for The Lost Art Of Flirting and How to Recapture It class.

As if I hadn't had my fill of dating for the day.

Delia had called and left a message on my answering machine that offered me a ride to the Center for the class. Shannon had played back the message and she, Chloe, and my grandmother had ganged up on me to pressure me to go.

And just in case I didn't want to impose on Delia again, Gramma threw in my grandfather's Chevy Nova for me to drive, sealing the deal and simultaneously canceling my plans for a leisurely evening of movie watching.

No doubt about it, some gifts can really be a pain.

So, once dinner was finished I left the three conspirators to do the dishes and went to the Center.

The class turned out to be a lot of fun. For me, at least. And only because of Bert Chumley.

As with dancing, he needed no tutoring on the subject of flirting but had come purely for the entertainment value. I had to give him credit, he got the most bang for his enrollment buck.

I was sure I wasn't who he had come to spend the evening with, though. Especially since there were several other women—younger and older than me— whom he greeted by name, waved to, or blew a kiss.

But because everyone else was already paired up when he and I happened to arrive at the same time, he got stuck with me.

Not that he showed any signs of disappointment. He made light of the whole nonsense of learning to flirt and had me laughing most of the evening while still adding to Diane's and Irene's lesson.

I liked Bert's methods better. He was more subtle and used humor rather than the slap-'em-up-the-side-of-the-head so-called charm that was the class curriculum. Not that I thought I'd ever use his methods, either, but it helped make the session bearable.

When the class was over, Bert was swept away by those other women eager to have a little of his attention and I was left to my own devices again. But not for long. Delia and Brenda worked their way through the folding chairs to where I was pulling my coat on preparing to leave.

"You looked like you were having a good time," Delia said.

"Bert's quite a character," I answered, unsure how Brenda would take it. But just because she disliked the elderly gentleman for some reason, didn't mean I had to.

"We just wanted to thank you again for last night," Delia said. "We had such a nice time."

"I'm glad. We enjoyed having you."

She was wearing a large lily in her hair tonight and another floor-length, brightly flowered sarong draped over a white blouse.

"Tell that cousin of yours that anytime he has a night free to give me a call," Delia added.

"I will," I said, but then I changed the focus from

Delia to Brenda before I had to make any more of a commitment on Danny's behalf. "How about you and Carl, Brenda? You guys seemed to hit it off. Any dates on the horizon for you?"

"I don't know. Maybe," she said without enthusiasm.

We were standing near the door that was open to the hallway and she was preoccupied with looking through it, particularly whenever anyone passed by.

She had on the same outfit she'd worn to dinner the night before—black slacks that were so old they'd turned ashy around all the seams and creases, and a gray V-neck sweater that had a mend near the bottom center as if it had been caught in her zipper at some point, torn, and repaired.

I didn't think her hair had been washed, either, because it hung even more limply than it had the previous evening, and I wondered if she'd had her makeover counseling yet or was planning to take the advice if she had. Surely Diane or Irene would send her to a hairstylist and recommend some new clothes even if they had to be inexpensive. I knew for a fact that the thrift shop Shannon liked to check out for some of her freakier outfits sold clothes in better shape than what Brenda had on. And for next to nothing.

Just then Diane passed by us on her way out and said good night.

Brenda tried to stop her, but Diane begged off, saying she was in a hurry to get to the bathroom but that Irene could help with anything we wanted.

That drew Irene's attention from where she was gathering papers on top of the schoolteacher's desk at the front of the room. "Who needs me?" she asked.

"I just wanted to know if Steve is here tonight," Brenda said, speaking up loudly enough to be heard, more loudly than I'd ever heard her before. So loudly, she even drew glances from Bert's group. Or maybe it was the urgency that seemed to underlie her tone.

Irene checked her wristwatch and then said, "Steve was gone earlier but he's probably back by now. He always uses the sauna at closing time while we clean up."

Brenda thanked her for the information and then turned to Delia. "I have to talk to him," she said with more of that almost panicky determination in her voice.

Delia watched her go, shaking her head as she did.

"Aren't things going well with Brenda and Steve?" I asked, trying not to sound too hopeful.

"I don't know. One minute he's sweet-talking her. The next he withdraws and she'll do anything to please him so he's nice to her again. I don't like it. But you know how it goes—I can't say anything."

"She'd be better off with Carl," I said, putting in a pitch for my neighbor.

But all I got in response was a vague "Mmm" that led me to think Carl might not be winning the competition with Steve.

Bert called a general good night to us then and left, which broke up his group of admirers, who all headed for the door too.

"Well, maybe I'll check out a few videos while I wait for Brenda," Delia said as the room emptied of all but the two of us and Irene. "Want to join me?"

About as much as I wanted to have pins stuck into my eyes.

But I didn't say that. Instead I said, "No, thanks

anyway. I saw Carl head for the weight room a while ago and I want to talk to him about my car."

"Oh that's right, he's helping you get a new one," she said as she adjusted the biggest fishnet purse I'd ever seen so it didn't fall off her shoulder. "But really, don't hesitate to call if you need a ride anyplace. I'd be happy to help."

I believed it. Delia seemed like a genuinely nice person. She probably always had been. Which made me feel bad for the times I'd overheard her made fun of in high school for her odd clothes and the flowers in her hair.

I knew Danny was dead serious about keeping her on the list of suspects, but the more I got to know her, the harder it was for me to see her as someone who might have picked up the still missing video camera and smashed Steffi Hargitay's head in with it. Even if Steffi had been unkind to her. And I certainly couldn't see Delia blowing up my Subaru.

Danny might be right that anything was possible, but I just didn't think Delia as a murderer and mad bomber was too likely.

" 'Night," she said to me and to Irene then.

"Good night," I responded as I bent over to drag my purse out from under the chair I'd been sitting on throughout the evening, intent on catching Carl before he left.

I didn't make it out of the room, though, before Irene said, "So. Are you seeing Bert Chumley?"

It took me a little off guard. I even glanced around in case I'd missed someone else in the room with us. But Irene and I were the only two there.

"No," I answered belatedly, ignoring the challenging

note in her voice. "Not outside the Center. You put us together yourself in dance class and tonight was just a coincidence. He's fun, though."

"Does that mean you'd be interested if he did want to see you outside of the Center?"

"Me? No." I said it with force but stopped short of explaining that not only wasn't I attracted to him, he was old enough to be my grandfather. The age thing might not have gone over too well with a woman who was probably in the same bracket.

Irene had come around to the front of the desk and she leaned against it, stretching out long legs to cross at the ankles. She had on a pair of white wool slacks and a white cashmere sweater set that gave her a sophisticated, casual appearance. Her silvery hair shimmered with highlights that might have been natural or might not have been, and her makeup was so flawless, her skin looked like velvet. She really was a striking woman. The kind we all wish we'd end up looking like at an advanced age. Or even a not so advanced one.

"Are you seeing Bert?" I asked, figuring one point-blank question deserved another.

"I don't seem to be getting anywhere with him, no. Apparently I'm too old for him," she said, making it clear she didn't appreciate that. Then she added, "He seems to like them no more than your age."

Just what Danny had said about Bert.

"Maybe you should try going younger too," I suggested.

"Younger men?" Irene smiled and I felt as if I'd finally broken the ice with her.

"It's not unheard of, you know. And if anyone could do it, I'd think you could. You're gorgeous. In great shape. Pulled together." I wasn't sucking up. It was all true.

Irene visually warmed. "I'm also sixty-eight years old. Besides, I can't see myself with anyone more than a few years younger. Ten or twenty or thirty years and I feel like their mothers. Or worse, their grandmothers," she confessed with a warm laugh.

"Do you have kids or grandkids?" I ventured.

Irene shook her head. "Bad for the career. I was a model and in my heyday things weren't the way they are today. A pregnancy canceled you out for good. Of course, not having kids cost me my first husband."

"Did you have more than one?"

"Four. And a live-in Latin lover for ten years, too, who ended up stealing me blind or I wouldn't have to be working here now."

I really did want to talk to Carl. But how could I ignore an opening like that?

"I understand Steffi Hargitay wasn't happy to have you working here," I said, figuring I could call Carl at home if I needed to.

"Steffi Hargitay," Irene repeated, partly as if she'd forgotten about her, partly as if she couldn't stand the sound of the name. "In a life that's put me into contact with more unpleasant women than I could count, she was the worst of them all. By far."

Since we were talking about a long life complete with four husbands and a Latin lover, I thought that was saying something.

"Wasn't Steffi in on the hiring when you got the job here?" I asked. I'd had the impression Steffi had been by Steve's side from the get-go and wondered why she hadn't stopped him from hiring Irene in the first place.

"Oh, she didn't mind having me work here at first. She even agreed with Steve that I would be a good draw for the older clientele. But then I had a little fling with her father and her tune changed."

"I heard she hadn't seen her father in over ten years," I said, confused.

"I don't know who you heard that from, but it's a lie. They'd been estranged for years, but the month before last he came to town and tried to patch things up with her. That was when I met him."

"He wasn't a lot younger than you?" I said carefully. After all, Steffi wasn't too much older than Chloe and my former husband was much too young for Irene's specifications.

"His relationship with Steffi's mother was another of the May–December things so he was closer to my age."

"But Steffi didn't like you dating him?" I prompted.

"You know, I think she was jealous," Irene said as if it had just occurred to her. "No, she didn't like me dating him. She didn't want me anywhere near him."

"So she thought if she got you fired it would keep you away?" I guessed.

"No, her trying to get me fired didn't start until after he left. She'd already won the battle but that wasn't enough for her."

"He stopped seeing you because she wanted him to?" Another guess.

"He stopped seeing me because she bribed him to."

So much for my guesses.

"What did she bribe him with?" I asked.

"There was an inheritance from his own father that bypassed him. The old man—he was ninety-three—hadn't approved of some of what Steffi's father had

done in his life and to get his point across, he'd left a
house and I'm not sure what all—nothing huge, but
what amounted to a plump little package—to Steffi
instead. And her father wanted to convince her that she
should give him half. That it was only fair. That's why
he came here in the first place."

"Did he need it?"

"I didn't think so at first. He lived well, had expensive taste, spent money freely. But later I found out that
living above his means had left him in some financial
trouble and he really did need the money. So when
Steffi gave him the choice of half the inheritance or me,
he opted for the inheritance. Of course, once he was
back in California, she didn't end up giving it to him.
She kept the whole thing for herself."

"She told you that?"

"He did. He called once he'd given up hope of getting any of the inheritance from her and asked me to
move out there with him. I might have gone except I
was worried that all he really wanted was my second
income. And to tell you the truth, I'm looking to quit
work and be taken care of myself."

Irene's honesty surprised me. I wondered if she
knew Bert Chumley was living only on social security.

But I didn't tell her. Instead I said, "And bribing her
father to stay away from you wasn't enough of a blow
to strike against you? Steffi wanted you out of the Center then too?"

"We'd never gotten along. Not that that was unusual. Steffi fought with a lot of people. But the business
with her father was the straw that broke the camel's
back. Getting Steve to fire me seemed to become a
sacred quest for her after that. She started saying I

made them all look bad. That counselors here should be young and attractive, not old prune-faced hags."

Irene was a long way from a prune-faced hag. But the bitterness she felt did etch some deeper lines into her photogenic face.

"Steffi must have known you needed the job."

"She did. She didn't care. In fact, I think that sweetened the pot—knowing just how badly I need the job. I honestly felt as if she would have had some satisfaction seeing me out on the streets."

"Luckily Steve didn't listen to her," I said. But something about Irene's expression told me differently, so I added, "Did he?"

"She wouldn't let up on him. And frankly, although I don't know any of the details, I was afraid she had something on him that gave her the same kind of leverage she'd used with her father. I think Steve was on the verge of giving in."

"Until she died."

"I thought I'd be out of the woods then. But he's still watching me as if he's thinking about everything Steffi planted in his mind. I may find myself out on my ear yet."

"So it didn't ease your mind to have Steffi out of the way."

I must not have put that right because it made Irene defensive. "I didn't kill her to get her *out of the way,* if that's what you're thinking."

Who me?

"I didn't say that."

"I'm a lot of things but I'm not a killer. And I certainly wouldn't have murdered anyone over a job."

"Especially when it didn't even insure it," I agreed,

hoping to get myself out of this before she got too angry. Because from the look of Irene, she had a pretty good temper of her own.

"I'm also not the only one around here who hated Steffi," she said as if she had the inside line.

"Who would get your vote?" I asked, careful to keep my tone merely conversational.

"Diane, for starters."

"Diane told me Steffi wasn't her greatest friend."

"That's an understatement. Steffi had Diane in tears at least once a week and raving mad more than that."

"Over what?"

"Everything. Steffi ridiculed every outfit Diane wore, every hairstyle, every word that came out of Diane's mouth. I've never seen anyone be as cruel as Steffi was to Diane. And without letting up. She was vicious. Knives couldn't have cut Diane more than Steffi's mouth."

"Why did Steffi hate Diane so much?"

"I'm not sure. But I know that just after Diane was hired Steffi asked her to be *extra* friendly to some of the members whether she was interested in them or not."

"How do you mean? She didn't want Diane to *sleep* with them, did she?"

Irene closed her eyes and raised her brows as if to say I could draw my own conclusions.

"That would be prostitution of sorts, wouldn't it?" I persisted.

Again Irene merely left it to me to decide.

"Did Steffi ask you to do anything like that?"

Irene laughed. "I'm hardly of an age where she would."

"And Diane wouldn't agree to it?"

"No. But that was when Steffi turned so venomous to her. If anybody could have been driven to kill Steffi, it would have been Diane and I wouldn't have blamed her. Of course, I wouldn't have blamed Gary, either, since Steffi dumped him in favor of *dating* members. And, like I said, I don't know what the leverage was that she had with Steve, but she's been riding him hard for a while now. I'm sure he's a happier man with her out of the picture."

Not a lot of loyalty among the New You Center ranks.

Irene looked at her wristwatch the way she had earlier, and pushed away from the desk to stand tall and straight and signal that our visit was over. "It's just about closing time. I'd better finish up so I can get home tonight."

I took my cue. "I wanted to catch Carl before he leaves, too," I said. Then I nodded in the direction of the door. "Good luck with Bert."

She let out a ladylike but still derisive snort of a laugh. "Oh, I think that dog is dead. There's no fool like an old fool, you know."

"I guess," I said, not too sure whether she was referring to Bert or to herself.

I also wasn't too sure if she'd instigated our conversation for the express purpose of planting seeds of doubt about her co-workers.

One thing was for sure, though, she was yet another woman who had hated Steffi. For good reason.

But as I left the classroom I tried to keep the image in my mind of the younger Steffi Hargitay, who had stood up for Carl against his high school tormentors.

I didn't know what had changed her into the super-bitch most women—and Steve Stivik—thought she'd been, but it was good to remember she'd once had enough heart to defend a homely, scrawny boy who'd adored her.

I would have liked to have gone home right after my chat with Irene, but I really did want to talk to Carl about the car. So when I stepped out into the hall, I turned left toward the weight room rather than heading for the lobby.

I nearly collided with Delia and Gary Oldershaw, who were standing a few feet outside the door. Apparently Delia hadn't made it to the video counter. Instead she was leaning against the corridor wall, apparently practicing some of what she'd learned in flirting class on Gary.

Gary didn't seem particularly impressed by it.

He looked at me as I came out and said, "Hi."

I returned it and then, since he was supposed to be working out with Carl, I asked, "Is Carl still here or have I missed him?"

Gary pointed down the hall. "He's still in the weight room."

"Thanks," I said, and left them to each other.

The lights were on in the aerobics/dance studio and I glanced in as I passed. Diane was there, setting out exercise mats for the morning class and playing one of the tapes we'd danced to on the boom box, a country western two-step.

I decided to take a shortcut to the weight room through the women's locker room, wondering as I did if Brenda had found Steve. There were no signs of her or him—or of anyone else for that matter—as I went down the center aisle between the locker rows. In fact, every step I took echoed through the empty space.

The utility room was at the same end as the facing doors to the weight room and the aerobics/dance studio. The utility room was also the only way to get to the sauna, so if Brenda had located Steve there—as Irene had suggested—I wouldn't have been able to see them anyway unless I went all the way into the utility room and peeked into the sauna. And since I didn't have any excuse for doing that—and since I couldn't hear the sound of any voices coming from there even though I strained a little trying—my curiosity had to go unquenched.

Instead I reached for the handle of the door to the weight room.

But I'd barely turned it when the utility room door flew open from the other side.

Not having expected it, I was slightly startled.

But not nearly as startled as I was a split second later.

Chapter Eighteen

"AY, YOU MEAN he's one of those kind who takes out his coglione in public?"

"I'm not really sure." In fact, I was unsure of exactly what had happened the previous night at the New You Center when the utility room door had opened suddenly. Sitting at lunch with my grandmother the next day was the first I'd said anything about it to anyone.

"Who is this old buzzard?"

"His name is Bert Chumley. He's about your age. A nice man—or so I thought. A lot of fun. I liked him. I'd just spent that whole class with him as my partner."

"And then when nobody else is around he shows you his thing?" Gramma was working up a head of steam about it and I was wondering if I'd picked the wrong person to tell.

"It was only a split second. I had the feeling that it wasn't me he was expecting to see in that locker room and when he realized who I was he shut the door in a hurry. Maybe he had a secret tryst planned with somebody and I was just the wrong somebody. But yes, for that split second, there he was with his pants open, flapping in the breeze."

"What kind of place is this we sent you to? People die. Men do this. Whatsa matter with it?"

"It isn't as if I haven't seen it before, but I could have lived forever not seeing it again like that."

"Tell Danny," Gramma concluded. "Report it."

"Tell Danny and report what?"

Gramma and I both jumped about a foot off our vinyl kitchen chairs. With the cherry wood door closed, Danny had come in silently from the back entrance and scared us, just the way Bert had scared me the night before.

Well, not *just* the way. Danny's brown dress pants were zipped.

"What're you doing home in the middle of the day?" Gramma asked.

Danny sniffed the air. "I could smell your minestrone from ten miles away so I came home for a bowl."

That was all it took for Gramma to get up and ladle some of the rich soup into a man-size bowl while I sliced him two thick pieces of the bread she'd baked the day before and filled a glass with ice and water.

When all three of us were sitting around the Formica-topped table again, Danny said, "Are you going to tell me what you were talking about when I came in?"

"Some old buzzard showed himself to Jimi last night at that dating place."

Danny got serious. His forehead beetled up and his eyebrows took a dip over the bridge of his nose. "What?"

I explained about taking a shortcut through the women's locker room to get to the weight room and what had happened before I'd managed to get there.

"You saw Bert Chumley in the utility room at what time?"

"Boy did I see Bert Chumley in the utility room," I joked, since Danny had gotten a little too serious too fast. "It must have been shortly before ten or maybe right at ten because I'd been talking to Irene—who had some things to say that you'll be interested in—and she'd looked at her watch and said it was closing time. And when I finally pulled myself together after the shock of seeing Bert Chumley's little wing-ding and went into the weight room, Carl was getting ready to leave too."

"Shouldn't somebody like that get arrested?" Gramma asked. "What if he shows it to little kids?"

Danny didn't address that. Instead he said to me, "Did you see anyone else in the women's locker room?"

"No. I didn't hear anyone else either. I'm reasonably sure I was the only one in there. Much to Bert's dismay, I think. And definitely to mine."

"What about behind Bert? Did you see anyone else in the utility room?"

"It all happened in a flash—literally—Danny. But I don't recall anyone standing behind him, no."

"What about the sauna, did you see it? Was the door open? Was anyone in there?"

This was getting stranger and stranger. "The sauna?"

"Did you notice anything about it?" he reiterated.

"What do you mean, like did I notice that there was some kind of orgy going on in the sauna and I just happened to come face-to-face—so to speak—with Bert and his unzipped pants when he went out for beer?"

Danny just gave me the hard cop-stare while he ate some of his soup. And waited for me to answer his question. I rolled my eyes at him. "No, I didn't notice that the sauna door was open. And there was no way for me to see if anyone was in it unless I'd gone into the utility room and pressed my eye to that three-inch square of glass that pretends to be a window in the sauna door. I didn't do that, so I don't have any idea if there was anybody in it. I do know that Irene had told Brenda earlier that she might find Steve there."

"What does any of that have to do with the price of tea in China, Danny?" Gramma demanded.

"There are just some things I need to know, Nellie," Danny said patiently. Then back to me he said, "Did Bert say anything to you?"

"He looked as much like a deer caught in headlights as I'm sure I did. That's why I said it was as if he expected me to be somebody else. There were about five women vying for his attention at the class, I thought maybe he had something set up with one of them and I just happened to be in the wrong place at the wrong time."

"Do you know any of the women he was with after class?"

I still didn't know what this had to do with anything.

"No, I've seen their faces here and there at the Center but I couldn't tell you who any of them were."

"What about you? Did you get mad? Did you do or say anything to him? Did you holler out?"

"I believe I said, 'Oh!' and then he was gone and I stood there for a minute like an idiot, wondering if I'd really just seen what I'd seen. Then I decided it must have been some kind of mistake and I went to talk to Carl in the weight room."

"Did you tell Carl what had happened?"

The cop who came to lunch. "No. What was I going to say—guess what I just saw?"

"Did you mention Bert Chumley to Carl at all? Or the fact that Bert was in the utility room?"

"What's going on, Danny?" Gramma tried again, proving that she was as suspicious as I was of this whole thing.

But rather than answering her question, he just repeated his to me. Apparently I was being interrogated for some reason neither I nor my grandmother could fathom. Or stop.

"No, I didn't mention Bert to Carl at all or tell Carl that Bert was anywhere around. I asked Carl if he'd talked to his brother-in-law. He said he had, just before leaving for the Center, and that we could go over to the lot as soon as he—Carl—could free up some time."

"Then what?"

"Then they danced the cha-cha! What the hell is going on, Danny?" Gramma said, obviously as tired of this one-sided game as I was.

But by then I knew it wouldn't get us anywhere not to answer Danny so I said, "Then Carl said he'd give me a call today to set it up and I left to come home."

"Did Carl leave with you? Hit the showers? What?"

"He left with me, we got as far as the lobby and Diane Samboro called him over to the video counter to tell him someone was interested in a date. He took the woman's videotape to watch at home and walked me out to my car. Then he went to his own."

"What about anyone else—did you talk to anybody else on your way out? Tell anybody what had happened with Bert?"

"I told you no. I didn't tell anybody but Gramma just now. I didn't talk to anybody. I just left." And it was time to dig in my heels. "And I'm not saying another word until you tell me what's up."

Danny had barely touched his soup, but he took a spoonful then. "Good batch, Nellie," he said as if I hadn't said a thing.

"You going to do something about this old fart who showed his cogliones to Jimi?" Gramma asked, ignoring the compliment and sounding as if she might take the soup back if he didn't give the right answer.

"Nothing for me to do," Danny said, sounding solemn again. Then he focused on me once more. "This morning when the Center was opened Bert Chumley was found dead in the sauna."

Chapter Nineteen

I HAD TO go to the police station with Danny after lunch to make a formal statement about the last time I'd seen Bert Chumley in the doorway of the utility room and the hours before that that I'd spent with him in the flirting class.

It took all afternoon. Not that I had much to say. Mostly I just waited for an interview room to become free, waited for the room to be cleared and set up for me, waited for the detectives who needed to question me to work me in, waited for my statement to be typed up so I could sign it, and then waited for Danny to take me home.

It gave me a lot of idle time to think and to wonder what had happened the night before with Bert and me, and to Bert later on. I didn't come up with any answers one way or another though.

It was nearly dark when Danny could finally leave for the day. Heather-gray clouds hung low in a sky that was turning charcoal, and it reflected my mood.

I couldn't be sure if Bert's exposing himself to me had been just that—a man with a proclivity who had acted it out for me to witness—or if it had been something else entirely. Something that I'd accidentally intruded upon somehow. My uncertainty left me not ready to condemn him, that was for sure.

I'd genuinely liked the old guy and enjoyed his company before the incident in the locker room, and I was sorry he was dead. More sorry still that he'd been murdered, which I was reasonably sure was the case even though no one had told me much of anything. I hadn't been interrogated first by Danny and then formally by two other cops because Bert had died of natural causes.

"So how did this happen?" I asked my cousin as he drove in silence.

Danny looked at me out of the corner of his eye and for a minute I wasn't sure he was going to let me in on the details. He can clam up sometimes and just leave me high and dry.

But then he watched the road again and said, "The cause of death looks to be a massive stroke. But the cause of the stroke was that Bert Chumley got locked in the sauna with the heat turned up as high as it would go. That warning on the outside of it about not staying in for longer than twenty minutes and not to use it at all if you have high blood pressure or heart problems isn't just for looks. We found high blood pressure

medicine at Chumley's apartment, so we know he had
that. The coroner hasn't set the time of death yet but
the old man was locked in somewhere between ten and
ten-forty—Steve Stivik checked to make sure no one
was in the sauna a little before ten and turned it off. He
didn't go back after that and everything was locked up
by ten-forty. This morning at nine Gary Oldershaw
found Chumley. That makes it a lot more than twenty
minutes in there."

"Gary found him?"

"Steve and Gary were the first arrivals this morning.
Gary went to work out, went into the utility room for
towels, and *voilà*."

"Could it have been an accident?" I asked, knowing
my hope that it had been was feeble.

"There was a broomstick stuck through the handle
jamming the door closed. I don't think it jumped two
and a half feet and landed horizontally through the
handle and stuck between the wall and the shelving on
the other side."

"Uh, no that doesn't sound like an accident," I
agreed.

"Looks like he went into the sauna, somebody put
the broom through the handle, turned up the heat, and
left. The old man tried to force the door open—there
were marks on his hands, shoulders, hips, and feet that
looked as if he'd hit and kicked the door and even tried
to break out the little window for ventilation. But none
of it did him any good."

"God." I hated to think of the panic and terror
Bert must have felt. Not to mention that picturing him
locked in that cedar box was enough to kick off my
claustrophobia.

I rolled down the window on my side of Danny's car just a fraction of an inch to let in some fresh air. I tried not to think about Bert frantic to break that tiny window in the sauna door to do the same thing.

"Do you think I was right about Bert expecting me to be somebody else when he opened the utility room door and maybe whoever it was showed up later and did this?" I asked.

"Could be. But so far no one is admitting to a plan to meet him and you seem to be the last person to have seen him alive."

"Except for the killer." I don't know why I kept having to say that so much lately. "What about the women he was talking to from the class?"

"I put my guys to work on that as soon as we got to the station this afternoon. Irene Oatman knew who the women were. She gave us their names and numbers. There were five of them and they all left the Center shortly after Bert said good night and headed for the sauna. He told them it helped him sleep. As for everybody else—Irene, Diane Samboro, Delia, and Brenda—they all said the last they saw of Chumley was in that class, they thought he'd gone home. Carl says he never saw Bert, that he didn't even know he was at the Center last night, and he left when you did—which you confirmed. Gary saw Chumley when the old man came in early in the evening, not after that. Steve was gone until about nine, claims he didn't know Chumley was there either."

Neither of us said anything for a few blocks. There didn't seem to be anything to say to that roll call of the people who had been at the Center the previous evening.

Then Danny said, "Tell me exactly where you remember everyone being when you left the Center last night."

I mentally retraced my steps after having seen Bert in the almost altogether. "I told you about Carl and me. When we left the weight room Diane was still in the aerobics/dance studio where she'd been when I'd passed by on my way to the locker room before. She was setting out exercise mats and listening to music. Delia was standing in the hallway, flirting with Gary—the same place the two of them had been when I'd headed for the weight room. Irene was at the reception desk, she's the one who told Carl somebody was interested in a date and handed him the videotape. There wasn't anyone else in the lobby. I don't know where Brenda or Steve were. There wasn't anybody in the parking lot."

Danny nodded. "Steve claims he was dodging Brenda, that she's getting too serious about him and he was trying to cool things with her."

"Delia said he sweet-talks Brenda, then withdraws until she does something to win him back," I said, thinking that Steve's side of things shouldn't be the only one aired.

"What does she do to win him back?"

"I don't know. Delia didn't say that. Maybe we don't want to know."

Danny agreed with a nod and an *mmm*. Then he went on. "Steve usually uses the sauna after all the members are gone, while everyone else—"

"Cleans up and then he's the last one to leave so he can lock the doors and turn on the alarm," I finished for my cousin. "I've already heard about the routine and Irene told Brenda again last night, when Brenda asked where Steve would be, that he always uses the sauna at closing."

"Except that last night," Danny said, picking up where I'd left off, "Stivik says he broke his pattern because he was afraid Brenda would track him down. He was hiding out in the conference room after shutting down the sauna for the night. He was going to stay there until the coast was clear and Brenda was gone. But apparently she searched until she found him. They argued. She ran out in tears. He decided to turn the sauna on again and use it after all to relax. He apparently even headed in that direction, then at the last minute he remembered that he needed to sign a check for an overdue bill, went back to his office to do that instead. By the time he'd finished at ten-forty everyone was gone—or so he thought—so he locked up as usual and went home himself."

"Without rechecking the sauna because he'd already turned it off earlier."

"Right," Danny confirmed.

"So it doesn't seem as if anybody would have known Bert was where he was except someone who was going to meet him in the locker room or the utility room or the sauna itself."

"Doesn't seem like it," Danny said.

"But nobody admits to having plans to meet him."

"Not a soul. We're running his background check now. There wasn't much information about him on the personal profile that went with his application to the Center—name, address, phone number, date of birth, social security number, and 'retired' as the answer to damn near every other question. And so far no one is saying they hated his guts because he was their long-lost grandfather who cheated the family out of millions."

Danny was being facetious, but he was also making it clear to me that he didn't know the one person I did who disliked Bert. It left me in the uncomfortable position of tattletale.

I didn't relish it and kept my mouth shut for about half a mile while I thought over whether or not I should squeal. I didn't want to, no doubt about that. But I thought I had to.

"I hate to say this and cast any aspersions, and it isn't as if I honestly think she'd do anything like this," I prefaced. "But Brenda didn't like Bert. A lot."

Danny took his eyes off the road only long enough to glance at me before he turned back and said, "She didn't mention that when I talked to her."

The suspicion in his tone made me regret all the more that I'd been responsible for turning the spotlight on Brenda.

"Did she tell you this outright?" Danny asked.

"When I invited her to dinner she wanted to know if he was coming because she wouldn't if he was."

"How come?"

"I don't know. Getting her to open up is not easy."

"Tell me about it," Danny agreed.

"She didn't say why she didn't like Bert. But I can't imagine that she'd lock him in the sauna to die. She just seemed to steer clear of him. Besides, she was going to the sauna to find Steve when she left the class and I thought I might come across them when I cut through the locker room, but I honestly don't think anybody was in either the locker room or the utility room except

Bert and me. Obviously Brenda didn't find Steve in the sauna, she may not have gone there at all or if she did, she left because he wasn't there, and then wouldn't have had any reason to go back once she'd found him in the conference room. And if she ran off crying after fighting with Steve, she probably would have just gone to find Delia to take her home."

"Unless she went into the locker room to cry or wash her face or blow her nose before she had to see anybody. From the conference room the closest face-washing-nose-blowing facility is the locker room, not the other rest room in the office wing. Then maybe she met up with Bert the same way you did, freaked out and locked him in the sauna."

"I don't think anybody *kills* some old guy for showing her his willy."

"Maybe not you, but you didn't hate him from the start either."

"And how would she have gotten him into the sauna? He was in the doorway from the utility room to the locker room when I saw him. That's a good five or six feet from the door to the sauna."

"Maybe she went berserk and he ran in there to get away from her."

"I just don't think so," I repeated.

I wanted to get Danny thinking in a different direction, so I said, "You know, the night of the dance class Bert was playing whodunit with me. When I became the possible suspect, he said maybe I'd killed Steffi, Gary Oldershaw had found out about it and blown up my car as retribution. You don't suppose that's the scenario that went on here, do you? That Bert killed Steffi, someone knew about it and returned the favor?"

"Anything's possible," Danny said, his favorite line.

I played with the idea for a while, thinking about Bert and Steffi and what Bert had said about her when I'd talked to him. As I did, I remembered something.

"Didn't you say that Carl's date with Steffi was for the night after she died?" I asked Danny.

"Yep. We have his voice on her home answering machine tape calling to confirm it."

"Bert told me that she'd agreed to go out with *him* that next night."

Danny looked at me again and I knew I'd told him something else he hadn't known before. "Bert claimed to have a date scheduled with Steffi Hargitay for the Saturday night after she was killed?"

"That's what he told me. But who was Steffi more likely to have accepted a date with? A man her own age, who she'd known and liked in high school, who's a nice guy and has bucks out the wazoo? Or someone old enough to be her grandfather, who's stretching his entertainment dollar by joining the Center in the first place so he can spend time with women without having to spring for dinner or a movie?"

"Obviously the answer there is Carl. She was more likely to have a date with Carl. Besides, we found a note on her calendar that confirmed it. But there was nothing about Bert."

"I thought he was teasing, but he even said maybe she'd turned him down and called him a shriveled-up old coot and maybe it had made him so mad he'd killed her." I didn't like casting aspersions on the dead, either, but it was better than casting them on the living. "He'd laughed then and said she hadn't turned him down, though, which was why he'd definitely wanted her alive and well for Saturday night. But what if he really did ask her out, she shot him down, he got mad and struck out at her?"

"And somebody knew about it and instead of telling the cops they killed him in return? I don't know, Jimi," Danny said dubiously.

"It's possible," I said, my own version of his line. "Anything is possible."

"It's also possible that there's a maniac on the loose who's targeted the Center. A disgruntled dater," Danny said facetiously again. "But it isn't probable. I think I'm better off sticking with the flesh-and-blood suspects and leaving the phantoms to you."

"I beg your pardon," I said as a verbal punch in the arm, which is what I would have done when we were kids to show my affront at his insult.

He made amends by confiding in me about another suspect. "There's Irene Oatman too. By all accounts she was bending over backward trying to make time with Bert Chumley and he was rejecting her right and left. And she hated Steffi, that's for sure. Steffi was a threat to her job and was insulting to her, to boot."

"Steffi's death didn't save her job, though," I said, to make sure Danny had all the information before he turned too serious an eye on Irene either. "Irene told me last night that she hasn't been able to stop worrying about it because Steve is still acting as if he might fire her."

I don't know why that turned the wheels in my head in a different direction, but it did.

I didn't tell Danny right away what I was thinking. I wanted to think about it for a minute to see if I was way off the beam or not.

But in the end, I started to believe I wasn't.

"Remember when I told you I thought maybe I was just in the wrong place at the wrong time last night when Bert exposed himself to me? What if the same was true of him?"

"You've lost me."

"What if he decided to use the sauna after all—the way he told those women he was going to. He turned it back on, got in, and that put him at the wrong place at the wrong time. What if whoever locked him in there thought they were really locking Steve in?"

"That's a pretty big leap, Jimi."

"Maybe not. It's common knowledge that Steve uses the sauna every night around closing time. Steve broke his pattern last night, but how many people knew it? Did you ask anybody that?"

"No," Danny answered with enough inflection in the single word to convey that he thought I was reaching into the ridiculous.

"Well maybe you should. That window in the sauna door is tiny. The killer could easily have barely glanced in it to make sure Steve—who the killer expected to be in there—was, without actually looking closely enough to see that it wasn't Steve at all. Or the killer might not have even looked and just assumed it was Steve, stuck the broomstick through the handle, jacked up the heat, and left, never realizing it was Bert in there instead."

Okay, maybe I did finish that with a victorious flourish as if I'd single-handedly solved the crime. But Danny didn't need to look at me as if I were on drugs.

"So you think the act was premeditated enough for the killer to learn Stivik's routine, wait for the opportune moment, but then not even make sure it was Stivik in the sauna?"

"Planning it out and actually doing it are two different things. When it came time to step up to the plate the killer was probably nervous and in a hurry to do the deed and get out of there. Yes, I think it's possible they might not have gone far enough to see exactly who was in the sauna."

"Okay, sure, Jimi."

"Don't give me 'okay, sure, Jimi' like I'm some kind of doofus." Both of our fuses were a bit short. Maybe it had something to do with the way we'd spent the day. Or with the frustration of having people dying right under our noses.

"I know you aren't any kind of doofus," Danny said, changing his tune. "I just don't think the killer's murdering Bert Chumley by mistake is the likeliest option."

"Steve and Steffi were more two of a kind than Steffi and Bert. There are more connections between them, a better chance that whoever went after one, went after the other," I reasoned.

"That's only true in the broadest sense. We don't *know* why Steffi was killed, and don't forget it looked like an act of passion—in that instance the idea of Bert killing her because she'd rejected him and called him a shriveled-up old coot is more likely."

"But you don't think someone turning around and killing Bert to get back at him is likely either. And if that isn't likely, then what's the connection between Bert's death and Steffi's death?"

"Who said there was one?"

"Come on. You don't think these deaths were coincidental," I said, giving back a little of that you've-got-to-be-kidding tone.

"Could be a maniac disgruntled dater," he repeated.

We'd arrived home by then and Danny pulled his car into the driveway that ran alongside the house, beside the main one where Chloe's car was parked.

"Okay, so there's probably a connection of some kind between Chumley's death and Hargitay's," he acknowledged as we got out of the car. "We just don't know what it is yet."

"Maybe because there isn't one because Bert wasn't the intended victim of the second killing." I really could dig in my heels when I wanted to. "And maybe you should warn Steve."

Danny sighed as we went up the porch steps to the house. "I can't call that guy and warn him when there's no evidence to support it. What do you want me to do? Tell him my Magic Eight Ball sent me a message?"

"You could just tell him to be careful, that it's possible he could be in danger."

"No, I couldn't." Danny unlocked the front door and held it open for me.

"Are you at least going to ask around and see if anybody knew Steve wasn't going to use the sauna last night?"

"That I'll do."

"But you won't warn Steve before that?"

"No, I won't." Danny made a sweeping motion with his arm to usher me inside.

I went, and the subject seemed at a natural conclusion as Lucy charged us for a hello-petting and the girls and Gramma all started bombarding us with questions.

But in my mind the subject of someone warning Steve Stivik was not closed.

And if that someone wasn't going to be Danny, then maybe it would have to be me.

"Are you closing the Center until you catch the killer?" I asked Danny, hoping I sounded as casual as I intended.

"It's tempting. But a few of my undercover cops are going to become members instead. We decided it might be better to keep things going under a watchful eye and hope our killer comes to us. Otherwise, we're out tracking down over a thousand members—if you count people who may just come in to use the video dating service—any one of whom might be our bad guy. Or girl. From here on, every hour the Center is open one of my people will be on the premises."

Seemed like a decent plan to me.

And with the Center still open, I wouldn't have any problem finding an opportunity to brush up against Steve Stivik. Which was what I was really interested in.

Chapter Twenty

AFTER THINKING ALL night and again in the morning about my theory that Bert Chumley might have been the wrong victim of the sauna murder, I wasn't totally convinced that I was right. But I still thought there was no harm in a word of warning to Steve Stivik. Maybe cold, hard evidence didn't warrant Danny's doing it in an official capacity, but I didn't have any official capacity to worry about. Or anything to stop me.

Except that I didn't have a car to get me to the Center to do it.

I'm not much of a morning person, but I didn't want to wait too long to caution Steve. So about ten-thirty I went downstairs and told my grandmother I had some errands to run and needed to use one of my grandfather's cars.

Gramma paused the Jack La Lanne exercise tape she was working out to and said, "Better take the '57. It hasn't been run in a long time."

The '57 was a '57 copper-and-white Chevy in mint condition that had belonged to my grandfather along with the Nova. Gramma had gotten her driver's license after a Sears training course when she turned sixty, but only for emergencies. She never drove, but she kept Grandpa's cars just in case she decided to start. And because they were his.

I wasn't interested in either of them as replacements for the Subaru, but I didn't mind driving them occasionally to keep them running. And today I was just glad they were there when I needed them and that Gramma hadn't asked any questions about where I was going.

I turned to leave her to Jack La Lanne, but before I got out of the room she said, "Maybe I'll take a little ride with you."

"Aren't you busy today?"

"Not too busy, no. And I'm wishing for that fish at that McDonald's. Let's have lunch there."

Sometimes I could swear my grandmother has a sixth sense about the things I have up my sleeve. But there was nothing I could—or would—do to stop her from coming with me. I don't refuse her anything, certainly not a McDonald's fish sandwich if she is in the mood for one. And definitely not when it was her car I was going to use to accomplish what I had up my sleeve.

I did think I should let her know ahead of time what she was getting into, though, if she was coming along.

"I'm stopping by the New You Center."

"Ooo, then for sure I'm going. I don't want you there without Delia or Carl or even that Brenda. Safety in numbers, Jimi." Off went Jack La Lanne and the television. "Just let me pull up my stockings and put on some lipstick."

Nylons and lipstick to eat at McDonald's. That's Gramma.

When she had her hose and garters in place, she bounced out of the chair with the agility and energy of a five-year-old and disappeared into the bathroom.

She came back two minutes later with her lipstick in place and her black fake-fur coat going on over her dress.

"Okay, I'm ready," she announced, and out we went.

I really had planned to run a few errands in addition to my stop at the Center, so I hadn't been lying about that. But we hit the Center first.

I asked Gramma if she wanted to wait in the car, but there was no way she was doing that when she was intent on protecting me. That wasn't going to make my task easier, but there was nothing I could do about it.

The Center was reasonably quiet at eleven on a Wednesday morning. Almost all of the members milling around were women who fit into two categories—elderly-postretirement and those who looked like middle-aged housewives who had probably received fat enough divorce settlements or insurance benefits to allow them not to work. But I didn't see any of the members I'd come to know.

Irene and Diane were both behind the reception counter, looking less cheery than usual even in their stark whites. I was reasonably sure Bert's death, along with Steffi's preceding it so closely, had cast a pall over their moods. Hard to stay upbeat when you were working in a place where two people had died in less than two weeks.

I introduced my grandmother and asked if Steve was around.

"He's in his office," Irene answered. Then, to my grandmother, she said, "Would you like a tour of the facilities while Jimi talks to Steve?"

I could have kissed her.

But it would have been for naught because Gramma declined the offer and stuck to me like glue.

She was talking about what beautiful women Diane and Irene were as we rounded the corner to the corridor on the right side of the building where the offices were. Even though I'd been down there since I found Steffi Hargitay dead, I still had a flashback of her slumped in that high-backed chair with her head bashed in.

I closed my eyes to clear the image and when I opened them again it was to a new view through the half-windowed wall of Steve Stivik's office.

He was sitting at his desk, in the act of closing a small black notebook that he slipped into a red-and-white athletic bag on his lap.

For a moment it all seemed a part of the mental picture I'd been trying to block out, but it didn't take long for me to realize it wasn't, that I really had seen what I'd seen.

Steve's door was closed and he'd been busy enough with his own interests not to notice our approach to his office. So I knocked and waited for him to call "Yeah."

I opened the door and let Gramma go in first, following close behind. Steve's expression went from
pleasant anticipation—as if he assumed Gramma was a
potential new member—to something else when his
gaze landed on me.

"Jimi," he said in a tone I couldn't quite put my finger on. But one thing was certain—he wasn't glad to
see me.

I ignored the unwarm welcome. "I want to talk to
you, Steve," I said after introducing my grandmother
and watching him lift the athletic bag from his lap to
set alongside him on the floor.

He didn't offer either of us a seat but we took the
visitors' chairs facing his desk anyway.

"I heard about Bert Chumley's death," I said. No
sense beating around the bush. I might feel an obligation to warn him, but I didn't feel the need to make
small talk.

"I'm sure you did," he said pointedly.

"The police are looking at it at face value but I'm
not so sure they're right and I wanted to talk to you
about it."

"The way you *talked* to me about Steffi's murder? I
don't think so. You're nobody and I've told the cops all
I had to tell."

I heard Gramma make a *humph* sound, but she
didn't say anything.

"The truth is, more than talking to you about Bert's
death, I came to warn you."

"Warn me? About what? That the cops think *I*
killed Bert? What is this? Some kind of game? You
think you'll scare me into confessing something?
Because you might as well save it, lady."

'"Who does this *bruto* think he is, talking to you like that?" Gramma asked me.

"It's okay, Gram," I assured her. Then I returned my attention to Steve. "I got to thinking that it was you who was supposed to be in the sauna when Bert was killed. It seems to be common knowledge that you use it every night at closing. The night Bert died you broke that pattern. I don't know who knew it or who didn't know it, but I think it could have been you the killer was after."

"Me?" he said as if I'd ventured into the absurd. "And you think what? That I should *beware*?" He gave a phony Halloweenish inflection to that.

"I think it couldn't do any harm to be careful."

He laughed. He leaned back in his chair like an overstuffed potentate and laughed. "You expect me to be afraid of some wimp who kills women with video cameras and locks old men in saunas? I don't think so."

"I think everybody should be afraid of someone who kills. Probably twice now."

"Oh, yeah, and we're talking about some big brave guy I should be terrified of."

"We might not be talking about a *guy* at all. It could be a woman. And if that's the case, she's especially likely to use cunning rather than physical force if she's after you. That's why I'm here—to tell you to watch out for yourself."

"That almost sounds like a threat," he said with another laugh, as if I was there purely for his entertainment and without the slightest indication that he was taking this seriously. "Maybe you know the killer is a woman because it's you."

"Aay!"

"Or maybe the reason you're so unconcerned," I countered, "is because you're the killer and you know Bert *was* the target. For that matter, maybe you killed Steffi, too." I could play the same game.

"They were both causing me enough trouble to deserve it," he muttered. "But I didn't do either of them. Not that I think that'll stop you from running back to your cop friend to tell him I did. So go ahead and see what it gets you."

I didn't know if that was a threat or just cockiness.

"I give up," I said. "I did what I came for. I warned you to be careful. Treat it like a joke if you want. It's your business."

"Gee, thanks," he said, pushing away from his desk to stand. "Now if you'll excuse me, I have a date for lunch."

Gramma and I stood, too, and let him usher us out.

But once the three of us were in the hallway I said, "Oh," as if something else had just occurred to me. "By the way, have you found your ledger yet?"

"No, I haven't. I gave up on that," he answered with even more of that cocky I-could-care-less attitude.

"Probably wise," I said, making him laugh again, this time with an echo to it that said he'd put something over on me and probably the rest of the world too.

I suggested that Gramma and I stop in at the bathroom as we passed it and said good-bye to Steve to let him know we weren't going any farther with him.

He didn't bother returning the sentiment, but I didn't care. I was only interested in making sure he actually rounded the corner to the lobby before Gramma and I went into the rest room.

I was banking on Gramma using the facilities if I got her in there, and that's just what she did. But rather than going into one of the other stalls myself, I said, "I left my purse in that office, Gram. I'll be right back."

And out I went again, alone.

From the hallway outside the bathroom I could see most of the lobby, including the three members who were standing in the middle of the waiting area talking. What I couldn't see was the reception desk.

Steve wasn't in the main part of the lobby, but I didn't want to take any chances that he might be near the counter, so I went to the corner and hazarded a quick glance around it.

Of course, I would have looked like an idiot if anyone had seen me, but I'd made sure none of the chatting members were looking and behind the counter Diane's and Irene's backs were to me. Steve wasn't there at all, so I considered that the all-clear and retraced my steps to his office, hoping he hadn't locked the door as we left. I didn't recall it, but I might have missed something.

With one hand on the knob, I looked up and down the hall, wishing my heartbeat weren't pounding in my ears.

Luck was with me—the door was unlocked and nobody from one end of the corridor to the other appeared to catch me in the act.

I slipped into the office as smooth as silk, shutting the door behind me but not tightly. I didn't want any telltale click to draw attention.

The hall wall of windows that had offered me my earlier view was now a liability. But like Gramma's

coming along on this little adventure, there was nothing
I could do about it.

So, with a glance through them out into the hall, I
wasted no time going to the far side of the desk chair to
find Steve's athletic bag.

I hoisted it to the desktop and reached for the
zipper.

I didn't know if the zipper was stubborn or stuck or
if my hand was shaking too much to get a good grip,
but I couldn't seem to open it.

"Come on," I whispered, jiggling the thing like crazy
until it finally gave way.

Once I had the top of the bag spread like a surgical
incision, it was no problem locating the notebook. It
was sitting right on top of the gym clothes. Unburied
treasure.

I took it out and set it on the desk beside the bag,
wondering as I did how it had turned up in the first
place.

I would have liked just to stuff it under my turtleneck and walk out with it so I could go through it at
my leisure and then hand it over to Danny if it was
incriminating, but that would be taking things a little
far. So, after another quick look outside the office to
make sure no one was standing in the corridor watching, I just opened the cover.

It didn't take me long to realize that Steve's refer-
ence to it as a ledger was a stretch of the imagination.
The pages did not have tables or figures listed on them.
No, this was something else.

I didn't know any of the names written on the first
several pages, and when I had the gist of what was in

the notebook I flipped ahead to the last pages, which showed two different types of handwriting. One was flowery script, the other was bolder, half printing, half cursive.

That was when it got interesting.

I spotted three names I recognized, only one of them entered in the flowery script, the other two in the bolder hand. But only the very last name shocked me.

It was one of those written in the more masculine writing, and even as I read the information that went with the name, I couldn't believe my eyes.

"Jimi!"

I nearly jumped out of my skin.

"What are you doing?" my grandmother whispered from the doorway.

I'd been so engrossed in the final entry of that notebook that I hadn't seen her coming or heard her open the office door. I was just grateful it wasn't Steve Stivik who'd sneaked up on me.

"This jerk has been accusing me of having this notebook and I thought that entitled me to a look at it," I said.

"Ooo, Jimi, I don't know. I don't like this. Let's get out of here."

I'd seen enough, so I gave up without a fight. "It's okay, I'm finished. Just keep a look out while I put it back," I advised since I knew it was a waste of breath to try to get her to wait for me in the lobby.

I closed the notebook and set it back in the athletic bag where I'd found it, then pulled the zipper closed.

Halfway at least. That was as far as it went before it stuck again.

By then my palms were more than damp and I dried them on the thighs of my jeans so I could get a better grip of the zipper pull for another go-round. My hands were really clumsy, and it suddenly seemed much too hot in that room.

"Just close, dammit," I whispered, thinking that my verbal command had worked earlier and maybe it would again.

But it didn't. And this time as I jiggled the zipper I lost my grip on it and knocked a pencil cup off the desk to spill all over the floor.

I had to get down on my hands and knees to pick up the pens and pencils, and just as I was standing again, Gramma hissed, "Jinx, Jimi! Jinx!" and I knew we were in trouble.

I jammed what I had of the writing implements into the pencil cup and stuck it on the desk. I didn't bother trying to close the bag's zipper the rest of the way. I just dropped it to the floor beside the desk chair and ran around to the one I'd been sitting in earlier just as Steve Stivik's angry voice stabbed the air like a knife.

"What the hell are you doing in here?"

"I forgot my purse," I answered him in a none too nice tone of my own, grabbing the leather hobo bag from where I'd purposely left it next to the visitor's chair. "We came back for it," I finished, hoping the heat I could feel in my face came from the temperature in the room and not from my cheeks turning red from the fright and the romp around the desk.

Stivik was still suspicious. And angry-looking. And I was actually glad Gramma was with me. I didn't know how dangerous he might be, but at least we outnumbered him and I didn't think he'd do anything to me with my grandmother as a witness.

"Got it," I announced, holding my purse aloft.

Then I made a beeline for the door, linked my arm through Gramma's, and took my racing heart and my grandmother out of there.

Chapter Twenty-one

EVERYBODY WAS HOME for dinner that night, which always makes for a lively meal.

Chloe was mad because her biology professor had already scheduled a big test only a week into the semester.

Shannon had met a new guy she liked. His name was Chris—which made him Chris-number-nine in a streak of Chrises. This one had more tattoos than the last one, fewer piercings than the one before that, but he didn't have B.O. the way Chris-number-six had.

Thank God for small favors.

Danny wanted to know how to get soy sauce out of a white shirt. Gramma offered to do it for him. And both Gramma and I put in our two cents' worth with the girls.

"Ben called you, Mom," Shannon said as we cleared the dishes afterward.

"Ben Barrows? Did Lucy get out again?" I asked.

"No. I took her up to see Barney between school and work this afternoon, but I kept her on the leash so she couldn't dig. They just nuzzled noses through the fence. It was like bringing her to jail to see her boyfriend. When I got home I played the messages on the machine and Ben was on it from earlier in the day."

I hadn't noticed the light flashing when Gramma and I had returned from our errands and lunch at McDonald's. "What did he want?"

"He didn't say. He wanted you to pick up if you were there. When you didn't, he said it wasn't important, he'd call back."

"He probably saw the work Vince did and wanted to let me know," I said, the only reason I could think of why he'd call, unless it was to complain or get me over there to retrieve Lucy from his yard.

With the table cleared and the girls making noises about wanting to get to their homework—which meant their respective telephones—I suggested they go ahead. I also suggested that Gramma watch the program she wanted to catch on TV, and that Danny and I do the rest of the kitchen cleanup.

Of course, I had an ulterior motive. But my ploy worked and within five minutes Danny and I were alone.

"I wanted to talk to you," I told him once we were.

"Big surprise. Bet nobody could have guessed that," he said facetiously.

The news of Bert's death had made me forget that I'd wanted to talk to my cousin about my chat with

Irene, so before I told him about my latest discovery, I thought I should backtrack. Besides, I like to save the best for last.

"I had a talk with Irene Oatman the other night, after the flirting class."

"And apparently you learned something interesting enough to make me do the dishes."

"As a matter of fact I know a couple of things interesting enough to make you do the dishes," I said with satisfaction. "But for starters, Irene told me it's a lie that Steffi Hargitay hadn't seen her father in ten years. He came here in November."

"Really . . ."

"Did you know that Steffi got an inheritance from her grandfather that should have gone to her father?" I asked after giving Danny a brief summary of my conversation with Irene.

"I knew Steffi had recently inherited just under forty thousand dollars, but not that it should have gone to someone else."

I explained the whys and wherefores of that. Then I said, "I'm wondering who the inheritance goes to now that she's dead."

"She didn't leave a will and she only has two living relatives—her sister and her father—that means everything she owns gets split between them."

"So her father wanted half the inheritance Steffi got from her grandfather—that's why he came here. She promised it to him, then reneged. But now he'll get his half after all," I summarized.

"I wonder why the sister didn't inherit anything from the grandfather? Why bypass the father to give to only one of the granddaughters?" Danny said, as if he were thinking out loud.

"Maybe he just liked Steffi better," I offered.

"Mmm. Or maybe the grandfather just caused trouble all the way around and the sister didn't like it any more than the father did," Danny mused.

"It's probably worth looking into," I said, pretending I hadn't been thinking that all along.

After a moment during which we discussed what container to save meatloaf in, he altered the subject slightly. "And Steffi broke up Irene's fling with the father, huh?"

"I don't think Irene held that against her, if you're figuring it points to Irene as Steffi's killer. Irene realized the guy was a jerk."

"Or so she says now."

"I didn't mean any of this to make Irene look bad," I said. "I thought you should know that there could be people outside the Center who might have had a grudge against Steffi."

"I'll look into the father and the sister a little more, but there's still Bert's murder—that makes an outsider less likely. And by the way, his exposing himself to you wasn't an accident. Well, it might have been an accident that he exposed himself to you specifically, but it seems he had a long string of indecent exposure charges."

"No!"

"Dating back to his twenties. He did minor jail time for it twice."

"That nice old man?"

"And the reason Brenda didn't like him? She's been

his most recent audience. Seems he was getting off on flashing to our mousy friend."

"He's been exposing himself to Brenda? *Only* to Brenda?"

"She's who's complained. Knowing what happened with you, my bet is he was lying in wait for her that night. You said yourself he was in the classroom when Irene told Brenda she could probably find Steve in the sauna. Looks to me like Bert hightailed it out of there, went to the sauna, and when Steve wasn't there, waited at the door to the women's locker room until he heard footsteps. When he did, he figured it was Brenda and did his thing. Only it was you in the locker room instead of Brenda, that's why it looked as if he was expecting somebody else. He was."

I knew the way Danny's mind worked, so it wasn't much of a leap to guess what he was thinking from there. "You're wondering if Brenda came in after I'd left, Bert did an encore, and she locked him in the sauna to kill him."

Danny raised one eyebrow and tilted his head to concede that that was exactly what he was thinking.

"Wouldn't it have been easier to just turn him in?" I asked.

"She had. Before that. To Steve, anyway. But Steve persuaded her not to call in the cops, said he'd handle it. Unfortunately he didn't handle it too effectively because when he confronted Bert about it, Bert said he wasn't doing any such thing, that Brenda was finding opportunities to peep at *him*. He said he'd pursue his own complaint to the police if she didn't leave him alone."

"A big bluff."

"Right. Because with his record nobody would have

bought that. But neither Steve nor Brenda knew he had a record. Steve judged it a toss-up as to who was doing what to whom."

"Nice."

"Isn't it, though? It left Brenda out in the cold. Not only didn't Steve do anything, but she couldn't even turn to the cops for fear Bert would tell his little tale and make her look bad. So, it could be that the other night she took matters into her own hands. Maybe our little mouse has a temper underneath all that shyness and when somebody pisses her off—like Steffi Hargitay and Bert Chumley—she goes ballistic. Maybe she even blew up your car, thinking it was mine, because she didn't like my questioning her."

I loaded the dishwasher. "I don't know about all that." But I did remember seeing what I'd thought at the time was a core of steel to Brenda, so I couldn't refute Danny's theory much more firmly.

"On the other hand," he said then, "it's likely Delia knew what Bert was doing to Brenda, that protective streak of hers could have come out, and she might have intervened on Brenda's behalf. Or, for that matter, maybe Bert exposed himself to Delia too. She knew complaining didn't get Brenda anything but an accusation of her own, so Delia took matters into *her* own hands and locked Bert in the sauna. Maybe she'd already killed Steffi for insulting her, and figured what was one more?"

"Or maybe Brenda and Delia committed both murders together to rid the world of evil," I said to underscore how far-fetched I thought any of that was.

"Or maybe Carl found out about Bert's tormenting Brenda and he did it."

I rolled my eyes. "Carl and Brenda haven't even been out on a date yet, but you think he *killed* for her? Not to mention that he left the Center with me that night, remember?"

"Okay, then maybe Bert was exposing himself to Diane, too, and *she* took care of it herself. Along with ridding herself of Steffi."

Danny rinsed the sponge he'd been using and set it on the window ledge as I washed the sink out.

I didn't look at him as I said, "Or Steve could have done the murders to rid himself of all his problems." Which led me neatly to my coup de grâce, so I added, "When I talked to him today he made a snide comment about Bert and Steffi both causing him enough trouble to want them dead."

Danny got quiet all of a sudden, and out of the corner of my eye I saw him lean back against the counter's edge and stare at me.

But it's hard to tell out of the corner of your eye if you're in trouble or not.

"You went to the Center and told him you thought he was the intended victim of the sauna killing, didn't you?"

I gave him a no-big-deal shrug. "I understood why you couldn't do it, but I thought somebody should. He didn't take it seriously, though. In fact, he thought it was all very funny. He got a kick out of accusing me of knowing Bert wasn't the real target because I was the killer. I accused him of being the murderer and knowing Bert *was* the target. That was when he said Bert and Steffi were big enough pains in the neck to deserve it."

"We know why Bert was a pain in the neck, but did he say why Steffi was?"

I knew I was out of the doghouse then. If Danny was asking reasonable questions, I wasn't in too much trouble.

As I shined the sinks I said, "Steve didn't say anything about why he was ticked off at Steffi, but maybe it had something to do with that notebook he's been so hot to get back. Which, by the way, he now has back."

I finished the cleanup at about the time I finished that announcement and turned to face Danny, finding his brow furrowed again.

"You were busy today, weren't you?"

I explained how I'd caught a glimpse of the notebook in the first place and then asked Steve about it later. "He denied having it and said he'd given up thinking he'd ever get it back. But I'd seen what I'd seen, so since he'd said he had a lunch date and left the office—"

"Don't tell me you went back and did a little B and E."

"Is it breaking and entering when the door is unlocked? In a public place?"

Danny closed his eyes and shook his head as if this was not stuff he wanted to hear.

But I knew better, so I skipped over that part and got to the part I knew he *did* want to hear. "Interesting material in that notebook."

My cousin took a deep breath and then sighed elaborately. When he opened his eyes again, he said, "Since Stivik has now probably buried the ledger so deep we'll never find it, I guess you better tell me what's in it."

"He may not have known I saw it. Gramma played lookout and warned me in time to put it back in the bag and get the bag back on the floor before he found us."

"This just gets better and better. I don't even want to know about that. Just tell me what was in the notebook."

"Names and information about what value certain members have to the Center. I thought about it and it's stuff that must have originated from those supposedly confidential personal profiles they make you fill out when you join. Income levels, assets, occupations— from what little I saw, it's basically a list of what certain members can do for the Center or Steve Stivik personally."

"How handy."

"Mmm. No wonder he missed it. There was the name of a woman who owns the apartment building where Steve apparently lives rent-free; a man who sold exercise equipment who gave the Center a seventy-five percent discount—that was written in a more flowery handwriting that I'm betting was Steffi's since Steve said that only the two of them had access to the ledger. There was video gear, *gifts* of money, cars, clothes, advertising, construction, landscaping, office furniture, computers, even Ben Barrows was in it with a notation for plastic surgery referrals, but he told me he'd nixed that idea."

"Don't tell me you talked to him about this today too? Is that why he called you?"

"No, he told me about that Sunday night at dinner."

"And he claims that he refused?"

"He said he isn't certified to do plastic surgery and he doesn't do kickbacks one way or another."

Danny nodded his head, but his expression was so ambiguous I couldn't tell what was on his mind.

Rather than try to read it, I just went on. "Carl was in the ledger, with a note about what he's worth and another one about suggesting he donate some free dinners and tokens for Cutler's Corner that could be used as incentive giveaways. And there were a lot of people Steve or Steffi got free wining and dining out of."

One person in particular, who I was still having trouble grasping as a part of that notebook.

"I, on the other hand," I added, "did not make the cut. But basically it's the vital financial statistics of the lonely and well-off. Or of the lonely and what services can be garnered from them."

"Seduced from them is more likely. But I don't know if that's a motive for murder, Jimi. I know I can't arrest Stivik for accepting *gifts*. No matter how lonely the giver or how adept a manipulator the taker is. There's no law against a beautiful woman wooing a man into a seventy-five percent discount on a weight machine or trying to get a doctor to give a referral fee, or a restaurateur to donate free dinners to give away. The fact that Steve and maybe Steffi preyed on the lonely to accomplish it is slimy, but it isn't illegal."

"But it's that slimy part that might be important. Maybe someone Steve or Steffi was working on figured out that their attentions weren't genuine. And maybe when that someone figured it out he or she got mad enough to go after the two of them."

"Presuming—again—that Steve was the intended victim in the sauna."

Which, from the tone of Danny's voice, he still felt was unlikely.

I ignored it and said, "There's also that business about Steffi being angry at Steve and saying that he owed her and she wanted what she had coming to her. Maybe she was blackmailing him or threatening to expose the seduction scams. Or maybe some of what's been going on is illegal—I didn't have time to go through every page or every entry. But I'm betting whatever trouble Steffi was causing Steve had something to do with that notebook and what's in it."

"Could be Steffi was sticking it to Stivik over the gift thing and the pity-fucks," Danny agreed. "She could have been threatening to warn members that Stivik was using them if he didn't give her the partnership Gary Oldershaw thinks she was working for, and he killed her because of it. Then maybe when Bert started causing trouble with the flashing stuff Stivik just decided that since he'd come this far, he might as well snuff out Bert too."

"Unless someone else knew Steve had killed Steffi and went after who he thought was Steve in the sauna," I said, reminding Danny of my earlier scenario. "Have you found out yet who did and didn't know Steve wasn't taking his usual sauna that night Bert died?"

"I put two guys on the phones for it today," Danny said as if I was stretching his patience. "Doesn't seem anybody was aware of what Steve was doing that night one way or another. But that still doesn't convince me that Chumley was locked in the sauna by mistake."

"Okay, maybe it isn't much, but it's something," I persisted.

Danny just shook his head at me as if he thought I was fighting windmills.

"I do think, though, that that ledger or something in it had something to do with Steffi's death even if not Bert's," I said, switching back to our prior subject.

"I'd like to get a look at it, that's for sure. So, if any-body asks you, here's your story: You knew about it because Stivik's been bugging you about seeing it in Steffi's office the day you found her dead. Today when you were at the Center you happened to see him look-ing through what you thought might be the ledger, then stick it in his gym bag, so you told me about it. Period. You didn't get into that bag. You didn't look in the notebook yourself."

"Fine."

"I'm going to try to get a search warrant and hope Stivik wasn't wise to your escapade today so he didn't hide or destroy it."

"And wouldn't it be nice to know where it was from the time Steffi was murdered, and how Steve got it back?" I put in, hoping my cousin might get an answer to the other question burning a hole in me.

"That's something I'd like to know, too, yeah."

Danny pushed away from the edge of the counter, making it clear our conversation was at an end. Still, he didn't leave until he said, "But regardless, I want you to be more careful about what the hell you're doing over at that Center, Jimi."

"I will," I assured him with full confidence.

Because the Center wasn't where my next chat would be held when I followed up on the one particu-lar name I'd been so surprised to find in Steve Stivik's ledger.

Chapter Twenty-two

I'M NOT PATIENT when it comes to having my curiosity satisfied. But the next day I had to postpone my plans to get satisfaction when Carl called and offered to take me to the dealership to pick out my new car.

We agreed to go just after noon, so I left home when Gramma and I had finished lunch to walk up to Carl's house.

Colorado is great for one or two gray days followed by a flood of sunshine-filled weeks, but we were in the midst of an unusually long period of unrelenting overcast skies. It was beginning to get to everyone. Even me, and I've always loved the occasional gloomy days.

As I headed up the street past Ben Barrows's house I made sure to check out the area around his gate—from the sidewalk. I didn't go into the yard. I wanted to be certain that Vince's handiwork hadn't been corrupted somehow. It hadn't. The walkway around the gate still looked nearly as good as new and I was more convinced that that was why the doctor had called the day before—to say he'd noticed the fix-up and appreciated it.

When I got to Carl's house and rang his doorbell, he called for me to come in. I did that and once I'd closed the front door behind me he hollered that he was in the kitchen. I went through the house to the back, finding him cleaning his own lunch mess.

"Are you all set for some new wheels?" he asked rather than saying hello, full of his usual energy and enthusiasm.

"Do you think I'll be able to drive one home today?"

"I don't know why not."

I admit I was a little excited. I hated digging into my nest egg for the difference between my insurance check and what a new car would cost, but it was always fun to get a new car. And I was going crazy without my own transportation.

"How's the shed coming?" I asked then, crossing the room to the French doors to look out at the backyard.

Carl laughed. "It isn't. Vince still hasn't been able to pour the cement. If the weather would cooperate and he could get that done he could do the framing, but he can't do anything without the pad."

There was lumber stacked near the site and covered with a tarp. Vince had finished smoothing the soil so that the whole area was a perfect, flat surface, but Carl was right, other than those two things, everything was just the way it had been before.

I was glad he was so easygoing and wasn't making a big deal about the delay. Even if it was out of Vince's control, I knew a lot of people who would have been getting irritated.

"Ready to go?" Carl asked as he dried his hands on a dishtowel.

"Yep."

I waited until we were on our way before I indulged the portion of my curiosity that included Carl. Granted it was the smaller portion, but at least I might get some satisfaction.

"Did Steve Stivik or Steffi approach you about donating free dinners and game tokens to the Center?" I asked.

"No," Carl said, sounding confused by the notion. Why?"

"I was just wondering. I've heard that they per-suaded several of the members to make contributions of one kind or another."

"As if the Center is some kind of charitable foundation?"

"Not quite. For instance, they might have made arrangements to recommend someone or some busi-ness for something and then received a kickback if the members took the recommendation. Or they might have gotten discounts on things or services members could provide. Or, for instance, if you let them have, say, coupons for free dinners and tokens, they could give the coupons away with new memberships—an incentive that would help draw business but not cost the Center anything."

"That wouldn't be a bad idea. The person with the coupon would probably come in with friends, so we'd make money on what the friends spent or on what was spent on more games when the free tokens were used up. And there's always the booze," Carl said as if I'd just presented him with a proposal worth considering.

"But this is the first you've heard about it?" I persisted.

"Nobody's said anything to me about anything like that before."

And obviously it wasn't something Carl would be opposed to so not everything in the notebook was a bad thing.

"Did Steffi mention that she might want to talk to you about something that Saturday night you were supposed to go out?" I asked.

"No. I asked her out, it wasn't the other way around. And she didn't say anything about the Center or wanting to talk to me about anything. She just said yes."

"Did she mention anything about Bert Chumley or his asking her out for that same night?"

Carl laughed. Not a cruel laugh, just a disbelieving one. "Bert Chumley? The old man who wears the bow ties and sucks his dentures all the time?"

Carl's tone and lighthearted comment seemed inappropriate under the circumstances, and it suddenly occurred to me that he might not be aware of what had happened to Bert. In a gentler voice, I said, "Did you know that Bert was killed the other night? In the sauna at the Center?"

Carl sobered up instantly and his expression showed his shock. "What?"

I repeated myself, adding the details of just what night it had been.

"Oh, my God."

"You didn't know."

"I've been swamped this week. My manager quit the morning after I saw you at the Center that night, I had plumbing problems and a dispute with one of the bartenders. I haven't been doing anything but dealing with work. I haven't been back to the Center and I guess I haven't even seen a newspaper or heard a news report. That's why I took today off—I needed a breather. God. Somebody *else* died there?"

I could hear a note of uneasiness in Carl's voice that was similar to my grandmother's new concerns about my going to the Center anymore. Death was not good for business.

"What's going on at that place?" Carl asked rhetorically.

I answered anyway. "I don't know. Nobody's figured it out yet. But did Steffi mention anything to you about Bert?"

Carl shrugged and shook his head. "No."

"Nothing at all? Not that he was causing trouble or that he was bothering her in any way?"

"She didn't mention anything about Bert Chumley. She and I hadn't talked that much before she died. We'd done some catching up, but not even a lot of that. That's why we were going out Saturday night."

Well, that and probably so Steffi could hit him up for the donation of free dinners and tokens for the Center. But I didn't say that. No sense bursting his bubble.

"Do the police think there's a connection between Steffi's death and this one?" Carl asked then.

"Seems possible but I'm not so sure. I just wondered if you knew of any connection."

"Not that I can think of." Carl took his eyes off the road long enough to frown at me. "Are you still digging around in the stuff that's going on at the Center?"

"I don't know if you'd call it digging around," I hedged.

"Don't you have enough on your plate with an exploding car?"

"You'd think, wouldn't you?" I said with a laugh, hoping to ease some of the tension that had come with telling him about Bert's death.

We turned into a Toyota dealership on 104th Avenue in Northglenn, and that changed the subject naturally.

But I hadn't come away from our conversation empty-handed.

Between the fact that Carl's name was written on Steffi's calendar for that Saturday night and was also in Steve Stivik's ledger as one of the *desirable* members, I didn't think there was any doubt that Carl was Steffi's date for that night. Which meant that Bert had lied.

I didn't know how that lie might factor into things one way or another. Maybe it didn't matter. Maybe he'd just been telling a little fib to make himself look better.

I did think, though, that it was important the old guy had not been what he'd appeared to be on any front.

And what kept sticking in my mind was that he wasn't the only one.

Chapter Twenty-three

I WAS SURPRISED to see that Danny was home when I got back at four that afternoon. But I didn't think much about it except to be glad he was there to see my new car.

I'd wanted a Rav 4 but had settled on a basic Corolla sedan because even at fleet prices it was what I could afford. But at least I'd gotten an automatic transmission and air conditioning—luxuries in my book.

The car was a nondescript beige color with tan interior and it seemed to fly when I hit the gas because it had way more power and pickup than the Subaru. I felt disloyal, but I liked it a lot more than the old diaper wagon.

I pulled into the driveway behind Chloe's car and honked like crazy until I had the whole household outside to ooh and aah over my new baby. Danny was the only one to hang back and between that and his being home at four in the afternoon, I knew something was up.

Something not too good, if the tightness in his face was any indication.

Both the girls wanted to drive the new car and Gramma was always willing to take a ride, in fact she said she could use a trip to the store. So I let the three of them go off in my new wheels and seized the time alone with Danny to pry.

"Spill it," I ordered as we went inside.

Danny didn't even acknowledge that I'd said anything.

So I added, "I know there's a reason you're home now and I can tell by the look on your face that it's not to tell me I won a raffle. What's the matter?"

I tossed my coat on the banister to be brought upstairs later, and when I turned around it was to find Danny walking into the kitchen.

Apparently he wasn't going to make this easy for me.

But I'm nothing if not tenacious. I followed him.

He'd gone all the way to the sink, where he threw back a drink of water as if it were cheap whiskey.

"Come on," I urged.

"I hate to spoil the moment for you," he finally said.

"What are you going to do, arrest me?"

"No. But I don't have good news."

"Oh, God," I said, echoing Carl from earlier. When Danny had bad news, it could really be bad. "Better to just say it and get it over with."

"You may have been right."

"About . . ."

"Steve Stivik. That he was the intended victim in the

sauna. He was found murdered in his apartment this morning."

Of all the things I'd ever wanted to be right about, that wasn't one of them. I hadn't liked the man, but predicting that someone wanted him dead was not something I could take any pleasure in.

"What happened?"

"It's not very nice. You might not want to know."

"What happened?"

"Looks like somebody broke in, probably late, after he was asleep. He lives on the ground floor and there was a broken pane of glass in his patio door. It was scheduled to be fixed but hadn't been yet. Whoever did this knocked the glass out, reached in and unlocked the door. Apparently they were pretty quiet about it and didn't wake Stivik. He was cuffed to the bed, probably before he even woke up."

"*Cuffed* to the bed?"

"His hands, to the headboard. His feet were tied to the legs of the bed frame, spread-eagle. And he was gagged so he couldn't make any noise."

"How was he killed?"

"Several blows to the head with a sports trophy he'd won in high school. It was left at the scene."

I flinched. "When I warned him that I thought Bert might have been mistaken for him when Bert was killed, Steve said he wasn't afraid of some wimp who would hit a woman with a video camera or lock an old man in a sauna."

"Well apparently this time the wimp didn't take any chances with Steve fighting back."

Chapter Twenty-four

MY CONVERSATION WITH Danny ended abruptly when Gramma and the girls came home from the store and the test drive of my new car. My excitement had fizzled with the news of Steve Stivik's death, but I tried to pretend it hadn't and spent the evening hoping my daughters' and my grandmother's talk about the Toyota might lighten my spirits.

It didn't. And when they finally said good night, Danny and I picked up where we'd left off.

It wasn't that I felt responsible for Steve's death, but throughout the evening I'd gone over and over in my mind what had happened between us the day I'd gone to see him. I couldn't help wondering whether I might have been more effective in alerting him if I hadn't let him get to me. I couldn't help wondering if

I could have been more forceful somehow. More convincing.

But I also couldn't help wavering between those feelings and wondering why he couldn't have just listened to me when I'd told him I thought he was in danger.

Okay, maybe nothing could have saved him from an attack like the one that had taken his life, maybe no amount of caution would have interfered with the killer's determination. But I just kept thinking that it might have helped if he had at least paid some attention to what I'd tried to tell him.

When I voiced all of that to Danny, he told me he didn't think that I could have been more convincing or more forceful, or that it would have made a difference if Steve had taken my warning to heart.

On the other hand, by then Danny was taking my theory that Bert had been killed because he'd been mistaken for Steve more seriously and kicking himself for not having put a guard on Steve.

Not that Danny was discounting Bert as the intended victim either. He was just keeping an open mind about both possibilities now. But if neither he nor Steve had put much weight into my hypothesis, he didn't think I should feel guilty and he assured me I'd done all I could to prevent what had happened from happening.

I was just having a hard time accepting it and ended up not getting much sleep once we called it a night.

Steve's death was still on my mind the next morning, so I couldn't concentrate on work. By eleven o'clock I gave up trying. Instead, I got into my new car and headed for The World Is Your Oyster travel agency where I now had two things I wanted to talk about.

Along the way I kept hashing and rehashing Steve's murder itself.

Apparently it was easier than I thought to get hold of a pair of handcuffs, so that wasn't as much of a lead for Danny as I'd originally assumed. He'd said that novelty stores, sex shops, costume shops, and mail-order houses all sold them without keeping records of who bought them.

The only fingerprints on the trophy had been Steve's. The handcuffs and everything else that had been used on him had been clean. Danny figured the killer had worn gloves.

We'd both found it strange that whoever had broken into Steve's apartment had come equipped with handcuffs but not a weapon. I thought that meant the murderer had been more worried about his or her own safety rather than about how to actually kill Steve. Or maybe the killer hadn't arrived with the intention of killing Steve. Maybe whatever the murderer had come for had gotten out of hand the way Steffi Hargitay's final meeting had.

Danny didn't buy the maybe-things-had-just-gotten-out-of-hand angle, but he did think that the killer could have arrived knowing an edge would be needed in dealing with Steve Stivik. It played into the fact that Danny was leaning heavily toward thoughts that the killer was a woman. He thought she might have shown up with the idea of seducing Steve into using the handcuffs, but that once she'd arrived and seen the broken glass in the door, she'd opted for breaking in instead and just getting down to business.

Danny's focus was definitely on the Center's surviving instructors and the handful of members I was acquainted with—male or female—but it was hard for me to believe that anyone I knew from the Center could have done what was done to Steve. Although it wasn't within the realm of my own reactions, I could understand a flash of rage so severe it had caused someone to pick up the nearest heavy object and hit Steffi with it. I could imagine someone sneaking up on Bert in the sauna—whether they'd meant it to be Bert or Steve—and locking the door.

But to bridle Steve to a bed and then inflict pain like that and watch him suffer? That I couldn't fathom, and I didn't know anybody I could picture doing it, no matter how angry or hate-filled. Barring some kind of mental disorder—which was something I thought I would have been able to spot in the people around me—why would anyone do such a thing? What purpose could it have served?

But once again I didn't have any answers, and my mind was still swimming in disbelief when I pulled into the parking lot of the strip mall.

I took a few deep breaths of frigid air as I got out of the car and studied the buttons on the inside of the door to figure out how to lock it. Then I went to the travel agency.

I wasn't too sure if Brenda or Delia would even be there or if Danny might have hauled them in for questioning. I knew from some of the things he'd said the night before that it was a distinct possibility.

But as I approached the glass storefront I could see them inside, at their respective desks.

There were no customers, and both Delia and Brenda looked up from what they were doing when I went in. Delia's smile was quick and welcoming. Brenda's expression didn't change and was as blank as a wax sculpture's.

We all exchanged greetings and I took a chair in front of Brenda's desk, turning it enough to include Delia in the conversation, even though Brenda was who I primarily wanted to talk to.

"I suppose you guys know about Steve," I said without any preliminaries.

Brenda's expression still didn't change and she didn't say a word.

Delia said, "Danny was here when we opened up this morning."

I nodded to acknowledge Delia's comment then looked at Brenda. "Are you okay?"

"Things weren't working out between us anyway," she said flatly.

I hoped she hadn't said that, like that, to Danny because it was void of grief or regret or sorrow or even sympathy. In fact, it was cold and wouldn't have served her well in light of my cousin's already strengthening suspicions of her.

"I know about Bert," I said then, assuming Steve's lack of support for Brenda was what had caused the rift and her attitude. "I know he was exposing himself to you. He exposed himself to me the night he died."

"That old son of a bitch," Delia said venomously, reminding me a little of my grandmother when I'd told her about Bert.

"Did he do it to you, too?" I asked Delia since it seemed I'd hit a nerve.

"Once. But not the way he was doing it with Brenda. He was tormenting her. Then he turns around and says *she* was peeping at *him*. And Steve believed him enough not to do anything. The old bastard even threatened to turn Brenda in to the police! But did Steve even kick him out of the Center? No. He wasn't going to part with a dime of membership money no matter what."

Brenda didn't react at all to Delia's angry tirade.

"That must have been frustrating," I said, still not getting a rise out of Brenda, even though I aimed the comment at her.

She was sitting there ramrod straight, and I again saw a glimmer of what I'd thought before was an iron core of strength running through her. She certainly didn't seem shaken by the recent events.

"Speaking of money," I said then. Delia's comment about Steve's not parting with any wasn't much of a segue, but I used it anyway. "I happened across some information about you, Brenda."

I got my first response from her with that. She gave me a dirty look.

I ignored it.

"I didn't know you were a wealthy woman," I added.

"My grandfather was in steel."

And the faded shirtdress she had on with its frayed collar and cuffs could have dated back to her grandmother, it looked so old and ratty.

"And he did well in it?" I said to encourage her.

"He called himself the king of steel," Delia answered. "He was a real-life magnate. It made him a millionaire many times over."

"And I'm the only one left of my family, so I inherited everything," Brenda finished.

"Brenda owns the agency. She even owns the whole mall," Delia put in with a suppressed pride, as if she were bursting to tell me more of what Brenda owned. Then she leaned over her desk slightly and said confidentially, "She only works for the fun of it."

"It must be nice to have that freedom," I said as Delia straightened back up and pushed at the gardenia she had in her hair today. She almost matched the Hawaiian girl in the poster advertisement hanging behind her chair except that she had on a crew-neck sweater under her pink and lavender sarong.

"I keep thinking about Steve's credit cards being at their limits when he took you out to dinner," I said to Brenda again. "Do you suppose that was his way of having you share the wealth?"

"Maybe," she admitted.

"It's part of why she doesn't like people to know how much money she has." Delia again.

"I hate it when people know," Brenda offered, almost as if there was a warning in it for me. "All of a sudden things change. They hit you up for things they leave other people alone about."

"Did Steve do that? I mean, besides the dinners?"

"He started hinting around about it. Talking about how much he'd like to expand the Center if only he had the capital. What a good investment it would be for someone. The dinners were one thing, but when he started that—"

"She wasn't going to go out with him anymore," Delia interjected, seeming proud of that fact.

"That night after the flirting class," I said. "Was that what you were mad at Steve about—his wanting you to invest in the Center?"

"I was mad because Steve wasn't going to do anything about Bert."

Delia picked up where Brenda had left off. "Because Steve was acting like maybe he *would* kick Bert out if Brenda paid what Steve lost by returning Bert's membership fee and then agreed to the investment too. Like blackmail or some kind of scam or something," Delia expounded.

"Did it seem as if Bert and Steve were in cahoots?"

"I think Steve just used the opportunity circumstances presented him with," Brenda said, toning down Delia's allusions to conspiracy.

"Did you see Bert at all that night of the flirting class? I had the impression when he exposed himself to me that I wasn't who he was expecting. Was he waiting for you, do you think?"

"Probably."

"So did you see him?"

"Do you mean did he expose himself to me and did I kill him over it?"

Now that was hostile.

"I wasn't insinuating—"

"No, you're grilling me just like your cousin did. I didn't kill anyone and I have a whole law firm I can get over here with one phone call if I have to do it to get the two of you to leave me alone about this."

Oh yeah, there was a whole different Brenda under the cover of that scraggly, oily hair and those bangs that hung in her eyes like half-drawn window shades. And the other Brenda wasn't anywhere near as shy or quiet or withdrawn. She had claws.

"Brenda wouldn't hurt a fly," Delia said as if she'd read my thoughts, sounding conciliatory but protective too. "Not that we think any of those three deaths were a great loss to humanity. Steffi Hargitay was a mean, nasty bitch. Bert was an exhibitionist. And Steve . . . he took advantage of Brenda's attraction to him and that filthy old man's threats and was trying to use it to get money out of her. If you ask us, it just looks like somebody is getting the bad apples out of the barrel."

I hoped Delia hadn't said *that* to Danny in that tone of voice either.

"Murder is a pretty harsh way to do it," I suggested.

Neither of them agreed with me.

Instead they just sat there, staring at me and making me as uncomfortable as a knock-kneed freshman who'd stumbled into the upperclassmen's courtyard to face a couple of senior superlatives.

I was sure I'd worn out my welcome when Brenda said, "If that's all you came here for, we have a lunch appointment."

To make it look as if I hadn't come only to nose around, I asked about the plane tickets my grandmother had ordered.

Delia checked the safe but didn't find the tickets and said she'd make a follow-up call after lunch and let us know when they were in. Then both Brenda and Delia just seemed to wait for me to leave.

I didn't have much choice but to say good-bye and grant them their wish.

But as I left a little uneasiness about the two of them came with me. Even though I didn't want to think it, I had to wonder if maybe my facetiousness before about their teaming up to fight evil hadn't been far off the mark.

Chapter Twenty-five

I SHOULD HAVE used Friday evening to catch up on the work I hadn't done during the day. But after virtually no sleep the night before, the pall of Steve Stivik's death, and my conversation with Delia and Brenda, I decided I needed a little down time. My plan was to make some chocolate cupcakes with cream cheese centers, watch a movie on tape, and go to bed at a reasonable hour.

So much for the New You Dating Center's transforming me and my life.

Chloe and Shannon were both out with friends and Gramma had gone to play bingo, which left Danny and me alone for the flick. He made popcorn to go along with the cupcakes and the movie we settled on was *The Birdcage* with Robin Williams because neither of us had seen it and we agreed we needed a laugh. We also agreed not to talk about any of the Center's murders or Danny's suspects and to just relax.

So, for about three hours, I didn't think about anything but keeping my feet up and my mouth full of comfort food. It was nice for a change, and as Danny and I said good night and headed to our respective levels of the house I was sure I was going to sleep like a baby.

But the minute my head hit the pillow the wheels of my mind started turning.

First I was just thinking about what I needed to accomplish over the weekend. About finishing the kitchen catalog and how much I had left to do on Carl's prospectus.

That led to thinking about Carl's invitation for the whole family to spend Saturday night with him at Cutler's Corner. His treat. The girls and Gramma and I were all looking forward to it even though Danny had made up an excuse not to go. Privately, he'd told me he couldn't because Carl was a suspect, and even though Carl was at the bottom of the list with an alibi for Steffi's murder, no motive for Steve's, and only the remote possibility that he'd killed Bert to spare Brenda the exhibitionism, Danny was afraid a free meal and entertainment at Cutler's Corner might appear to be a bribe to look the other way.

That was when I began to consider who besides Carl was the least likely to have committed the murders, and since I was getting progressively more awake rather than falling asleep, I opted for turning on the lights and fixing a cup of tea.

And while I was at it, I let Lucy outside. The later

she goes out for that last time at night, the later she sleeps in the morning. Which means the later *I* can sleep in the morning.

As I filled the kettle with just enough water for one cup and put it on my mini two-burner stove, I thought that Gary Oldershaw was only slightly more apt to be the killer than Carl was. Sure, Gary could have killed Steffi out of anger, hurt, and frustration for breaking up with him, but he still seemed to love her and I didn't think he was likely to have crossed over that line to end her life.

As for Bert and Steve, Gary could have been after Steve because Steve had been instrumental in the breakup, killed Bert by mistake, and then gone after Steve a second time at home. Or he might even have believed Bert killed Steffi, exacted revenge, then decided to get back at Steve, too, while he was at it.

But Gary could have held his own with Steve and somehow I couldn't picture him incapacitating another man with handcuffs rather than just going after him hand to hand. Plus, with all that might behind the swing of a trophy, surely one blow would have done the job and Danny had said it had taken several blows to the head to kill Steve.

Diane and Irene both had motives all the way down the line. Steffi had made their lives miserable at work and put Irene, in particular, at risk of losing her livelihood. It was possible Bert had been exposing himself to Diane, and certainly Bert's rejection of Irene could have driven her to lock the sauna door behind him. As for Steve, he had had Irene still fearing for her job at the same time he wouldn't let Diane out of hers.

Those were all motives, but they didn't strike me as strong enough to actually indict either of the Center's remaining female employees.

There were Brenda and Delia, together or alone. My talk with them that afternoon had left a slightly bad taste in my mouth and I'd been wondering a lot of things since then. Like how far Delia might go to protect Brenda. Like how far she might go to even the score for her. Like just how tough Brenda really was deep down. Like what the two of them teamed up might be able to pull off. And whether Brenda's shyness and Delia's flowery persona hid some not too nice traits.

But despite how my conversation with them had gone, I just couldn't believe that either of them, alone or together, was responsible for getting the rotten apples out of the barrel the way Delia had suggested someone was doing.

My water was boiling, so I poured it into a mug and dipped a tea bag. As I did I was thinking that that business about getting the bad apples out of the barrel was true. Of the people I'd met at the Center—instructors and members—the three worst of the lot were the ones who were dead.

Beyond the one good deed Steffi had done for Carl years and years ago, by every account she was a mean, vindictive, cruel manipulator. She was helping Steve to prey on the insecurities of members and then apparently holding it over Steve's head in order to gain a stronger position or possibly joint ownership in the Center, essentially blackmailing him.

She'd been nasty and hurtful to Delia. She'd threatened Brenda. She'd dumped Gary in favor of the scams

she and Steve were working on members. She'd been
awful to Diane. Worse to Irene. She'd likely rejected
Bert and, if her pattern had remained the same, had
probably not been kind about it.

If she hadn't been killed herself, she'd no doubt
have made a good suspect in both Bert's death and
Steve's, especially since Steve was apparently not complying with what she wanted and she'd been reduced to
threatening him.

Bert, whom I'd liked, had proven to have a much
darker side. He'd lied about having a date with Steffi
and might even have been her killer. Then, not only
had he been an exhibitionist, he'd clearly taken some
delight in choosing the most socially inept of women—
Brenda—to target, track, and torment. There was cruelty to that too. Maybe even the kind of cruelty that
could have handcuffed Steve to a bed before killing
him. Except that Bert had already been out of the picture by that time.

And as for Steve, I've rarely met anyone I disliked
more. Cocky, sarcastic, snide, smug, egotistical, cruel,
and worse than just manipulative in his mercenary bed-
ding practices and veiled blackmail of Brenda and in
plotting to subtly extort from his clients. He was a
schoolyard bully grown up to carry his bullying to new
heights.

He'd used Steffi and still had almost no regard for
her, ruining the one good relationship she'd had with
Gary. He'd held Diane prisoner in a job she didn't
want. He'd kept Irene on edge with the threat of firing
her. He'd toyed with Brenda and her emotions and
used Bert's antics in an attempt to force an investment
out of her. He'd just been a world-class creep.

But if the bad guys were dead, who among the good guys had killed them?

My tea was so strong by the time I realized I was still dipping my bag that it was nearly black. I usually drain the leaves the way my grandfather taught me—by lifting the bag out of the cup with a spoon and wrapping the string around spoon and bag at once—but this time I just threw the bag away and added more water to the mug. Then I took the mug to set on my nightstand and went to the door to let Lucy in.

She wasn't out on the landing the way I'd expected her to be, so I made the kissing noise and whistled for her. But there was no answering clicks of her nails on the wooden steps to let me know she was coming. In fact, there was no sound at all.

"Dammit."

We'd gotten lax about going out to watch her so she didn't dig under the fence anymore. She hadn't been making any attempts, and we all had the impression she'd lost interest in it or forgotten about it.

Little did we know she was just waiting until we dropped our guard.

"Lucy!" I tried again, hoping she was just being stubborn.

But she didn't come then, either, and I knew she'd beat a path to Barney.

I pulled on my sweat suit in a hurry, hoping I could get to her before she did too much damage at the doctor's. Then I went out into the night air that was actually warmer than the daytime had been. Apparently our cold snap had broken.

As I hightailed it up the street I had a flash of memory that Ben Barrows's name had been in Steve Stivik's notebook, and that Danny thought the doctor might have had a grudge against Steffi and Steve for trying to get him to agree to kickbacks. Certainly I'd seen signs of resentment for insulting his integrity and ethics. That put him on the suspect list, too, I thought as I reached his house.

The place was dark, and since he kept his car in the garage I couldn't tell if he was out for a late evening or just in bed the way the rest of the block seemed to be. In case he was in bed, I didn't want to go up to the door and announce that my dog was paying a midnight visit, so once again I just went up the driveway and around the side of the house.

Sure enough, Lucy was there, digging for China and tearing the hell out of his walkway again, destroying all my cousin Vince's hard work.

I would have liked to sneak up on her, but between Ben's security lights all blazing to life and Barney spotting me and barking his head off, that was impossible.

Lucy tried to dig even faster, but I managed to grab her before she got under the fence—just barely.

"Bad dog!" I scolded.

In my hurry to get to her I hadn't taken her leash with me, and it occurred to me then that I should have. That without it I didn't have a way to hang on to her while I tried to repair the mess she'd made. About the only thing I could do was push stones back into a semblance of their order with my foot and stomp them down some.

Then I headed for home again before Barney's barking woke everybody for miles, figuring I'd have to call Ben first thing in the morning, explain and apologize again, and go over to do the real repair work.

Or maybe I'd get lucky, my cousin would be able to pour Carl's cement the next day and I could hit Vince up for a redo of what he'd done for me at Ben's before.

I was making a mental note to call Vince at the crack of dawn as I let Lucy and myself into the attic. And that's when a bunch of strangely disjointed thoughts started to pop into my head and connect themselves—thoughts of Vince smoothing out Ben's walkway, thoughts of Steve's notebook and what, and who, had been in it, of people not being what they seemed to be, of who knew the truth. . . .

And what was coming out of all those disjointed thoughts stopped me in my tracks.

I didn't like what I was thinking, but as one thing fell into place alongside another it was as if a light had been turned on in a closet to reveal what couldn't be seen before through the darkness.

And I knew I had to follow up on the ugly hunch that struck me like a bolt of lightning.

I crossed the loft and went out through the interior door, going down the stairs past the girls' bedrooms all the way to the main level, through the living room and kitchen to the cherry wood door that separated the rest of the house from Danny's basement apartment.

Unfortunately, I could hear my cousin snoring from the top of the stairs and that kept me from going any farther.

I knew he'd had a long, hard week and I didn't have the heart to go down and wake him. Especially not when his voice suddenly started to sound in my head, telling me how far-fetched my newest theory was. How there wasn't any evidence. How it was all supposition and speculation.

I knew that he'd tell me to go back to bed. He'd say that he'd ask around tomorrow or the next day. That maybe he'd get a search warrant.

But anything later than first thing the next morning might be too late.

I closed the cherry wood door softly and headed back to the attic, trying the whole time to talk myself out of what I was considering doing.

But it didn't work, and by the time I reached the attic again I knew I was sunk.

I retraced my steps across the loft and for the second time tonight, I went outside.

Hoping I wasn't doing something really stupid . . .

Chapter Twenty-six

I WANTED TO be wrong. And the whole way up the street I hoped I was. I hoped I would come out of this feeling like an idiot and having two apologies to make in the morning.

Barney started barking the minute I neared Ben Barrows's house. I shushed him but it didn't matter, he went right on with a booming bark that bounced off the houses and echoed through the quiet of the night.

He kept it up even after I went past the doctor's big Tudor, and I could still hear him as I approached the bend in the road.

Only then did he stop. Oddly, I was almost sorry. At least as long as the animal was making a ruckus I didn't feel so alone. But in the silence that was left, an uneasiness settled over me.

I tried to ignore it. I told myself the uneasiness was natural. It came from being out alone, at night, without the best intentions. It didn't help, but even so I couldn't convince myself to turn around and go home rather than do what I'd come to do.

Neither Carl's house nor the house built on the curve of the road had fences, so I took a shortcut across the backyard of the corner house right into Carl's backyard. There were no lights shining through his windows. I didn't know if that meant a late date, late work, or that he was sleeping. I was counting on his being asleep because if he was out, that meant he could come home at any time and catch me. Not a prospect I relished.

The sky was full of bright white clouds rather than the ominous gray ones that had been hovering overhead for so long. They made a ceiling that reflected the earth's lights and that, coupled with the streetlight just across the neighbor's yard, helped me see where I was going.

Not that even the two factors together were as good as a flashlight, but in my eagerness to get there I hadn't thought to bring one.

Keeping a wary eye on Carl's house, I followed a path through the stacked lumber and tools to the site of the shed my cousin was going to build. Along the way I grabbed a shovel I knew I'd need.

I had a vivid image in my mind of that first day I'd been to Carl's house, of looking out at the graded plot of ground ready for the shed and seeing that one spot that wasn't as smooth as the rest. Vince did good work. He wouldn't have left one section rough while the remainder was as hard and flat as granite.

Of course, a neighborhood dog or cat could have made a midnight foray to dig like Lucy had been doing—like I was going to do—and I kept a good thought that that was the case even as I went to that resmoothed corner of the site.

A reasonable explanation. Surely there was a reasonable explanation for everything, I kept telling myself.

It was amazing how loud that initial stab of spade into earth sounded to me. I'd never realized before that digging could actually make so much noise, and I couldn't be sure if it was just amplified by my own tension and guilty conscience or if the sound really might carry. But by the third jab I decided it was better to do this with my hands than take the risk. Besides, it also occurred to me that the shovel might do some damage if I hit what I was looking for.

With another quick glance at the house to make sure no light had come on since my last look, I laid the shovel quietly on the ground and got down on my knees.

The earth wasn't quite frozen, but it took some effort to get through it anyway. Luckily—or maybe not so luckily—I didn't have to go too deep before I hit pay dirt.

"Oh, Carl . . ." I whispered to myself as I touched cold, hard metal.

It took more work to free it, but in the end I lifted the video camera out of the ground. The video camera that had no doubt been used to kill Steffi Hargitay.

"You just couldn't leave it alone, could you?"

It's a good thing I have a strong heart because if I didn't, I would have had a heart attack on the spot. As it was, I lunged to my feet and spun around to find Carl standing a few feet away.

He was dressed like I was in a gray sweat suit rather than a navy blue one, his hair was sleep-mussed, and he'd slipped his feet into tennis shoes. The only difference between us was that I was holding a soil-slogged video camera and he was carrying a butcher's knife.

I didn't know what to say. *Hi, Carl* didn't seem appropriate. I just stood there, caught in the act, waiting for whatever was going to happen next.

"It's funny," he said then. "You're who I've been the most afraid of all along. Not the cops, even with their forensics and questions. You. Somehow I knew you were the real trouble. God damn you, Jimi, doesn't anything stop you? I even blew up your car to give you something else to think about and here you are, still sticking your nose in where it doesn't belong."

An apology didn't seem in order either. But I finally found my voice through the fright he'd caused me. "Why, Carl? I thought you were one of the few people Steffi had ever been kind to."

"Me too. I guess that makes us both pretty gullible."

"She *wasn't* kind to you?"

"Not like I thought. Not for my sake. Not because she liked me. Not even because she felt sorry for me."

"Why then?"

Carl shrugged. "Let me see if I can remember it all. In high school she stopped those pricks from running me up the flagpole because her boyfriend at the time would have been kicked off the football team for it. He'd had too many infractions and one more would be the end for him. It didn't have anything to do with me, the way I thought. In fact, her being friendly to me was all just a big joke to Steffi. I was really just the geek she could lead around by the nose and get to do her math homework."

"But you didn't realize that then."

"No," he said with a sad laugh. "You know, she was always my fantasy. Not just when I was a kid. All along. It was the kind of thing you do—like with a movie star or a pinup girl or something. When I had the plastic surgery, when I made money, there was always this fantasy in the back of my mind of meeting Steffi Hargitay again. Of her seeing I wasn't as homely as before. That I was successful. Of her taking a second look and liking what she saw, of my ending up with her. I wouldn't have ever gone after her purposely or anything. It was just a fantasy. Not really what I thought could happen. And then I joined the Center and there she was. I was sure it was fate telling me something."

I was listening to him, wanting to keep him talking because as long as he was, there was some distance between us. But I was also on the alert for a way out of this.

"Wasn't Steffi nice to you when you met up with her at the Center?" I asked.

"Sure. That's what suckered me in. She acted like she was glad to see me, you'd have thought we were old friends, just the way I imagined we were. From the minute she did my orientation I started thinking of reasons to go to the Center, to meet up with her. I started thinking that maybe the fantasy would actually come true. And every time I managed to make our paths cross she was warm and wonderful. More than she'd even been in school. So warm and wonderful and sweet that I got up my courage to ask her out."

"For that Saturday night."

"And she accepted. I was so excited I couldn't sleep. I bought a two-thousand-dollar suit. I was going to wow her. But I was so jazzed, I couldn't wait. I honest to God couldn't wait. Friday night I hung around the Center as late as I could. I even hid in the conference room, in the dark, in the shadow where I could see the lobby through those hall windows, to watch for her. I was going to go out when I saw her leaving, as if I was just leaving, too, and ask her for coffee or a drink."

"Wouldn't she go with you?"

He did that laugh again. There was something about it that was manic. And made me know just how much danger I was in.

"I saw everybody leave but her. Well, not Steve, he'd left early that night. But when Steffi still wasn't coming out I decided to see if she was in her office. Poke my head in, make a crack about how late she was working, tell her she'd earned a drink or the coffee."

I inched backward, hoping Carl was engrossed enough in his tale not to notice.

He didn't seem to.

"Steffi was at her desk, looking in a notebook," he said. "I went in. Played it cool, even kind of propped a hip on her desk—enough to see my name in that notebook just before she closed it as if I wasn't supposed to. I made a joke about it being her diary. She didn't get it. I thought I was being so smooth, but she just didn't seem to be getting any of it."

I took another small step as he went on with what he was saying.

"Don't ask me why, but I started to tell her about my crush on her in school, my fantasies through the years, how much she meant to me, that I hoped we could get serious about each other. And do you know what she did? She acted like I made her sick. She said she just couldn't play this game with me no matter how much money I had or how much Steve was offering her to do it. She said she'd done enough for him and for what? He wasn't holding up his end of the bargain and having to have anything to do with me wasn't worth it."

"That was when she told you what had really gone on in high school," I guessed, so I'd seem involved and not as if I was subtly putting more space between us.

"She said a geek was a geek, rich or poor, and I made her skin crawl. Then and now."

"I'm sorry, Carl," I said, meaning it because his voice rang with the disillusionment and pain he'd felt, and as afraid as I was at that moment of him and of the knife he was wielding, there was still a part of me that sympathized.

"I just . . . I just lost it," he went on. "All those years of humiliation weren't as bad as that one moment. And I was so mad. I had this flash of anger that somebody could make me feel like that again. That somebody could do that to me even now. The video camera was on her desk, too, and she started to laugh at me, to tell me how I'd wasted my money on plastic surgery because I was still homely and inept and . . ."

"You hit her with the camera."

"I just wanted to shut her up, to stop her from going on and on about what a loser I am. I just . . . hit her."

He took a step toward me, as if he was going to hit me too. But he had that knife in his hand, so I knew he could do a lot more if he got close enough.

"But you had an alibi," I said in a hurry, as if I was impressed. "That threw me off the track."

He laughed a little once more, sounding proud of himself and stalling his approach again. "It was amazing how clear-headed I was afterward," he explained. "I turned the chair to face the wall so nobody could see what I'd done to her. I even remembered seeing my name in that notebook and thought to grab it to take with me when I ran out so I could see what was in it later. Then I realized no one else knew I was there at the Center at that hour and if I could say I was somewhere else where people would see me, that when the police asked, I'd be better off. So I went to Laddy's. It's only five minutes away. I had to leave my jacket in the car because there was blood on it, but I went in, ordered a beer, and went into the rest room to wash my hands. When I came out I called Steffi's home number so my voice would be on her machine and then I made sure the bartender would remember me and the phone call by talking to him about it, about Steffi, and by giving him a big tip. So I'd have an alibi."

"That was pretty fast thinking."

"I know. I couldn't believe myself."

"And it might have worked if that was all you'd done."

He nodded, and I had the sense that I'd somehow managed to refocus his interest on me rather than on his own adventures of the past couple of weeks. Big mistake.

"How'd you figure it out, anyway?" he asked.

I couldn't go through the whole process, so I cut to the clincher. "It occurred to me that maybe you weren't just making small talk with Brenda about franchising Cutler's Corner, that maybe you were trying to interest her in it. You wouldn't have been doing that unless you knew she had money. And since she did everything to keep her wealth a secret it seemed likely that you'd seen the notebook and what was in it in order to know. Steffi was the last person to have it before she was killed. Steve kept bugging me about it. He thought I'd picked it up when I found her Saturday morning. But I hadn't. So that meant it was likely that her killer had taken it. One thing fed into the other."

Carl sighed and shook his head as if he couldn't believe his bad fortune. "Steve. God. What a nightmare. He figured out the same thing you did, only a lot earlier. Brenda let him know I was pitching the idea of her buying a franchise and that tipped him off that I had the notebook and had taken it from Steffi's office."

"So Steve knew you'd killed Steffi?" Maybe I shouldn't have been surprised at anything Steve Stivik did, but to know Carl was a murderer and not turn him in to the police? I can't say I'd expected that.

"He was blackmailing me," Carl said. "He saw it as his ace in the hole. I was going to be his own private source of cash from then on."

Nice.

"And if that wasn't bad enough, the demands for money came with the same kind of abuse I'd suffered from people like him as a kid."

"Bullying," I guessed. It wasn't too much of a stretch.

"More like degradation—that's what people like him thrive on. It wasn't enough that he was forcing money out of me, he wanted me jumping through hoops to do it. I wasn't going to put up with it, Jimi. I couldn't."

"You decided to kill him too."

"He didn't realize it until you told him, though."

There was venom in that and I knew that despite the amiability of this chat, I really was in trouble. I was on the same list of enemies as Steffi and Steve.

I didn't dare move anymore because Carl was watching me more closely now, but I kept my eyes open for any opportunity.

As I did, I tried to buy time with another apology. "I'm sorry. But Steve acted as if I was crazy when I said that to him. He didn't seem afraid at all."

Wrong thing to say. It raised Carl's hackles. "No, he wasn't afraid. He said I was a goddamned wimp. A chicken-shit. That I was too fucking scared to come after him like a man. The guy had no conscience. He didn't even care that the old man had died, it was just more ammunition against me, to tell me what a stupid asshole I was."

Imagine that, a guy with no conscience.

"So killing Bert really was only an accident," I said as if that absolved Carl.

"It should have been Steve in that sauna. I thought it was. Everybody said he used it every night. But not the stinking night I locked the sauna door. No, then it has to be some old man in there."

"And the next time you went after Steve you made sure it was him." In all too grizzly a fashion.

"It wasn't like I didn't try to avoid having to do it at all. I paid him the money he wanted. I would have given him the franchise for the next Cutler's Corner. I did everything he told me to do. I even gave back that damn notebook that was so important to him," Carl went on in defense of himself. "We could have both gone our separate ways, put it all behind us, forgotten about it. But was he willing to do that?"

"Bullies are never satisfied."

"Well, he should have been. Because look what he got instead. I showed him," Carl said with satisfaction. "I showed him who was a wimp and who wasn't."

I didn't like the smile on Carl's face and I didn't encourage him to say more. I didn't want to hear him brag about killing Steve Stivik.

But it didn't matter.

"You'll have the last laugh," Carl said then in a voice that mimicked someone else's. "That's what my grandmother used to tell me. Every time something mortifying happened to me, that's what she'd say. I didn't believe her. I didn't even want the last laugh. I just wanted to be left alone. But having it was a rush, I'll tell you that. Watching him beg. Squirm like his kind always made me squirm."

Carl glanced off into the distance, enjoying his memory, and I took the only chance I was afraid I might get.

I dropped the video camera where I stood and took off like a shot.

I ran faster than I've ever run in my life, across the corner house's yard again and back onto the sidewalk of my section of the street.

I could hear Carl behind me, so I knew his reaction had been quick and I didn't have much of a head start. I also knew he had longer legs and was in better shape than I was.

"Barney!" I shouted as I ran, thinking that if the dog was still outside and I could incite him to bark again, it might rouse someone who could help.

One yell was all it took to get the big dog going, joined by a smaller yip I knew was Lucy's.

I didn't know how she'd gotten out again, but it didn't make much difference at that point. That was the least of my worries. Carl was gaining on me and even though he wasn't near enough to make it real, it seemed I could actually feel him on my heels.

Too close. He was too close. And I was giving the run all I had as it was.

My house had never looked so far away, and I knew I wouldn't get to it before Carl caught me. But Ben's place was right there, complete with two noise-making dogs. Hopefully Ben himself was inside and if he was, he was the most apt to be lured out by Barney's barking and my calling for help.

It wasn't a great plan, but it was the best I could come up with. I made a quick jag into his yard, using what air I had left to scream for him, for Barney, for Lucy, as I reached the wrought-iron gate.

Lucy had been out long enough to finish her dig under the fence because she was in the backyard with the Doberman. Hoping Barney wouldn't attack me, I yanked open the gate and nearly fell through it into the backyard.

Carl was right behind me, and he grabbed the hood of my sweat suit. I lost my footing and stumbled to the ground. He lunged for me as I did and something sliced through my sleeve and arm at once.

Lucy went for him then, clamping on to his leg with her teeth while Barney kept on barking ferociously.

Carl hit Lucy, knocking her off his leg and I used that moment to roll away.

Only I didn't get far. Carl was fast and pumped up. He caught my ankle, pulling so hard, my leg nearly came out of the socket.

"What the hell is this?" I heard Ben Barrows shout from somewhere not far away.

But it didn't do me any good. Carl was intent and he suddenly had me pinned to the ground, sitting on my hips, the knife poised for a downward strike.

I looked up into his face and saw rage that was ages old, that tuned out everything else, and I held my breath for the attack.

That was when Ben Barrows threw a body tackle at Carl, knocking him off me.

It should have been enough to put an end to things. But Carl turned on Ben with the knife, diving for him vengefully.

The two men struggled. I didn't know enough about the dermatologist to know what kind of power or strength or ability he had. But I did know that Carl was desperate and wouldn't stop at anything to save himself.

I got to my feet, ignoring the pain that shot through my arm, through my leg and hip, and grabbed the nearest thing I could reach—a snow shovel braced against the rear of the garage.

And that was when I learned just how much damage you can do when you hit a man in the head with one.

Chapter Twenty-seven

I SPENT THE remainder of that night at the hospital having my arm stitched, my hip X-rayed and answering a million questions posed to me by three different cops who streamed in and out of every room I was sent to for medical care.

Anyone in the neighborhood who had slept through the dogs' barking and my yelling from Ben Barrows's backyard hadn't made it through the sirens of police cars and ambulances when Ben had dialed 911 and I'd called Danny. That included my grandmother, who had ridden with me to the hospital and stayed by my side every minute until I was released at 6:00 A.M.

Then a uniformed officer drove us home.

The block was peaceful again except for the distant static that could be heard coming from a police radio around the bend in the road. I didn't have to see it to know investigators were still working at Carl's house. But on the straightaway the paperboy was tossing plastic-wrapped newspapers from his bicycle as the sun began to peek through the clouds and all was right with the world once more.

Too bad I didn't feel that way.

Once we were inside I assured Gramma that I was fine, that my arm was still numb from the Novocain and my leg and hip were sore but nothing I couldn't live through, so she could relax and go back to bed for a few hours. Then I winced my way up two flights of stairs to my attic room, where Lucy was waiting for me, none the worse for wear.

I stripped off my torn and tattered sweat suit and crawled into my own bed, patting the mattress next to me to invite her up. She snuggled against my side and I fell asleep petting her warm, furry head.

The next thing I knew Shannon was opening my door and saying, "Mom? Are you all right?"

I opened my eyes to the green display of numbers on my clock radio. It was after four in the afternoon.

I rolled to my back, keeping my groan to myself and said, "I'm fine. Good thing you woke me up. I was out like a light."

"Do you want to stay in bed?"

"No. I'll take a quick bath and come downstairs."

"You're sure you're okay?"

"Positive."

Even though I didn't feel like hurrying—or even like talking—I made good on my word because I knew my family would be worried until they saw me. With that in mind, I put on makeup and combed my hair along

with gritting my teeth through pulling on a pair of jeans
and one of my dressier turtlenecks.

Then I went downstairs and into the smell of my
grandmother's homemade chicken soup simmering on
the stove.

Gramma, Danny, Chloe, and Shannon were all sitting at the kitchen table sipping out of steaming mugs.

"There she is!" Gramma said as if I were royalty,
spotting me first and following up with "We're having
tea just like Grandpa liked it. Sit down and I'll bring
you a cup."

Just like Grandpa liked it meant tea with lemon,
honey, and plenty of brandy. I knew because he taught
me to make it for him. But I didn't balk. It sounded
good. And maybe it would chase away the chill I couldn't
seem to shake.

"The whole cop shop's joking about putting you on
the squad's payroll," Danny said as I eased myself into
a chair across from him.

"Great. I can use the extra income."

"I told them no. You're too much of a hotdog."

"Who me?"

"Why the hell didn't you wake me up and tell me
what you thought instead of going out to dig around
yourself in the middle of the night, Jimi?"

The reprimand. I was expecting it.

"Yeah, Mom," Shannon chimed in. "You'd ground
us for the rest of our lives if we did something like
that."

"Ground us? She'd kill us herself," Chloe said to
put in her two cents' worth.

Apparently they'd been told the whole story of my
midnight adventure.

I didn't answer either of my daughters' chastisements, but I did address my cousin's question. "You were asleep, Danny. I wasn't sure if I was right or not, but I didn't want to wait until morning when Vince might pour cement. And besides, this way, if I'd been wrong, all Carl would have had to contend with was my apology. If I'd told you ahead of time and been wrong, there would have been cops all over Carl and his house and his yard, digging everything up, making a mess and a nuisance and embarrassing him, and all for nothing."

"Too bad he wasn't as concerned about saving face for you," Danny said facetiously.

Gramma set a mug in front of me and sat with the rest of us. "That dirty bugger tried to make the police think you were burying that video camera in his yard. Planting it to make him look bad," she informed me.

"Ah. He does think fast in a crisis. He told me he did. Does that mean I'll have to answer even more questions?"

Danny shook his head as he sipped his toddy. "I told him your fingerprints were on the outside of the dirt. His were underneath it. I don't know if that's true or not, but when I said it he gave up the ghost and filled out a full statement."

"I heard most of it last night," I said so Danny wouldn't have to go through it all.

"I also got more information out of Steffi Hargitay's father and sister," he said then. "Her father lied about not having seen her in ten years because he figured after what had gone down over the inheritance he'd be a likely suspect. I guess he thought we'd never figure out he'd been here."

"And the sister?" I prompted.

"I sent a couple of investigators to talk to her personally and found out she was closer to Steffi than she'd originally led us to believe. She didn't *like* her, but they talked on the telephone often enough for the sister to know most of what was going on."

"And she finally told the investigators?"

"Better late than never." Danny took another drink of his spiked tea and filled me in. "The reason the grandfather left everything to Steffi was that she buttered him up the same way she apparently did with the Center's desirable members. She did some back-stabbing along with it and basically won the whole pot for herself."

"Why stop at the job when you can put your true talents to work on relatives, too?" I said.

"Makes sense I suppose. And we were right about what Steffi wanted from Steve—he apparently started his con jobs on the rich and lonely at the gym where he and Steffi met. That was how he managed a fair portion of the bankroll for the Center in the first place—there are more lifetime members running around out there than we've been able to tally yet. When Steffi realized what Steve had going, she told her sister about it. Then she dealt herself a hand with Steve so he'd take her with him when he left by threatening to tell his investors he was pity . . . well, you know," Danny said, catching himself before saying the F-word in front of the girls and Gramma.

"When did Steffi start contributing to the seductions?" I asked.

"At the Center. But Steve was basically doing the same thing to her that he did with everyone else—he kept making promises to give her a share of the Center in return for what she was schmoozing out of the male members, but never coming through. She was sick of it and planned to take the notebook as evidence as soon as the opportunity presented itself—probably the night she died. But before that she'd bragged to her sister that the notebook was going to be her upper hand. Steffi had already threatened to go public with what Steve was doing if he didn't make good on his promises to her but he wasn't taking that any more seriously than he took your warning to him. That left the notebook as Steffi's ace in the hole."

"And was what Steve was doing legal or not?"

"Mmm, I'd say it was borderline. But since none of the people he took *gifts* from went after him, Steffi didn't think he was in any legal jeopardy. But letting word out to the newspapers and news stations would have definitely hurt the Center, if not ruined it."

"The two of them really were sweethearts, weren't they?" I said. Then I thought of one other thing I didn't have an answer to. "What about the dynamite Carl used to blow up the Subaru? Where did that come from?"

"He stole it from the Forest Service. He worked avalanche control with them just after college, knew some people who still do. Apparently he paid them a little visit. Somehow managed to get hold of a stick up there. We were checking construction sites, landscapers, things around town. Hadn't thought to look into the mountains."

"Why'd he blow up our car?" Chloe asked.

"To distract me, I guess. Slow me down. So I'd have something more to think about and do than stick my nose into things."

"It also gave him a way of getting closer to you by offering you a ride and helping you replace the car, a way to keep tabs on you in the process," Danny offered. "Carl is no dummy."

"Do you think his brother-in-law will take the new car back now?" Shannon asked.

I laughed and looked at Danny. "The brother-in-law couldn't do that, could he?"

"I wouldn't worry about it."

"Let somebody try to come here and take that car. I'll let them know what I think about that bastard and what he did."

Gramma had had a severe change of heart about Carl, but I couldn't find the same anger and resentment in myself.

I kept picturing a scrawny, homely kid who'd lost his parents and been uprooted from his only friend to be tormented—tortured—in a new school. I thought of the pain and loneliness of that. Of the hell of getting up every morning to face merciless bullies. Of believing Steffi Hargitay was his angel and then finding out she was just another devil. Of having that same kind of torment inflicted on him all over again by Steve Stivik.

Maybe the wonder of it was just that something hadn't snapped in Carl earlier. But mostly I just felt sorry for him in spite of what had played out the night before.

"He did kill Bert by mistake," I told Danny then because it popped into my head.

Danny made a face at me. "Couldn't resist the I-told-you-so, could you?"

I just gave him a Cheshire cat smile.

"Do you think he'll get the death penalty?" Chloe asked.

Danny shrugged. "He can afford some big-gun defense attorneys. I wouldn't be surprised at a plea of insanity. For now, he's in the hospital. Your mother hit him with a snow shovel and broke his cheek and jaw-bone, and crushed his ear."

"Way to go, Mom," Shannon cheered.

"Ben told us you saved his life," Danny said.

"Not before he saved mine. He must have played football somewhere along the line because for a derma-tologist he has a mean tackle."

Then Danny wanted to know how I'd come to the conclusion that Carl was the killer, and I told him.

"I just don't understand why that Carl waited all those years and then killed some girl for what she did in high school," Gramma said when I'd gone through the whole disjointed thought process that had led me to my theory.

I explained that Carl had only found out the truth about Steffi when he'd met her again at the Center. I added, "He said he thought fate had brought them together and I guess that's true. But it was certainly fickle fate."

"Here we sent you to that dating center to meet somebody nice and this is what happens," Gramma concluded.

"It just wasn't my fate to meet anyone there," I said. "If I'm going to meet someone it'll just happen, Gram. Nobody can *make* it happen."

"God helps those who help themselves," Danny put in, getting me back for my I-told-you-so.

"I think I'd rather leave it to fate." I stood then, careful not to show how much it hurt, and announced my need for a trip to the bathroom. I wanted to put a moratorium on any more talk about dating.

As I passed through the living room I thought I heard a knock on the front door, so I took a detour to answer it.

I half expected more cops with more questions, but when I opened the door it was Ben Barrows standing outside.

"Hi," I said, pushing the screen open to let him in.

I'd lost track of him at the hospital, but he'd ridden over with Gramma and me in the ambulance and made sure the emergency room staff had been told to take special care of me. It helps to know people.

He came in, looking none the worse for wear, too, in jeans and a turtleneck sweater—a man after my own heart.

"I wanted to see how you're doing," he said once he was inside.

"I'm fine. It could have been a lot worse if not for you."

"I could say the same thing about you. I think it makes us even."

Except that he wouldn't have been in that predicament if I hadn't led Carl up into his yard in the first place. But I didn't say that. Instead I said, "We're all having tea, how about joining us?"

He glanced toward the kitchen, where apparently no one had heard his knock because not even Gramma had come to see who was there. "Uh, no, thanks. I, uh, had called you Wednesday and left a message on your machine."

"That's right. Shannon told me." I braced for something less friendly than things had been since last night. No doubt a complaint about Lucy. I decided to head him off at the pass.

"I'm sorry about Lucy tearing up your walkway again. I'll get my cousin over to fix it and I swear we won't take our eyes off her no matter what time of the day or night we let her out from here on."

"That's no big deal. Hard to keep the Romeo and Juliet of dogs apart. Anyway, that's not what I called about."

"Something worse?" I said with a laugh, wondering what other trouble I'd inadvertently gotten into.

"I hope not," he answered. "What I was going to ask you was if you'd have dinner with me. Not tonight—I know that under the circumstances it can't be tonight, but how about next weekend? Friday or Saturday?"

"You mean like a *date*?"

Okay, so blurting that out was not too smooth. But he'd taken me by surprise.

"Not *like* a date. I was thinking a real date."

"Oh."

I'm not too often at a loss for words and this was a lousy time for it to happen. But there I was, with a million things going through my mind, and none of it making any sense.

Then I heard myself say, "Sure. Okay. That sounds good."

"Great. How about Friday night? Say seven? Maybe we can get to a movie too."

"Friday night. Seven. Dinner and a movie. A date," I parroted, not quite believing what I was agreeing to even as I was agreeing to it.

A date?

Me and Barney the Doberman's doctor dad the dermatologist?

I was never going to live this down with my family.

But it was too late to back out—even though I considered it.

And all I could think of as Ben Barrows started to suggest restaurants was: funny, but that knock on the door hadn't *sounded* like fate. . . .